BREAKER

BREAKER

KAT ELLIS

RP|TEENS
PHILADELPHIA • LONDON

For

IAN

Books published by Running Press are available at special discounts for
bulk purchases in the United States by corporations, institutions, and other
organizations. For more information, please contact the Special Markets
Department at the Perseus Books Group, 2300 Chestnut Street, Suite 200,
Philadelphia, PA 19103, or call (800) 810-4145, ext. 5000,
or e-mail special.markets@perseusbooks.com.

ISBN 978-0-7624-5908-7
Library of Congress Control Number: 2015951853
E-book ISBN 978-0-7624-5909-4

9 8 7 6 5 4 3 2 1
Digit on the right indicates the number of this printing

Front cover images: Owl © Thinkstock Images/Eric Gevaert;
Twilight © Thinkstock Images/Gromovataya; Sky © T.L. Bonaddio
Back cover images: Victorian Reflection © Thinkstock Images/Feldore; Eerie
Night Sky © Thinkstock Images/Jupiterimages

Designed by T.L. Bonaddio
Edited by Lisa Cheng
Typography: Fairfield, Woodie, and Univers

Published by Running Press Teens
An Imprint of Running Press Book Publishers
A Member of the Perseus Books Group
2300 Chestnut Street
Philadelphia, PA 19103-4371

Visit us on the web!
www.runningpress.com/rpkids

CHAPTER ONE

BURTY'S WORLD TURNS UPSIDE DOWN

Naomi

The rope around my ankles burned, but it was a good burn. It meant I wouldn't plunge head-first onto the cobblestones four stories below—at least, as long as the rope didn't break.

Light glinted somewhere down on the quad. Kit was already standing there, his blond hair catching the sun. Another glint, and his camera lens was pointed up at me.

"Ready?" Fletch said behind me.

I touched my throat where Mom's sunflower pendant used to be.

"Ready," I said.

I let myself fall backward, and the world turned upside down.

The rope around my ankles tightened; everything tightened. The blood rushed behind my eardrums. My back bounced once off the bricks—not even hard enough to knock the wind out of me, really—and I settled into a dangle with my heels just below the window ledge.

"Are you okay?" Kit sounded like he was underwater. Or I was.

I waved down at him and he pretended to fumble the camera, trying to get me to crack a smile. Instead I mouthed the word *dick*, nice and clear, and he shook his head and started snapping away. I forced my body to relax into position. The shot had to be perfect, and I didn't want Kit to miss it. I tucked my arms behind my head, leaned straight back against the rough brick of the building. The slow-moving clouds drifting high above the Academy looked like they were under me now, one toe of my shoe nudging the hazy outline of the sun.

A tug on the rope told me Fletch was already getting impatient.

"Just a minute," I called up to him. Blood roared in my head, probably turning my face purple. I'd have to fix that in the photo.

"Don't struggle! You'll only make it hurt more."

The voice sliced into me, through the pressure building in my skull. The memory of a monster, that was all.

I wasn't scared. Definitely not scared.

"Stop fighting."

My elbows scraped against the wall as I panicked.

"Don't worry, I got it!"

Kit's cheerful yell reminded me what I was doing—the photo for the scrapbook. He wasn't looking at me now, busy flicking through the images on his camera.

I craned my neck to find Fletcher leaning through the window, hands stretched down toward me.

"Naomi?" he said. Fletcher's expression was flat, but the knuckles stood out pale under his skin. I got ready to swing up and catch Fletch's hands so he could pull me in the rest of the way, but stopped when a shadow moved behind Kit below.

Had Principal Kincaid seen us? If so, we were all in a big, steaming pile of trouble. But the shadow wasn't the right shape, and certainly wasn't stepping forward to yell at us. He—and I was sure it was a man—edged back farther into the shadows on the opposite side of the quad.

"Fletch, who's that guy down there with Kit?" I asked.

"There's nobody there. Only Kit."

"I saw—"

The shadows behind Kit were still now. Whoever had been there was gone.

Probably gone to rat us out to Kincaid.

I swung up, and Fletch grabbed my hands and yanked me back in. The pressure in my skull receded to somewhere near normal, and everything that was knotted up so tight inside loosened.

Fletch shook his head and started working on the knot tied at my ankles. Once I was free, I marched in place, sloshing blood back into my numb feet.

"Why are you laughing?" he asked.

I shrugged. "Adrenaline, I guess."

He rocked back on his heels. "Nothing truly scares you, does it?"

Fletch's questions were never just questions. Why wasn't I afraid to hang upside down out of a top-floor window? Wouldn't it be normal to be scared of something like that?

But you were afraid.

I shook it off, my brain still a little confused about which way was up.

It was the blood pounding in your head, reminding you of having hands wrapped around your throat. That's all.

Perfectly logical. There were no more monsters out there waiting for me.

Fletch sat with his elbows propped on his knees, waiting.

"Nah. What is there to be scared of anymore?" I said.

CHAPTER TWO

BURTY AT THE FRONT DOOR

Kyle

Mama kept staring at my head. She'd turn away as soon as I looked at her, going back to rolling the shopping cart along next to me, but not quick enough.

"Aluminum foil," she muttered, making like she was frowning at her grocery list instead of my freshly shaved head. I rubbed one hand over the stubble and waited for her to look at me. Mama pursed her lips, but said nothing. She was on edge shopping in an unfamiliar store, but I had my reasons for wanting to stop at this one on our way out of town.

I hopped up onto the front of the moving cart and her hand fluttered to her chest.

"Kyle Henry Bluchevsky, get down from—"

Bluchevsky. The name was a boulder strapped to my back.

I winced and glanced around the store. Nobody had heard.

"You'll have to remember not to do that when we get to Killdeer." My voice was lower than dirt. I took the handle of the cart from her and pushed it farther down the aisle. "Mama, you promised. It'll only take one slip, and we'll be right back where we started."

She made a pissy noise in the back of her throat, but I didn't care. We were getting out of this hole just as soon as Mama had picked up her corn syrup or baking soda or whatever the hell else she figured we'd need in the new house. And after I'd said a real goodbye to the town of Whistler—and one resident asshole in particular.

I pointed the cart toward the checkout, riding the thing like a scooter while Mama dipped her head. I knew she wasn't embarrassed to be seen with me, though. Things didn't register with her that way.

The checkout girl was a senior I kinda recognized. When she caught sight of Mama, her eyes became circles, adjusting to Mama's size. I knocked twice on the counter with my knuckles.

"We could use some help bagging, please."

The girl looked me up and down, a spark of recognition lighting up her face as she no doubt thought over every ugly thing she'd heard about me and my family. But then she caught her lower lip between her teeth and smiled at me. An invitation. One I'd normally have considered taking her up on.

This time, I did nothing. Didn't frown or smile or react in any way. I waited until she gave up gnawing on her lip and packed our shit into the plastic grocery bags like I asked, her movements jerky and cross. She didn't look at me at all after that, just took the cash Mama held out to her without a word.

I grabbed the bags as soon as we hit the exit and kicked the empty cart in the direction of the depot. A cart-snaker saw me do it, but he loitered over by the smokers rather than make a big thing out of it. He was just a kid, fourteen at the most, with a ratty mustache growing in patches across his lip. Not the guy I was looking for.

I searched for Tyler's greasy blond head among the smokers. If that asshole had called in sick today, I'd have to leave town without settling up with him. *Dammit.*

Mama tutted and fussed the cart in line with the others, then hurried on ahead to unlock the car.

"Fat bitch."

Tyler's voice came from behind the stack of crates she'd just walked by. The tiny hitch in Mama's step told me she'd heard him, but she didn't turn around. He leaned up against the concrete wall of the store, his neon vest looking like he'd driven over it a couple times before putting it on. Tyler took a drag of the cigarette hanging between his fingers. The muscle in his jaw ticked when he saw me.

I kept walking behind Mama. The weight of the bags kept my fists curled at my sides until I reached the open trunk of the car. It closed with a final-sounding *thunk.*

"You look real pretty today, Mama, you hear?" I held her door open and pretended not to hear her grunt as she got in. "Mama?" She acted like I hadn't spoken. "Oh, hey, I forgot to get a pack of gum for the ride. Sit tight while I run back in and grab some, okay?"

A couple minutes later I was back at the car. I revved the engine and pointed us toward Killdeer. The tires ate up the road like the car was as eager to get the hell out of Whistler as I was.

"You hurt your hand," Mama said after a while.

I looked down at my hands resting against the steering wheel. I'd skinned two of my knuckles raw, pale blue bruises starting to blossom underneath the graze. A dark red patch stained the leather strap of my wristwatch. "Must've caught it on something."

She probably heard the lie for what it was. It didn't matter. Not now.

"Will you wake me when we get there?" she said.

"Yes, ma'am."

She'd already closed her eyes, and didn't open them again for a real long time.

~~~~~~~~~

The sun peaked and faded, and by the time it rose again it didn't hold any real heat. I let the GPS guide me across the state line into Pennsylvania, only stopping when I had to. Maple and aspen trees mingled with cedar and dogwood, spiky shapes like cobwebs hanging from the sunrise.

"One mile to destination."

My palms grew clammy in spite of the cold. I'd thought it would happen when we passed the sign leaving Whistler, with the COME BACK SOON! that wasn't fooling nobody. Mama and I wouldn't be going back there, and I'd barely cast a glance at it as we drove past. I started paying closer attention once we were on the Delaware Expressway, passing exits for Brookhaven, Camden, Mayfair, each exit sign really telling me we were getting closer.

We were almost at the edge of Pennypack Park by the time WELCOME TO KILLDEER flashed by on the roadside. Tasteful lettering against a deep green sign was my first clue that Killdeer was a money town, like it would've been bad form to make the lettering *too* easy to see as you rolled by.

There were so many things about Killdeer I was looking forward to. Basketball. Parties. Friends. Normal stuff, I guess. Maybe I'd even find a girl. A nice girl, not like the ones back home who only wanted to piss off their daddies.

"Mama," I squeezed her shoulder one-handed. I knew she'd been awake for a while. She just didn't want to talk to me. She'd barely said five words the entire trip. "We're almost there now."

She opened her eyes and took in the roads leading us to the new house. There was a mix of old houses and modern houses built to look old, set back against thickset trees like they'd grown up out of the ground right alongside them.

The trees thinned out and became streets, neighborhoods. I crawled along, rolling the window down so I could lean out. The air didn't smell like Whistler air. It smelled of rain, but not our rain. This was clean and heavy and held the threat of snow to come. And it was ours now.

"Right turn ahead."

Mama reached out and snapped the GPS out of its holster, poking at the screen so fast I couldn't see what she was doing.

"Mama, we're not there just yet. I need to see where we're going."

She didn't look at me. She fumbled the GPS back onto the dash like her fingers were shaking. "We're making a stop on the way."

I knew there wasn't any point asking more questions. Instead I followed the directions the GPS gave me, the houses spreading farther apart as we drove, trees stretching up on either side of the road until the sunlight hardly reached the pavement.

"Left turn ahead."

I peered into the gloom. I couldn't see any kind of turn in the road ahead of us.

"Mama, where—"

I didn't get to finish the question. A sharp break in the trees showed great iron gates set back a ways from the road, gold lettering spelling out KILLDEER ACADEMY before they drifted apart to let us drive through. A tiny red dot up high on the gatepost showed me where the camera was hidden, and how someone had known to open the gates.

The driveway was narrow, winding a path that hid whatever kind of place lay waiting for us at the end.

"So this is my new school?"

I knew it was. I'd known the name of it before seeing it spelled out across the iron gates.

"Are we taking a look around before we go to the new house?" I said.

Mama fixed her eyes front as I inched the car along. I didn't break the silence even when we reached the edge of a gravel turnaround.

A clock above the main entrance showed it was nine thirty, though it was actually closer to five. The minute hand of the clock stretched downward, bleeding a murky rust stain over the faded bricks below.

The rest of the building was half smothered in ivy, three floors with raised turrets at each corner, dozens of tall, narrow windows peering out in between like the eyes of some great horned spider. A cloud passed in front of the sun, making the eyes go dark.

"You have reached your destination."

CHAPTER THREE

BURTY SWINGS A HOME RUN

Naomi

The photo had started to curl, so I took it out from under the heat lamp and shook it. I flicked on the lamp by the window, leaning back against the ledge while I inspected it.

Not too shabby.

Just as I'd asked, Kit had framed the shot so only half my body was visible, like I was chilling way up there on the wall of the Academy. After printing, I'd dried it for a couple of hours in kitty litter to make the photo paper brittle, then dried it out some more with a heat lamp. I'd need to leave it on my windowsill to fade for a few days, and then it'd be ready to go into Grandpa's scrapbook.

A light flicked on across the quad. The new guy was back in his room again, pacing like he didn't know what to do with himself.

The new-looking sedan had pulled to a stop in the quad the day before. The windows were tinted so it was impossible to see who was driving until he got out. Even then, all I saw was a tall guy who had to practically hoist a lady out of the passenger side, she was so big.

I could tell they were arguing. She didn't say a word, just stood there while he yelled at her. No, yelled wasn't the right word. He never once raised his voice loud enough for it to carry through my open window. It was the way he stood, with his big arms making jerky, stabbing motions as he talked.

Another surprise drop-off.

After a little while the woman started shouting back, pointy finger all up in his face. It was weird, almost as though they were taking turns at it. Then he said something and the woman snapped. Or slapped, to be more accurate. A real stinger across his face with one of her meaty hands, and he didn't move a muscle. Just took it, like it was what he'd been waiting for.

I wanted to reach out and hug him. Or maybe tell his mother to go to hell.

She got into the car and drove away then, and I noticed he didn't have any bags with him. She hadn't even taken him inside to meet with Principal Kincaid, just ditched him outside like he was nothing.

I would have gone down to rescue him, but the guy turned and stalked away. He was headed either for the main entrance to the Academy or the driveway leading away from it, so I figured he knew where he was going.

The window to his room was on the second floor of South Wing—directly across from mine—which gave me plenty of opportunity to get a look at him. Feeling like a creep, I turned off the lamp so he wouldn't catch me spying.

My phone buzzed in my pocket, and I jumped.

"Hey, Kit. What's up?"

The sound of crunching answered me before he spoke. "What do you make of the new guy?"

Kit's room was next to Fletch's in the southeastern tower—a privilege granted only to those whose parents made a *significant* donation to the Academy's deep pockets—which meant he had a stellar view of pretty much every window facing into the quad.

"Quit watching me, perv."

"Says she who is currently stalking a guy with her light out."

"Touché."

Kit chewed—chips? popcorn?—loudly in my ear.

"So?" he said. "What's the verdict?"

I studied the new guy, who had opened his laptop on his standard-issue study desk before shutting it again. I hadn't seen his mom come back, although she must have dropped off his stuff. He didn't have much, except a stack of books lined up the desk and whatever else he'd packed away in the teensy closet.

He was tall and solid, and packing a lot of muscle under his boring gray shirt. Something about that and the too-neat row of books made me wonder if he'd transferred from a military school.

"He's got to be some kind of jock," I said. "Big guns. No poser outfit, though. And a buzz cut. Army wannabe, probably. What do you think?"

"He could have lice—oh!"

I peered through our new neighbor's window, trying to see what Kit had seen, and thought for a second that the guy had caught me staring. New Neighbor Guy leaned against his windowsill, head tilted forward. But he wasn't looking at me, or up at Kit's window, either. I traced the path of his gaze into the darkness of the quad.

Someone was down there.

My fingers tightened and the photograph crackled, so I placed it carefully on the window ledge while I leaned in for a better look.

I could barely make out the person's shape at first. Whoever it was had tucked themselves into the ivy at the base of the wall right below me. I wouldn't have seen him at all if New Neighbor Guy hadn't angled his own reading lamp to shine in that direction. It cast the faintest trickle of yellow light down in the courtyard.

White guy, hair down to his collar . . .

I wouldn't be telling Principal Kincaid or the cops or anyone else who was out there. But knowing who it was didn't make me any happier about it.

"It's only Jackson. He's taking out the trash or something," I said.

"He needs to watch himself. If Kincaid catches him peeping, she'll fire his ass quicker than blinking," Kit muttered. He was the only one who knew what had happened between me and Jackson, and the way he pitched his words told me Fletcher was within earshot.

But then Kit's volume increased. "Not that anyone would take their eyes off that ass long enough to blink, eh, Fletch? Oh, *now* he's listening. Five seconds ago he was all, 'Shut up, Kit, you handsome bastard, and let me watch this gangster movie I've forced you to sit through a thousand times already.' Honestly, he thinks he's like an actual mob boss. Oh shit, Nai, he's coming for me! I think he's going to give me the kiss of death! Save me, please! Or at least tell my grieving fans that I died a hero . . . " Kit tapered off long enough for the sharp *click* of his bedroom door to carry down the line. "Okay, he's taken the laptop back to his room. Are you all right?"

"I'm fine, Kit. And you didn't need to chase Fletch away like that."

"Only saving you from weeks of interrogation," Kit said, and I nodded, then felt ridiculous for nodding into a phone. "Seriously, though, do you want me to go tell someone about Jackson being a dick? I wouldn't even need to mention your name, I could just tell Kincaid he's hanging around outside the dorms. Stranger-dangering and shit."

Principal Kincaid was a hardass when it came to anything that would threaten the Academy's income, and complaints about the new custodian spying on students would definitely qualify as a threat.

"I dunno," I said. As much as it bugged me that Jackson wouldn't take the hint that I wasn't interested, I didn't want him to get fired. "Maybe I should just get one of the proctors to go down there and talk to him, maybe just *say* they'll get the principal involved. He might be more worried if there was any chance Kincaid would catch him."

When she'd started at Killdeer Academy the previous year, Principal Kincaid had moved into one of the old staff cottages at the edge of the campus instead of living in the main building like the previous principal had. It wasn't like she'd walk by and see him lurking down there.

I hung up the phone—more to give myself the illusion of privacy than because it would hamper Kit's spying in any way—and opened my bedroom window. I grazed my fingertips over the old indentations in the brick where the bars had been back in the asylum days. Until the 1940s, Killdeer Academy was home to a hundred or so crazy kids—crazier even than the ones living here now—when one of them set fire to South Wing, killing everyone in there. After that, there hadn't been enough crazy kids to keep the place open, so they'd rebuilt South Wing and turned it into a private school. There really wasn't a whole lot of difference, when you thought about it.

Even my grandparents weren't old enough to remember the fire, but I felt like I did. I'd imagined it so many times, peering across the quad to where the kids had been trapped. I'd seen violence, knew the scars it gave you. The thought of being burned held a whole new level of terror, though. As much as I tried to make myself believe otherwise, there were still things to be afraid of out there. Surviving one monster didn't make me immune to all the rest.

"Jackson," I hissed. Principal Kincaid might not be within hearing distance, but the night staff were. "What are you doing down there?"

He stepped out of the shadows, staggering before he came to a wobbly stop. He'd either been drinking or he was high. Maybe both. *Yay.*

"Naomi! Why won't you . . . why won't you talk to me no more?"

Something fell from his hand and hit the cobbled courtyard with a clatter. Drunk, then.

"Jackson, go away! Stop bugging me, for God's sake."

Five times in the past month he'd done this—five times since I'd explained why us dating was a bad idea. Jackson had been working at the movie theater in town when I met him over the summer, but dating him now that he worked at my school didn't feel right, especially when I could feel Gram's eyes on me all the time.

Jackson disagreed. His late-night visits started out sort of sweet, I guess. The first time, he'd laid out a bunch of Christmas decorations on the cobblestones so they spelled out my name. It'd been pretty funny when he had to grab it all together and get the heck out of there when one of the proctors shone a flashlight down at him. The next time Jackson brought flowers, but he'd ended up tossing them one by one at my window when I refused to go down to talk to him. It'd gone downhill from there.

I reached out to pull the window closed, and the photo fluttered merrily through the gap and landed at Jackson's feet. He reached down and picked it up. I saw his look of triumph even in the dim light.

"You'll have to come and talk to me if you want your photo back!"

I fought the urge to throw something bigger and sharper down at Jackson. It had taken me hours to get the right finish for the scrapbook, and I didn't want to do it all again.

"Fine. Gimme two minutes." I leaned back from the window, then ducked my head out again. "And don't crease it!"

I'd have to creep out past the proctor. Casey was on evening duty, which was good. Like me, she was at the Academy because her mom, Anna, was on the staff, and actually worked with Gram in the kitchens. I think that's why she'd always been nice to me—some kind of underprivileged-solidarity thing.

I slipped on my sneaks and cracked open the bedroom door. There was a glow seeping out from under the door to the proctor's room, although that didn't necessarily mean Casey was in there. I waited thirty seconds, listening for sounds of water boiling or a toilet flushing. There was only the general murmuring of late-night life from the other girls' rooms along the hall.

The door leading out onto the fire escape was almost directly opposite my bedroom, but I didn't dare use it because of the alarm. I lemur-skipped as quietly as possible down the hallway, freezing in Ginny Ogden's doorway when I heard a sound, then continued all the way to the back stairway.

The proctor's door swung open, and I lemured straight into Casey on her way out.

"Naomi!" she squeaked.

"Hey, Case. How's it going?"

Casual, act superdefinitely casual.

"Someone's screwing around on the roof again. Probably up there smoking or something. This is the third time this week." Her eyes drifted to the ceiling, as though she might see the perp right through the drywall. "How come you're not in your room?"

"I knocked a page of my English assignment out of the window." I gave her a cheerful *duh* face. "Mind if I go downstairs and grab it real quick?"

She yawned, her eyes tracing upward again. "Fine. I'd better go deal with whoever's up there. But come straight back—you know the rules."

Nobody was allowed to leave their wing after dark. Getting caught meant you risked being expelled, and I couldn't do that to my grandparents. They'd worked at the Academy their whole lives, Grandpa overseeing the stables back when there'd been horses and Gram still in charge of the kitchens. They lived in a staff cottage near Principal Kincaid's, and it would kill them if their only granddaughter got kicked out of their beloved Academy.

"I'll be right back," I said.

Casey held my wrist for a second. "Hey, if you see Fletcher, could you tell him I'm running low? I know he said he couldn't help me out last time, but he'll have more by now, right?" She looked shiftily up and down the corridor, but there was no need. We were alone.

"Sure," I said, even though she didn't look like she was running low. Her eyes were bloodshot, and I could smell weed smoke on her breath. "I'll ask him to hook you up."

I ran down the back stairs and out into the quad. I'd expected Jackson to be waiting underneath my window, but he wasn't there. South Wing's staff door stood open, and in the glow I saw my new neighbor hugging Jackson up against the wall.

No, not hugging him. He had Jackson by the throat. The new guy's other arm hung down at his side, like he was being very casual about throttling the guy. Or holding something in his other hand, maybe.

I picked my way carefully over the cobblestones, but the guy met my eye, just for a second.

Eyes full of secrets.

He turned his attention back to Jackson, saying something so low I only caught a part of it.

" . . . knock you so hard . . . tomorrow today. Got it?"

I wasn't sure whether I should intervene, until Jackson nodded awkwardly against the guy's hold and was released. Jackson staggered away a few feet before pausing long enough to hurl a few curses.

"Jackson, give me my photo back," I said.

He'd obviously forgotten I was there. He crumpled the photo up in his fist and tossed it at my feet.

"Here, take it."

I stooped to pick it up, hoping the redness in my face wasn't visible in the dim light. When I looked up again, Jackson was gone. It was only the new guy and me, unless you counted the baseball bat hanging loosely from his hand.

"Kind of hard to see the ball at night," I said. I couldn't see his face, but I could feel him staring at me. The tension still ran under the skin of his forearms, curling his fingers into fists. But somehow it didn't feel threatening, like it wasn't meant for me. From the way he hadn't even bothered to glance after Jackson, it wasn't really meant for him, either. "You know, if you were planning on playing baseball."

He made a sound that might have been a laugh or a cough. "Thanks for the tip." His voice was deep, and there was something very controlled about it. There was definitely some kind of accent there. "D'ya know that guy?"

"Jackson's one of the custodians here. Don't worry, he's not going to say anything to Principal Kincaid. He's new, but he knows he's not meant to be anywhere near the dorms at night. We shouldn't be out here, either, really. Do you always rush out to tackle strange guys lurking outside?"

He seemed to study me then.

"More often than I'd like," he said finally.

I opened my mouth, but the words stalled as he turned and disappeared into South Wing. The door closed with a click behind him.

"Welcome to the Academy," I said to the empty quad.

CHAPTER FOUR

BURTY'S NEW BLAZER

Kyle

I'd been fighting the urge to call Uncle Coby ever since Mama left me standing like an idiot outside the school block. Mama would definitely have had his help getting me into Killdeer Academy, so he had to have known I was going to be boarding here, but he hadn't said a damn thing to me about it.

I didn't think he'd have told Mama to toss me outside the school like a bag of hot trash, though. It wasn't Uncle Coby's style, but I couldn't see Mama coming up with the idea on her own, either. She'd never liked being alone, and now she was in a new town where she didn't know anybody.

I'd said some ugly things to her before she took off. It didn't take me long to cool off and see that leaving me at Killdeer Academy was probably the best thing she could do for me—even if I didn't like the way she'd gone about it. But it was too late by then.

I tried to look friendly as I followed a group of kids in red blazers around the side of the building to the front entrance of the school, my own blazer stiff and tight across the shoulders. When I'd first arrived, there'd been nobody at the reception desk and I didn't know what to do until some girl called Casey wandered by and gave me sad eyes. She must've got someone to call Mama, seeing as my bags showed up a couple hours later—not that I saw Mama at all. She probably just slowed the car to a roll and pitched them out the window.

Casey told me I'd need to report to the principal first thing on Monday morning, so after asking one of the red blazers to point me in the right direction, I wound my way through the old building up to Principal Kincaid's office. I knocked, and a voice shouted at me to wait.

A strong smell of perfume hit me when the door finally opened. Principal Kincaid was a well put-together lady: smooth, dark skin and hair slicked up in a twisty thing, her clothes so crisp I expected her to crackle when she moved. She waved me in and shut the door, staring at me for a strong minute before she spoke.

"Welcome to Killdeer Academy, Kyle. Now, first things first: a few ground rules . . . "

I tuned out what I knew would be the same old lecture and looked around the office. The walls were mostly hidden by shelves full of old-looking leather books, doing nothing more useful than soundproofing the room. On the patches of wall around them, the paint was peeling away from the plaster like dead skin.

It didn't sit right next to the lady in front of me.

" . . . see you changed your name recently. Lots of redaction in your transcripts, most unusual. Your mother told me about your father passing last year—condolences—I assume that had something to do with it?"

She looked at me expectantly.

I almost choked. "Uh, yes, ma'am. That's right."

Principal Kincaid kept right on looking at me, but I wasn't about to volunteer any more than what she already knew.

"There were a number of incidents at your last school, Kyle. Unpleasantness. I trust that is all behind you now."

"Yes, ma'am."

"Good." Her smile was no more than a showing of teeth. "Your uncle has been extremely generous with your tuition, Kyle. That isn't something the Academy overlooks."

And can't afford to lose. I brushed a stray paint chip off my sleeve and scratched my new signature onto the forms the principal shoved at me—some kind of "honor agreement" for all seniors at the Academy.

"You are not to leave campus without a permission slip, even on weekends. You are representing the Academy whether you're on our campus or not, and must behave appropriately. Good manners and a positive attitude aren't optional. No piercings, tattoos, or dyed hair allowed," she said. "Although I suppose hair dye is not really an issue for you, is it?"

I shook my head, and she followed the movement over the rims of her glasses. Then her eyes fixed on something else. "You will need to find a new blazer, Mr. Henry. That one appears to be the wrong size for you."

I followed Principal Kincaid's glare to the ugly seams at my shoulders. Mama had ordered it a couple months before we moved out to Killdeer, and I'd added an inch or two across the shoulders since then. It figured, since I'd hardly left my weight bench in the garage all that time.

The principal didn't escort me to homeroom, thank God. She gave me a map of the entire school, with each room color-coded. I'd have to wait until last period to experience the brown room, whatever that was.

Homeroom was coded yellow on the map, and after getting turned around more times than I cared to admit, I found the door marked G16 and knocked on it. The door flew open.

"Ah, Kyle Henry!"

Every pair of eyes in the room turned toward me. I cleared my throat, looking for an open seat.

"Everyone, this is Kyle Henry! He's just transferred here! Kyle, won't you tell everyone something about yourself!"

I guessed from all the hollering that my homeroom teacher was excited to see me.

"Uh, yes, sir. Well, hey, I'm Kyle . . . Kyle Henry." I'd almost slipped and used my real last name. "Moved here from North Carolina this past weekend." I wasn't going to be more specific than I had to be. I didn't need anybody digging around online to see what dirt they could find on the new kid.

The teacher made a go on gesture.

"I play basketball. Used to be on the team in my old school, so I'll be trying out here," I said.

This was not entirely true. Even though I played well enough, I'd been on permanent bench duty at West Whistler High because nobody on the team wanted me on the court. Coach Davis just couldn't bring himself to kick me off the team.

"You play baseball, too, right?"

I'd been taking a long look at my shoes, but jerked my head up at that.

Huge dark eyes peered out from under a short crop of black hair, and the sleeves of her school blazer were rolled up to her elbows. I hadn't gotten a good look at her from across the courtyard last night, but it was definitely the same girl. And then under the stark striplight of homeroom, I felt like I'd been sucker punched.

I recognized her.

I could see she was waiting on an answer, so I nodded, with no idea what I was agreeing to.

"This seat's free if you want to take it," she said. Her hand flashed to one side before she tucked it away under the desk again.

"Yes, Kyle, why don't you take a seat and we'll continue with roll call?" the teacher said behind me.

The only other free seat was right in front of some guy who had already sneezed open-mouthed twice while I'd been standing there. So I sat down next to the girl.

"Hi, I'm Naomi Steadman. I thought I heard an accent last night—I used to live in North Carolina, too. Just outside Asheville."

Naomi Steadman.

I felt all my insides shrivel up.

Oh hell no.

It couldn't be her.

Except she had the same eyes. The same name. From the same place. And she was the right age.

It's her.

These two words screamed over and over inside my skull, telling me to get the hell out of Killdeer Academy.

Article from Whistler Tribune, June 20, 2014

BONEBREAKER STILL AT LARGE?
New evidence suggests man on death row may be innocent

Robert Kyle Bluchevsky awaits his execution on death row in Durham, North Carolina, convicted of what have been described as "the most brutal serial killings in US history"—a string of murders in the Asheville area almost nine years ago. Six women were beaten to death in their own homes, leading to the killer being dubbed "the Bonebreaker" due to his use of brass knuckles, baseball bats, and other blunt objects to bludgeon the victims beyond recognition.

FBI agents reviewing the case files yesterday revealed conflicting evidence, largely overlooked in the original trial.

Bluchevsky's wife had suffered minor brain damage as a result of a car accident three years prior to Bluchevsky's arrest, and the prosecution claimed that tending to his wife's medical care was a critical factor in triggering the Bonebreaker's killing spree. This was contrary to the initial profile, which stated that the killer would be in his early twenties, with a history of violent crime. Bluchevsky was 39 when police arrested him, married with a young son, and co-owner of the Asheville-based Big Blue Excavating Company. Prior to his arrest, Bluchevsky had never had so much as a speeding ticket.

New evidence submitted to the court also includes previously undisclosed security footage from a property near the residence of the final victim, Annabel Steadman, showing a man much shorter than Bluchevsky's 6 feet 6 inches fleeing the scene. . . .

CHAPTER FIVE

BURTY TAP-DANCES ACROSS THE COBBLES

Naomi

Kyle's face changed the second I spoke to him. He mouthed something that probably wasn't *whole leaf hug*, and didn't say another word after that. Didn't even look at me, which was kind of rude after I saved him from Viral Pete three rows over.

Had he recognized my name? Steadman was a common enough last name even in North Carolina, and he'd only have been six or seven when my mom was killed, so I couldn't see why that would freak him out.

Maybe Kyle was worried I'd be mad or upset about what had happened with Jackson. Maybe he thought I'd rat him out to Kincaid once I'd slept on it. Maybe Kyle was, after all, a douche.

The *maybes* bugged me all morning, but there was no way for me to find out which was the right one as I didn't see him again until lunchtime.

The tables in the cafeteria at the Academy weren't arranged in military rows. Principal Kincaid had made a bunch of changes when she was first put in charge, like making the cafeteria "less regimented." This involved offsetting every other table by three feet so that you had to walk in a zigzag to get from one side of the room to the other.

She didn't bother changing stuff around like that anymore.

I'd already taken my usual seat next to Kit on the safe side of our table when Kyle Henry walked into the room. His head turned slowly, taking everything in. Then with the same determined look he'd worn while avoiding looking at me in homeroom, he began to zigzag.

Addison headed back to our table, face scrunched in a way that said she'd failed to find anything at the lunch counter she could eat. Most people assumed she was a calorie-counter type, but that wasn't it. I knew from the few times I'd been to Addy's house what mealtimes were like with her mom and older sister.

"You're so funny, Addy, the way you hold your sandwich—just like a little chipmunk, isn't she, Mom?"

"Jesus, Addy, could you make more gross noises while you eat that pudding?"

"Oh, Addy! You've got sauce all over you! Honestly, it's like having a toddler at home again."

The weird thing was, Addy snarked right back at them like their comments didn't faze her at all—until you saw her eating in public.

She never mentioned it, but I could almost hear what she was thinking: *An apple might leave gross stuff in my teeth. I'm wearing a white shirt so I can't have pasta. I'll look stupid eating that.*

I caught her eye and held my breath, but she looked away a heartbeat later. Things hadn't been right between us since the end of summer, but I'd just have to wait it out if we were going to get back to being friends.

A kid pushed his chair out, getting up to take his leftovers to the trash—right into Addy's path. Her mouth rounded into an O as she tripped over the chair, arms flying up and to the sides like she was cliff-diving.

The new guy caught her before she'd even had a chance to squeak, as though it was some old-school swing-dance move they'd rehearsed. Addison disengaged without saying a word to the guy, and continued to our table like nothing had happened, black ponytail swinging behind her.

Kyle Henry's blazer hung by the seams on both shoulders, like he'd *Bruce Banner*-ed right out of his uniform. He looked down at the damage, paused, then shrugged out of the blazer right in the middle of the cafeteria.

"How *embarrassing*," Addison said, shoving my tray back over to my side of the table and sending an apple rolling into my lap. "And who was that guy who had his hands all over me?"

Kyle Henry seemed oblivious to all the stares he was getting. He ditched his doubly amputated blazer in the trash and joined the lunch line, not bothering to pick up a tray.

"He could be hot . . . in a totally *thug* sort of way," Addison said as she sized him up. "He needs to grow some hair, though. Bonehead isn't a good look for anybody."

She tossed her hair, looking just like her sister for that moment. It was a very obvious kind of move, one that exposed the long curve of her neck and pushed out her boobs. The Addison Effect rippled outward across the cafeteria. Chewing slowed to a stop, then a hard swallow. Chatter dimmed to simmering silence. It only lasted a few seconds—just long enough for whatever the guys and girls staring at her were imagining to draw to a natural end—and they went back to their chewing and laughing, and generally forgot about her completely. The Addison Effect was a spark, quick and sharp and then gone.

I checked to see if Kyle had noticed, but he was staring at the sandwich display.

Kit prodded my knee under the table as he pointed his fork at Addy. "He actually looks really pissed about you dive-bombing him," he said. "There's a big smear of your lipstick on his shirt."

Addy bristled, but the smirk was soon back. "I bet he'll be keeping that shirt and sniffing it when he . . . "

Addison shut up as Fletcher sat down next to her. "When he what?" he said.

"Nothing, Fletch."

Fletcher tilted his head to one side while he looked at me, his version of a wink. I started picking at my salad again. This had somehow become *my* conspiracy. Maybe Fletch had seen something written on my stupid face.

"We'd make such a cute couple," Addy said. "Maybe his hair will have grown enough by Thanksgiving for me to take him home to meet my folks."

My folks. That was what she called her mom and her mom's new husband, Paolo. She couldn't call them *Mom and Paolo*, because then everyone would figure out that the *Paolo* she'd been in love with all last year—the older guy she'd been "seeing" and telling us all the most detailed stories about—was her stepfather. And that none of those stories were true.

I stabbed my fork into a tomato, splattering dressing onto the table.

"We'd look great together. Perfect," Addy said, to nobody in particular.

I could almost see the image she was conjuring inside her head—Addy and Kyle wearing coordinating sweaters while they walked their matching purse dogs, laughing and kicking up piles of fallen leaves for the dogs to play in. The things she'd liked to do with her last imaginary boyfriend, but which would actually bore the crap out of her within thirty seconds in reality.

Kyle yanked his tie loose and stomped across the cafeteria with a sandwich in his fist, looking like he'd rather hurl the tables out of the way than zigzag. I pretended to cough to hide my laugh. There was no way he'd have a purse dog.

"What do you think, Fletch?" Addy batted her eyelashes. "Can I keep him?"

Fletcher didn't look at Addison or Kyle, and instead focused on the pasta bowl in front of him. "I'll invite him over on Friday, check him out. Make sure he's the kind of guy we want to have around." I didn't miss his glance in my direction at that last part.

Addy squealed like she'd won a prize. If Fletcher was thinking of asking Kyle to his party on Friday night, there had to be something about Kyle that had caught Fletcher's attention. But what?

Fletch had had a freaky upbringing. His mom had been a soap-star-turned-cult-follower for a while, and Fletch was there when it all got shot to pieces—literally—when he was six. The FBI stormed the place after the cult leader caught wind of their investigation, and there'd been an hours-long shootout that had ended with a body count of eighteen. Fletch was caught in the middle of it, had seen things no little kid should ever see, and barely got out of there with his mom.

We'd met sitting outside the nurse's office in the Academy, where the visiting therapist saw us both every week. Fletch stopped talking for a couple months after the shooting, but I just assumed he was shy, and jabber-jabber-jabbered at him until he finally gave me one of his ground-leveling looks and said, "Don't you ever shut up?"

We'd been tight ever since. He'd been the one person I even tried to talk to about Mom, but stopped when I realized it wasn't getting any easier. Some wounds fester if you leave them alone, but that doesn't mean they'll get better if you pick at them. Fletcher understood that. Our circle of friends was glued together by our secrets, and it was Fletcher who kept that circle airtight.

Kyle walked right past our table and out of the cafeteria.

"Think I'll go grab a few minutes on the court," Kit said, scruffing up my hair as he left.

"I'm heading out, too," I said. I'd already grabbed my bag and was on my feet.

"Working on your scrapbook?" Fletcher asked.

"Yeah," I said, glad of the excuse to get out of there. "I've got a free period after lunch. I'll catch up with you guys later."

CHAPTER SIX

BURTY'S BIG MATCH

Kyle

I knew I looked like a loser, leaning up against some random car and stuffing the dry sandwich into my mouth. It'd been so suffocating in there, though, surrounded by red blazers and everyone whispering about me, that I'd just had to get out.

Naomi Steadman walked out of the cafeteria behind me, and I ducked out of sight. She had her bag slung over her shoulder, sunglasses propped on her head even though it looked like rain was coming.

Walking in the opposite direction, I skirted around the corner of the school until I couldn't see her anymore. I hunched into my shirt, following a path that curved around the flower beds and between the school and a fenced-off section of the campus. Beyond the tall mesh sides, I found what I hadn't even consciously been looking for: a basketball court.

The court was empty except for one guy shooting hoops by himself. He was about my height, and skinny, like he'd been stretched too far. I couldn't see his face, but he had shaggy hair like mine had been before I buzzed it so I wouldn't look so much like Dad. It hadn't worked as well as I'd hoped, but at least the bristly feel of it was kinda nice. I wished I'd thought to bring a damn hat out with me, though.

The guy was shooting one after another, and he sank nine in a row before he missed a basket. Then he looked around.

"You weren't meant to see that," he said.

"Nine in a row's pretty good."

He offered me the ball and I dropped my bag by the fence, jogged over, and took it from him.

"Niiiiiice," the guy said when my first shot sailed into the basket. He picked up the ball and threw it back to me. I nailed another three. "I should've known."

I deliberately missed the next one. This wasn't West Whistler High. I was new here, and I didn't need to play the asshole card.

"I'm Christopher, by the way," he said. "But nobody will know who you're talking about unless you call me Kit. That, or *that handsome bastard with the mad basketball skills.*"

He would've seemed cocky if he hadn't been so damn good-humored about it.

"Kyle Henry. Just moved here," I said.

Kit shook his head before fetching the ball from where it'd rolled behind the post. "Yeah, I guessed that. I hear you're the new guy who moved here from NC."

"Wasn't expecting to find myself at some fancy-ass boarding school, though." I quietly cussed myself out. "Sorry. I didn't mean that the way it sounded."

Kit shrugged, but it felt like he'd heard more than I wanted to share.

"There are worse places you could end up," he said. "Like Gilchrist Academy—the seniors there all wear cravats, for God's sake. And they make transfer students sign up for like a whole year of glee club. I mean, can you imagine anything worse?"

"No. No, I cannot."

I stepped aside so he could claim back his spot, but Kit tossed the ball to me again and said, "For real this time."

I sank ten in a row before he stopped me.

"Please tell me you're not this good at everything," Kit said.

"I'm not this good at everything."

"You an A student?"

"Nope."

"Have girls throwing themselves at your feet?"

I snorted before I could stop myself.

"Then I guess I don't need to hate you."

~~~~~~~~~~

I'd never had to share a bathroom before, and I found I hated the clamor of naked guys sliding around me in the mornings. That's why I was up at the butt crack of dawn—so that would be the *only* butt crack I'd be faced with.

I leaned over the basin and splashed water on my face. Although I was used to much warmer nights back home, I'd spent a restless night sweating up my sheets, trying not to think about *her*.

I didn't even notice the guy standing behind me until I heard a shuffle of feet. Movement flickered in the mirror above the washbasin, a flash of dark hair and coveralls with the Academy logo stitched onto them. It was that custodian guy who'd been creeping around outside my window Sunday night. Jackson, she'd called him.

I didn't like the look of him. Too slick, with greased-up black hair you could smell from clear across the room.

"How's the hangover treating you?" I said, turning around so he wouldn't catch me off-balance.

He stepped back a couple inches. I knew what people saw when they looked at me. The buzz cut, hard eyes like my old man's, a scar running up through my eyebrow from when someone had thrown half a brick through the front window of our old house.

"Who do you think you're talking to, you little prick?" he said.

Jackson's fist smashed into the corner of my mouth. Pain shot deep into my eye socket when my head hit the hard tile above the basin. I threw myself at him, using my whole weight to pin him down on the floor for a strong minute while I waited for my head to stop screaming. He wasn't as winded as I'd hoped, and he had his arm pulled back ready to take another swing before I could blink. I reared back. The hit glanced off my shoulder, and I slammed my head down onto the asshole's face.

There was a crunch—this time not inside my skull, praise Jesus—and Jackson groaned and choked on the blood gushing out of his busted nose. I groaned, too.

"What the hell is going on?"

There were two guys leaning in the doorway. The one nearest me looked so serious I'd have sworn he was a teacher if he wasn't wearing a red blazer. Kit—the kid from the basketball court—stood next to him, hands in his pockets and his legs sort of crossed, so relaxed it was easier to imagine him lazing on a raft than calling time on a fight in a school bathroom.

I rolled off Jackson and got to my feet, trying to ignore the way the room tipped and swayed.

"Oh God, the blood," the guy said to Kit, swallowing hard as I went by. Kit said something, reaching for my shoulder, but I shrugged him off, staggering a little as I headed out the door. I had to keep my feet moving, one in front of the other. I kept going until I reached my room, locked the door, and passed out cold.

CHAPTER SEVEN

BURTY PEERS THROUGH THE BROKEN WINDOW

Naomi

It had taken a while to get the process right, but I was now pretty good at conning Grandpa into believing the photos were real. I shook the kitty litter off my reprinted photo and set it under the heat lamp. I had to wait an hour for the new print to be ready, so I grabbed the scrapbook to go sit with Grandpa until it was done.

When I reached the cottage, he was sitting on the back porch with a blanket tucked firmly over his legs and another around his shoulders. There was a cup of coffee on the side table next to him. It looked like he'd forgotten about it, and a fly had kamikazed its way in there. Grandpa didn't care. He was too busy staring across the fields at the back of the campus. There were no horses there now, not like when he'd been the stable manager. Now it was all long grass, the wind trailing through it like invisible fingers.

"What are you thinking about, Grandpa?"

He looked up. His pearly false teeth stood out against his yellowed skin, too big, like they were trying to escape. "Oh, I didn't hear you come up. That Jake kid came by again earlier. He's been calling here an awful lot lately."

"Jake?" I said gently. Pushing didn't help Grandpa's sketchy memory. "Are you talking about Crazy Jake from the ghost story?"

"You know who Jake is." He shook his head like I was being an idiot. "He's bad news, Burty."

"It's Naomi, Grandpa. Remember?" I tried not to hope this time would be different. I always tried. "Burt is *your* name."

Grandpa looked at me strangely. The dementia was a tendril in his brain, reaching out and warping his mind until he didn't know he was looking at his granddaughter, didn't understand how insane it was he was talking to himself as a teenager. Or maybe he didn't even know who he was anymore, and was only a nameless observer in his own life.

He'd first called me Burty after I cut my hair short. I'd done it to stop Grandpa sliding into calling me Annabel—my mom's name. Changing the way I dressed and taking off the old silver sunflower necklace of my mom's that I'd always worn hadn't worked. I hadn't even missed my hair, just cut it off, gone, there you go. Except then he started calling me Burty as a joke when Gram commented on the resemblance, and it'd stopped being a joke after a while. The tendril had caught hold and twisted, until Naomi no longer existed for him. I'd been erased.

Being Burty was better than being nothing.

Grandpa's face started to slacken.

"I brought the scrapbook down. I thought we could look at it together."

I scooted my chair closer to his, ignoring how he looked at the book like he'd never seen it before. It was dog-eared by now, the blue cover faded.

"Well, look at you, you handsome devil," Grandpa said, sounding weirdly like Kit as he pointed at a photo of me wearing a mortarboard I'd borrowed from a senior the year before. It was almost identical to a photo he'd had in one of his original scrapbooks—except that I was in this one, and not Grandpa.

Grandpa had spent hours showing his scrapbooks to me, each photo accompanied by a few notes in his looping handwriting.

Burty goes ape at the zoo. . . .

Burty takes to the skies. . . .

Burty gets old and forgets the person he used to be.

It was only after I'd been living with them for a while and Grandpa's memory started to fritz that the specialist suggested we show him old photos to try and refire whatever synapses had crapped out. When I'd gone down to the basement with Gram to haul the scrapbooks upstairs, we'd found a box full of soggy paper. A leaky pipe in the old house had gone to town on the scrapbooks, warping the photographs and regluing them wrong-side-up to the pages. Grandpa's handwritten captions had all smudged and faded, the paper dotted with mold like canker sores.

There'd been nothing left to show Grandpa from before all the bad stuff happened. But I thought maybe if I recreated some of it, brought his memories back to life—I might get my grandpa back. Even if it was only for a little while.

He turned the page with his papery-skinned fingers. The next photo showed me covered head-to-toe in mud. Beneath it, I was wearing a borrowed jersey, a football cradled under one arm.

"Tri-county play-offs. We slaughtered the Red Creek Hawks that year," I said.

The next picture showed me dressed in Grandpa's old military fatigues, sitting in the cockpit of a jet. Or actually the pilot's seat of Fletcher's dad's helicopter that time he'd landed in the field behind the Academy.

"When was this, did you say, Burty?" he asked, and I sucked my front teeth.

"Right before we shipped out in '68." I knew my lines.

Grandpa smiled.

"How about this one?"

It hadn't started out this way. In the beginning, he'd recognized me in the photos. We'd laughed about it, and the pictures were enough to jog his memory. *Naomi standing on the back of Jackson's motorcycle* was close enough to *Burty standing on his friend's crappy Vespa* to make the gears slide into place. But then the occasional *Burty* had slipped out, and I'd seen him grow more and more confused.

We flipped through the scrapbook until he got tired and even my made-up stories couldn't hold Grandpa's fuzzy mind any longer. When he went back to staring out across the fields, I slid the scrapbook from his hands and kissed him on the forehead.

"You go on inside before it gets too cold out here, okay? I'll be back to see you and Gram tomorrow."

I was about to turn for the steps when his fingers fastened around my wrist, hard like a claw.

"Grandpa, what is it?"

"Jake was here. Did I say that already?" His eyes were clearer than I'd seen them in months. "There's badness in that one, running through him like a wick."

Grandpa let go of my arm and sank back into his chair, once again mesmerized by the swaying grass.

"Crazy Jake isn't real, Grandpa. It's just a story."

He didn't respond. I tucked the book under my arm and watched my feet until I rounded the corner of the house.

Sunlight glinted off the upstairs window at the front of the cottage. That had been my window before Grandpa got really bad and started wandering the house at night, yelling at people who weren't there.

The house was my own scrapbook, with the photos on the walls, the crocheted throws Gram had draped over anything that didn't walk away fast enough, and the woodsy smell that always clung to Grandpa's cable-knit sweaters.

But it didn't feel like mine anymore. It'd only taken a few weeks of living at the Academy for the cottage to stop feeling like home, a faded copy of a life that wasn't mine anymore.

Gram was right: it was easier.

Transcript of 911 call made by Naomi Steadman, age 7

Operator: 9–1-1, what is your emergency?

NS: Someone hurt my mom.

Operator: Are you at home?

NS: Yes. Someone broke in and they hurt her.

Operator: I have your address, and I'm sending someone over to you right now. Stay on the line, okay, sweetie?

NS: Okay. But my mom . . . [crying]

Operator: What is your name?

NS: Naomi.

Operator: Hi, Naomi, I'm Margie. I need you to tell me, is the person who hurt your mom still there?

NS: No. They went away. I went back inside the house. I didn't mean to leave her by herself but I got scared and he told me to run.

Operator: That's okay, sweetie. Is your mom awake?

NS: No. I don't think so. But her eyes are open.

Operator: Can you tell me if she's breathing? Is her chest moving even a little?

NS: I'm going to check. [Pause] No. They hurt her real bad.

Operator: Did they hurt you, too, sweetie?

NS: He squeezed my neck, but then he said . . . he told me to run and I runned away. [Crying]

Operator: It's all right, sweetie. Someone should be with you in just a few minutes. Stay on the line with me, okay?

NS: Okay.

CHAPTER EIGHT

Kyle

The hallways of Killdeer Academy echoed even when they were packed with bodies. There were only a few hundred students at the Academy, but the blazers made even a dozen of them—us— look legion.

A recessed shelf sat up high on every wall, and every now and then a stuffed bird appeared on it as I passed. A goshawk, a white-tailed kite, a couple peregrine falcon chicks. They were sentries staring down with their dead eyes. There'd been one in the principal's office, I was pretty sure. Ugly, creepy things, with no life about them. They reminded me of the screech owl on top of the fireplace back home, with the tiny mouse caught in its claws—the one Mama wouldn't throw out because it reminded her of *him*, when that was the exact same reason I wanted it gone.

"There's always eyes on you, boy." Those words would usually come right before a rough night in our house, his temper a slow burn I was smart enough to back away from before it ratcheted

all the way up to crazy. But Mama didn't have any sense for trouble, least not when it came to him, so when she kept on fussing around my father like she did, not seeing that badness building in his eyes, I couldn't run and hide. There was nothing I could do back then to keep him away from my mama except take his rage on me instead.

The mouse's black-eyed gaze had never flinched, never blinked, not even after—when the newscaster was telling me all about how my daddy was the monster everybody called the Bonebreaker. I sat next to Uncle Coby on the couch that afternoon, his big arm over my shoulders, the smell of Dad's cigarettes hanging thick in the air like he was still there, sitting in that high-backed chair of his and watching the news with us. I was determined I wasn't going to cry it out like a little wuss. I kept my eyes fixed tight on that mouse, and I never flinched, never blinked, while my life fell apart.

"Coming through!"

A scrawny kid ran past as I climbed the staircase into one of the towers, his voice way too loud. Or maybe I was still punch-drunk from getting my head slammed in the bathroom the day before.

A wide wooden door stood open on the third landing, waiting to swallow us all. Even though I'd all but run out of homeroom ahead of her, I still scanned the faces for Naomi.

I churned it over and over in my head: Did Mama know Naomi Steadman was here? What did it mean that we'd moved here, of all places? How was I meant to act now, with an ugly lie hanging over me like a cloud of locusts?

I found my way to an empty desk, and exchanged a nod and a shrug with the guy one seat over.

(Nod) Anyone sitting here?

(Shrug) Nope, go ahead.

Even that short, silent exchange was better than what I'd gotten used to back home, and I was fine with leaving it there.

I'd seen some of the girls looking at me in Killdeer Academy, the way that checkout girl in Whistler had looked at me before she caught on to who I was. Maybe I could be that guy—the one girls would scribble notes to in the backs of their textbooks and get all shy around when I walked by?

Naw. I didn't have the face to be *that* guy. Mine was the face of someone you might wave off to war with a tear in your eye, but probably wouldn't lend your car to.

Kit stretched out at his desk next to mine. He zeroed in on the bruise upside my head.

"That looks painful," he said.

The teacher up front was some wrinkled old guy with half-circle glasses he probably thought made him stand out from the rest of the gray heads in the faculty lounge. He looked over at us and cleared his throat.

"Pay attention, Kit," the teacher said. Kit straightened up in his seat the tiniest little bit, and the teacher turned back to his chalkboard. He was using actual chalk.

A guy on Kit's other side was leaning forward to stare at me. He had deep-set eyes that looked a little too hard, and tight afro hair cut so close it was nearly as short as mine.

"I'm Fletcher," he said. He was the other guy from the bathroom, the one I'd stumbled past after messing up Jackson's face. "How are you finding Killdeer Academy? Head injuries aside."

"All right, I guess."

He was still staring at me, and it was getting to the point where I hoped the teacher would turn around again and cut me a break. "Why were you fighting with the custodian?"

"It was nothing," I said. "I don't know what his problem is, all right?"

"We're not trying to give you a hard time," Kit whispered so that the teacher wouldn't hear him. "Just checking you're okay."

"I'm fine," I said from between my teeth. "I can handle it."

Fletcher somehow loomed closer than Kit, even though he was sitting farther away. My head swam, and I closed my eyes. The clash with the bathroom tiles had done a number on my skull all right.

"I'm sure you can. It didn't look like that was the first time someone's taken a swing at you." When I opened my eyes again, Fletcher's face was back where it ought to be. "You broke his nose, you know. Two of his teeth, as well." He smiled, and it was like strings had pulled tight at the back of his head instead of there being any feeling behind it. "I'd be interested to see you in a real fight, Kyle. You look like you'd inflict some real damage."

Real damage?

They were both staring at me now.

"Look, whatever you two are into, that's not—"

"Not what I meant." Fletcher clipped his words. "You just look like you can . . . well, *break* things."

"Oh yeah, I can totally see that. Kyle Henry, breaker of heads and hearts," Kit drawled.

I felt sick. I didn't want to be *that* guy.

Fletcher turned to Kit. "*Breaker?* Yes, I like that. We could use a Breaker, don't you think?"

"Oh, definitely," Kit said.

"Stop it," I said.

"It suits him much better than *Kyle*. I mean, *Kyle* doesn't exactly fill you with dread, does it?" Fletcher smiled that lip-flex smile again. "Right. It's settled, then. Breaker."

"Stop calling me that!"

The teacher turned around, and the room got real quiet, real fast.

"Is there a problem . . . " The old guy searched his memory, came up short, and had to check the register to find my name. "Is there a problem, Kyle?"

"No, sir." I kept my eyes fixed on a spot two inches north of the guy's glasses. He sighed and went back to his chalkboard, the noise of the rest of the class gradually bubbling up to where it had left off.

Kit nudged me with a bony elbow. "Why?"

"Why what?" I said, face front.

"Why can't we call you Breaker? Not the worst nickname you could get in this place, trust me. See him?" He pointed one long finger at a kid two rows along. "Stinkrod." Kit raised an eyebrow at me, like the name should explain itself.

You can't call me Breaker because it's too close to what they called my dad.

I couldn't say that. I couldn't even hint at it. And I couldn't think of a convincing lie, either.

I sighed. "Whatever."

The bell rang and everyone bolted for the door, chairs screeching. Kit cut his eyes at Fletcher, who caught my arm.

"Before you disappear, *Breaker*," Fletcher stressed the word,

"I'm having some friends over on Friday night. You should come."

He kept right on talking as he and Kit walked with me to my next class, and I'd somehow been railed into step with them whether I liked it or not.

CHAPTER NINE

Naomi

Addison was alone when I reached the cafeteria for breakfast. It wasn't unusual for her to be early—all the better to eat without hordes of students around—but Fletcher, at least, was usually there before me. Kit shared my love of the snooze button, so I wasn't all that surprised he wasn't up yet.

There were only a few other students dotted around the room at various tables, most too bleary-eyed to talk, but a table of younger girls in the far corner were doing what I felt was an unnecessary amount of giggling for that time in the morning.

I hesitated just a second before joining Addy at our table. I hadn't meant to, but she looked up with a raised eyebrow as I sat down.

"I thought you were going to go sit with those eighth graders in the corner," she said, setting aside her half-empty cereal bowl.

"No, I—"

"How come you're up so early? Off on another of *Burty's Bold Adventures?*"

I ignored the snarky tone, running my finger over the letters someone had carved into the edge of the table. The wood had been reclaimed from the chapel that stood in the grounds back in the asylum days, the surface of the former pews pitted and marked from decades of use. I didn't know whether the "SAVE ME" had been carved into it before or after it became a table, but someone else had added "a sloppy joe" in shallower letters right underneath it, undermining the dramatic sentiment.

"Just scouting somewhere to recreate the photo of Grandpa in all his hunting gear."

But Addy wasn't listening. Her hand had clenched into a fist against the table as she looked at something over my shoulder. I followed the line of her gaze to the noisy table in the corner.

The girls kept nudging each other, darting glances at a smaller kid picking at a slice of toast at the end of their table. The little girl was ten at the most, sitting just slightly apart from the others, even though she could have taken a whole table for herself if she'd wanted.

"What's going on over there?" I asked Addy, but she just shook her head slightly. A girl at the other end of the group—one who looked remarkably like an older version of the little girl sitting hunched over her breakfast—shoved her tray into the one next to her, creating a cascade right down the length of the table. At the end of it, the little girl's breakfast shot sideways, plate and all, the whole thing clattering on the floor next to her. The rest of the kids cackled while she crouched down and started to clear up the mess.

That had been me for a while when I'd first started at the Academy. When the whispers and the jokes had made it feel like I'd been branded the world's punching bag overnight. Not that the proctors had ever allowed it to become *actual* punching—there was an honor code that meant proctors could never turn a blind eye to bullying—but there was only so much they could do to keep the nasty words from reaching me. I'd never understood how having something terrible happen to you made you less human to some people, but I'd seen it. I'd felt it.

"Hey!" Addy was on her feet, scaring the girls into silence. Even the little one froze, a limp crust in her hand. "You," she pointed at the girl crouching over her ruined breakfast. "Go get yourself a new tray. And you," Addy said, nailing Shover-Girl with a look, "can clear that up."

There was a second where I thought the little rats might turn on Addy, but I should've known better. Shit's not known to roll uphill, and Killdeer Academy wasn't exempt from the laws of gravity.

"Aww, come on," Shover-Girl whined. "She's just my little sister." This was the wrong thing to say to Addy. Her eyes narrowed to slits.

"She could use a better sister, then."

The girl scurried to do as she'd been told.

It was only when Addy nodded over to Casey standing in the cafeteria doorway that I realized the proctor was even there. Casey scanned the room, taking in the whole scene as she came over.

"All good?" she said, and Addy gave a sarcastic thumbs-up. Casey went over to the food line, resting her hand on the shoulder of the little girl who'd just started reassembling her breakfast.

Addison had her phone out when I looked back at her, not giving a crap about the "no phones outside the dorms" rule. She knew Casey would never bust her for it. The two weren't exactly friends, but I got the feeling they would have been if Addy had allowed it.

"What are you grinning at?" Addy snapped. But seeing her stick up for the little girl reminded me why we became friends in the first place. She'd stood up for me when I needed her to, told the gawkers to go crawl up their own asses, and made me laugh for the first time since before Mom died.

"Just thinking about how awesome you can be when you want to," I said.

Addy looked from me to the little girl in the food line, and I knew she'd made the same connection.

"Whatever." She rolled her eyes, but I could see her mouth twitch upward. "Don't you have some weird cross-dressing photos to take?"

CHAPTER TEN

BURTY'S SECRET ADMIRER

Kyle

Fletcher and Kit were my shadows from then on, appearing from out of nowhere between classes and steering me into their group. That wasn't so bad—I wanted to fit in and not have people staring at me like I was bad news. But the way Kit and Fletcher had laid claim left me feeling real uncomfortable, so I stayed away from them at mealtimes, hiding out in the moldy-smelling library or eating out in the yard.

That's what I was doing when I spotted Naomi Steadman sneaking out through a fire exit. I tugged my beanie down lower over my ears, like that would keep her from noticing me. But she didn't even look my way.

Naomi crept toward the trees lining the school property, took a last look over her shoulder, and disappeared into the woods. I tossed the last of my breakfast burrito in the trash and set off after her.

Annabel Steadman is survived by her daughter, Naomi. . . .

Big eyes, staring at me from the printout someone had glued to my locker back in Whistler. It was years later by then, while Dad was sitting out his time on death row. Those weren't eyes you forgot easily.

I didn't want her to know who I was, any more than she'd want to know it. It was like Uncle Coby said: *"People will always expect things from you, Kyle. It's up to you what you give 'em."*

Uncle Coby knew all about dealing with folks and their shitty expectations. Before Uncle Coby moved to Whistler and became Dad's business partner, Big Blue Excavating Company was just another tiny company fighting for a chunk of a market that didn't trust small firms. Uncle Coby was from old money, and my dad had been working up on this big ol' place outside of Asheville when he decided to see if the rich kid who owned it couldn't be talked out of some hard cash. That was how Dad told it, although I was pretty sure Uncle Coby wouldn't have been conned into investing in Dad's business if he hadn't thought it would go big. Between the two of them, they grew Big Blue until there were yards with the company's banner in eighteen counties, and both Dad and Uncle Coby were rolling in it.

Then the news about Dad broke, and almost bankrupted them both. But Uncle Coby turned it around.

"You got a fresh start now, and I know myself how changing

your name or moving to a new town can be freeing, Kyle. I promise, this is the best thing for you. Go make a bunch of friends, tear it up some. You know I'll see you right through college, and then when you're ready, and if you *want* to come back, there'll be a future for you at Big Blue."

Even after everything Dad had done, Uncle Coby had promised me that. Promised me a future, when everyone else was so sure I didn't have one. And he acted like it was no big thing, when he'd probably saved me from turning into something I didn't want to be.

I ducked low to avoid a branch, wincing at the sharp crack of a twig breaking under my foot. My breath misted out in front of me, and the air smelled damp.

I glimpsed Naomi Steadman moving through the trees up ahead. She wasn't being careful anymore, now that she was out of sight of any teachers who might bust her for leaving campus during the day. There was no one around to see her. Anyone with a lick of sense had stayed inside.

Naomi disappeared for a second. As I got closer I saw she was sitting with her back to one of the taller maples, her bag set aside. She wore gray uniform shorts instead of the pleated skirts the other girls seemed to prefer, socks pulled up almost to her knees so that only a few inches of her legs showed. She had to be freezing. I sure as hell was. One of her hands rested against that bare strip of skin, palm turned up like she was waiting for rain to fall, absolutely still.

She looked like a corpse.

Get the hell out of here.

I ought to have steered clear of the girl, convinced Mama I had to move to a different school, a new town. Maybe I still could. She probably hadn't even unpacked the house yet.

But I just stood there, watching. Minutes passed, only occasional gusts of wind swaying the grass. Then there was a scuttle of movement, something darting along the trunk she leaned against. A squirrel, fat and jittery, jumped into her lap and buried its face in her hand. Naomi stayed real still, like she'd been waiting on it.

Then a light flashed. The squirrel startled, jumped for the tree, and slipped. It clung to the front of Naomi's blazer, claws fixed to the stitching like some tiny, furry bull rider. The girl squealed through gritted teeth, scrambled to her feet, and swatted at her chest to try and shuck it off.

Her eyes widened when she saw me, but only for a second— like I was less of a threat than the squirrel. Then she went back to hopping around, still making that closed-mouth squealing sound. I turned Naomi to face me, grabbed hold of the squirrel by the tail, and tossed it. It landed in a clump of grass and ran off in an angry blur.

Naomi was breathing hard when I looked at her, with her face all pink.

"You okay?" I said.

She leaned back against the tree and broke down into a fit, and right then I wished I could go back to that moment in home-room before I knew who she was. She had the kind of laugh where you wanted to laugh with her, to be a part of it.

"Oh my God, I can't believe that just happened! It took ages to . . . Anyway, thanks for getting it off me." She straightened up and slow-punched my arm like we'd known each other forever. I tensed, but she'd already turned away to shove something in her bag. Her shorts stretched tight as she bent over, and I focused real hard on counting the leaves between my shoes. "I've been working on that squirrel for weeks to try and get it to eat from my hand. The flash must've scared it or something and it went nuts. Ha! Nuts." Naomi caught her breath. "Sorry, I didn't mean to word-vom all of that onto you."

I stepped back. I wasn't meant to be anywhere near this girl. Not only was it ten kinds of stupid to be around her at all, but here I was alone with her in the woods. Without witnesses.

"No, it's fine. I just . . . I gotta go."

I walked away, ignoring her when she called out. I'd been freezing a minute earlier in only my shirtsleeves. Now I was too hot. I yanked at my tie until it loosened. It didn't help any.

I ran, busting through the school door, the kids staring and the teacher yelling after me to slow down.

But being in the school was worse. I needed out. Someplace, just away from *her*. Only there was no place I could go, no place where she wasn't already there. Nowhere I could escape when I couldn't keep my thoughts from running right back to her.

UNITED STATES DISTRICT COURT
for the Western District of North Carolina

Case no. 13428780

Case title: **The State versus Robert Bluchevsky**

EXHIBIT NUMBER	DESCRIPTION	ADMITTED IN EVIDENCE (Y/N)
1	Brass knuckles, 2 sets, recovered from property of victim #6, Annabel Steadman.	Y
2	DNA analysis reports (compiled) for victims #1–6.	Y
3	Photograph of defendant's tire tread in comparison with imprint taken at crime scene of victim #4, Vanessa Hardy.	Y
4	Defendant's footwear, stained with blood matching DNA sample of victim #6, Annabel Steadman.	Y
5	Clothing worn by victim #6, Annabel Steadman, at time of death: 1 pair of gray cotton pajama pants, 1 white cotton T-shirt, 1 silver sunflower pendant. All items bearing fingerprints of defendant, Robert Bluchevsky, in victim's blood.	Y
6	Crime scene photograph: point of entry at home of victim #6, Annabel Steadman (broken window at rear of property).	Y
7	Crime scene photograph: blood spatter on bedroom wall of victim #6, Annabel Steadman.	Y
8	Crime scene photograph: blood trail from upstairs landing into bedroom of victim #6, Annabel Steadman.	Y
9	Crime scene photograph: body of victim #6, Annabel Steadman, on top of divan bed.	Y
10	Crime scene photograph: bloody imprint of victim's face on bedroom wall (victim #6, Annabel Steadman).	Y
11	Postmortem photograph: injuries to hands and wrists of victim #6, Annabel Steadman.	Y
12	Postmortem photograph: injuries to feet and ankles of victim #6, Annabel Steadman.	Y

CHAPTER ELEVEN

BURTY DIVES FROM THE BRIDGE

Naomi

The coast was clear, so I could have sneaked down the back-stairs. But there was something greasy about sneaking out after curfew to go see a guy who was obviously in two minds about whether I was a dick. So instead I went about it the *official* way, which meant strolling up to the proctor's open door and waving hello when Freddie tore his eyes from his video game long enough to see who it was. I turned off my iPod and realized he'd been playing the game with the sound muted—probably so he'd hear if Kincaid or one of the other staff came by. Not a brilliant plan, seeing as I'd walked right in, but brilliant wasn't really happening.

"Hey, Freddie."

He grunted, and I continued along the corridor. My stomach felt jittery, which didn't make sense. I'd been in South Wing a bunch of times, and going to knock on Kyle's door wasn't wrong. I was just being friendly.

It smelled different in the boys' wing, like dirty socks and bare skin. I had to double-check the number of rooms I walked past before I figured out which one was Kyle's. I knocked, and his voice carried through the door a moment later.

"What?"

I waited, bopping and miming along to a song that wasn't even playing. When the door opened, Kyle looked at me like I was crazy. So I kept right on shuffling my feet, using my pointer-fingers like antennae, all the while holding his eye and mouthing nonsense words until he couldn't just stand there any longer.

"What are you listening to?" he said loudly, then rubbed his head where the dark bruises were still in bloom.

I slid my headphones down around my neck. "Nothing. I was seeing how long you could hold out before you talked to me."

He was still looking at me like I was nuts when he started laughing. And I *wanted* to make him laugh. He looked like he could use it, especially with the great big purple-ass bruise on his head.

I looked too long.

"What can I do for you?" he said.

"I wanted to come and apologize. And see if you're okay. I mean, you said that you're okay, but are you *really* okay, you know?"

He squared his shoulders, nearly filling the doorway. "Say what?"

"Kit told me about you and Jackson fighting the other day."

When Kit had told me about the ambush in the toilets, it all made sense, though Kyle had saved me from the Terminator Squirrel, so he obviously didn't completely hate my guts.

He screwed up one side of his face like he was chewing the inside of his cheek. His mouth was slightly swollen in one corner, and I reached up to touch it—like *that* was something a normal person would do—and felt like an idiot when he looked at me like I was going to rub spit on him or something. I stuffed my stupid hand in my pocket.

"All that stuff with Jackson is kinda my fault, so I'm sorry you got caught up in the middle of it. We've got history. Me and Jackson, I mean. Nobody at the Academy knows—well, apart from Kit—so I'm hoping you'll keep this to yourself. It wasn't a big deal or anything, we only went out a few times, but he wanted to hook up when he started working here. I wasn't into it. Anyway, if Kincaid finds out, he'll get fired and stuff, and I don't need the bad karma."

Kyle looked puzzled.

"I wanted to explain what happened. And why he's being a dick to you. And stuff. Does your head still hurt?" I said.

I was surprised when Kyle smiled again. His whole face changed with it. I liked it.

"My head's just fine," he said, "and I'm pretty sure he's being a dick to me because I broke his face, but I appreciate the explanation."

"Oh. Okay. I just wanted to say I was sorry."

I knew I should probably shut up, but I could see Kyle relaxing a little. His shoulders had lost some of their tension, and his arms were crossed loosely over his chest as he leaned against the doorjamb.

"And if you ever want to hang out or something, give me a yell. I'm right across the quad, so I'll probably hear you," I said.

Kyle looked over his shoulder toward the window. It was dark out, so the windows in North Wing were mostly lit up, including mine. His whole body suddenly went rigid, like he'd had ice water tipped down his shorts. Then he ran out of the room.

"Hey! Where are you going?"

I sprinted after him down the stairs and across the quad, back into North Wing and past a couple of squealing juniors to my room.

I jogged the last part of the way and almost crashed into Kyle. He stood in the doorway to my room, staring at something.

"Jeez, Kyle, they should call you *Bolt*, not Breaker."

"What's that?" he said, and I followed the line of his finger.

At first I thought a bird had flown in through the window, until I saw how still it was. And that the window was closed.

I stepped past him into the room, peering at the dusty back

feathers of the owl sitting on my windowsill. It faced outward, like it was watching over the quad, but I could see its unnatural amber eyes reflected back in the darkened glass.

"Wh-what the hell is that thing doing there?" Kyle said.

Wrinkling my nose, I covered my hand with my sleeve and turned it around. "Ew."

I sidestepped Kyle again, poking my head out into the hallway. I could hear the sounds of some of the other girls chattering behind closed doors, the early evening noises of the dorm.

"*Ew?*" he said. "Is that all?"

"*Ew* with a side of *blech*, if you like." I grabbed the bird and held it out at arm's length. "You must've noticed these in the hallways?"

"Yes, but what is it doing in your room?" he said.

"Just chillin', I guess."

Kyle glared at me. Not in the mood for jokes, apparently.

"Did you know these were made decades ago, back when this place was an asylum? The inmates used to stuff them as some kind of occupational therapy, then sell them to folks in the local community. Except for some reason, they weren't all that popular," I said. "Crazy, right? So now there are tons of them still here, rotting away to dust."

I carried the owl out of my room, with Kyle practically pasting himself to the wall to avoid touching it as I went past. I stood on tiptoes to put it back in its spot on the high shelf in the hallway.

"I saw someone in here," Kyle said as I walked back in. He held my eye, his words measured. "It was just for a second, so I didn't get a good look. Do you know who it could've been? Like Jackson, maybe?"

"No! I mean, I don't know. Why the hell would he be in here?" I let out a breath. "It's just someone's idea of a joke. Like *ha ha, here's a dead bird, let's freak Naomi out with it.* I don't even think Jackson is working this afternoon."

They'd played pranks like this on me before, back when I was new and everyone was still talking about my mom. But I wasn't a little kid now, and I wasn't going to let anyone scare me with a stupid stuffed animal.

"Why would someone do that as a joke? And I bet Jackson's not meant to be in here whether he's working or not, so I don't see how that makes any difference."

He was right about that. But playing pranks wasn't exactly Jackson's thing, and he'd be in serious shit if he got caught.

"Kyle, it's nothing, okay?" I touched my throat, but Mom's necklace still wasn't there.

"You gotta tell the principal about this."

"No way! My door was unlocked, so anyone in North Wing could have put it in here. And even if Jackson did it, I'm not explaining to Kincaid what Jackson's problem is with me, or about us dating last summer. There's no way she'd believe me if I told her it was all over before he started working here."

Kyle frowned. "Wouldn't *he* be the one to get into trouble?"

"We both would. She punishes *anyone* who brings the slightest hint of negative attention to the Academy." I sighed, and Kyle looked distinctly uncomfortable. "Gram will have a fit if she hears about any of this. I can't tell Kincaid, it'd be a major pain in the ass. And I promise you, it's just some buttsquirt ninth grader's idea of a joke. They're probably hiding in their room right now, scared to death they'll be found out."

I went over to the washbasin and cleaned the dead owl funk off my hands.

"You can't always tell what a person will do," Kyle said at last. He looked so serious I wanted to poke him in the eye.

"Or a stuffed owl. Maybe the ghost of the Terminator Squirrel poltergeisted his dusty friend in here? It looked like it had evil in its squirrely little heart. What if you're next on its revenge list?" I turned around, making my eyes go huge. "Fear the wrath of Squirrelgeist!"

Kyle tried to keep a straight face, but his mouth twitched up at one corner. "Girl, you batshit crazy, you know that?"

Banging sounded from somewhere nearby, and we both

stopped to listen. It came from somewhere above our heads. It seemed like Casey's phantom smoker was up on the roof again.

"Doesn't anybody keep an eye on who comes and goes from your wing?" Kyle said as a squeal of laughter echoed down the corridor. "Isn't there a proctor on duty tonight?"

"Yeah, I think it's . . . "

Over his shoulder, something flashed past right outside the window. A black shape, outlined by the lights shining faintly across the quad, dropped like a rock and was gone.

I rushed over to the window. The dark shape had landed hard and broken against the cobbles, a darker shadow spreading out from beneath it, like some kind of liquid.

I screamed.

CHAPTER TWELVE

BURTY TAKES THE WIDOW'S WALK

Kyle

A girl lay on the stones, blonde hair turned dark red where she'd landed. I didn't need to take her pulse to know she was dead. Her eyes were staring at nothing, neck twisted so far I couldn't tell if she was lying on her front or her back. And then I recognized her. It was Casey, the girl who'd helped me when I first arrived at the Academy.

I stood over her, wanting to throw up.

There's always eyes on you, boy.

It was like that owl had been waiting for her to fall.

Naomi was gripping on to my sleeve like she wanted to hide behind me. It was about the only thing that kept me from getting the hell out of there.

"Oh no no no! Casey!" Naomi gasped. I pulled her against me so she couldn't keep looking down at her friend.

"We need to call an ambulance. Or the police, I guess. The principal, too," I said. That was what people did, wasn't it? I'd thought about it plenty—what a person did when they found something like this. My instinct was still hollering at me to run, to not let myself be seen with the thing that wasn't Casey anymore, but I didn't trust that it wasn't something wrong in me, passed down in my blood.

Looking up at the lit windows of North Wing, I could see shadows starting to gather. Some of the girls had heard Naomi scream, and peered down at us in the dark.

"Can you find a phone while I get something to cover the . . . something to cover her with?" I said. I was worried she'd shut herself down, like Mama did sometimes, except Naomi's hands were still shaking, her pulse beating so hard I could actually see it under her skin. She was trying real hard to hold it together.

"Phone. Yes. Right." She hurried back to the staff door, and I walked over to where the recycling crates were stored. There was an old tarp tied over the crates to keep the rain out, and I dragged it over to Casey's body.

I crouched over her, getting a good look at her for the first time. Her hands were battered and bloodied up, even worse than the rest of her—probably from the fall. Yeah, probably.

He always started with the hands. They couldn't claw at you with broken fingers, couldn't scrape away your DNA for the Feds to find. Then he'd break their legs, their feet, to stop them getting away.

That banging we'd heard from Naomi's room, had it come from up on the roof? Had those squeals really been girls screwing around in the dorm, or the muted sound of someone screaming? I sank into a crouch, needing to hold my head between my knees.

"Kincaid's on her way," Naomi said, breathless. "Cops, too." She hugged my arm as I got back to my feet. She wasn't shaking now as she looked down at the tarp covering Casey.

Naomi rested her cheek against my shoulder. "Thank you for taking care of her, Kyle."

~~~~~~~~~

All the girls were ordered to their rooms, Kincaid snapping at them to keep their curtains drawn, even after there wasn't anything to see outside. I took off back to South Wing before the cops arrived—before Kincaid really noticed I was there.

Back in my room, I sank down on the bed and took a hard look at the ceiling. My head pounded, and not just from the beating Jackson had given me. Something hot and toxic rose in my throat, and I rolled onto my side, expecting to hurl.

My doorknob rattled, and then someone knocked.

"Breaker?"

Fletcher. I unlocked the door, not surprised to see Kit standing behind him as Fletcher pushed past me into my room. He strode over to the window and made a gap in the curtains just wide enough for his head to poke through. Kit threw me a "Hey" before closing the door and leaning back against it.

"What's going on?" I asked Kit, but it was Fletcher who answered, his gaze still fixed on the window.

"I thought you'd have a clear view of what's happening from up here, but it looks like they've already covered everything over."

"You know what happened, right?" Kit said, and I got the feeling he was embarrassed at Fletcher acting like a goddamn vulture. "Casey Grimshaw fell off the roof."

"I heard," I said.

"Well, did you see anything?" Fletcher closed the gap in the curtains.

"No." Maybe Naomi would tell them about me being there, but I was in no mood to go over it all again right now.

Fletcher studied me a while longer before I got the feeling I'd been measured and found wanting. "Let's go and see if Randall saw anything from his window." Randall was the wiry kid in the room next to mine, though I hadn't said more than two words to him since I'd arrived.

Kit stepped aside to let Fletcher pass, and waited until he was out of earshot before looking me right in the eye. It was different than how Fletch did it, but I still wanted to shove him out of the room.

"Are you all right?"

"Peachy keen," I said.

He stepped back out into the hallway. "Okay then. Catch you tomorrow, Breaker."

I sank down onto the bed again after they'd left. What did it mean? First the owl, so like the one my dad had kept in the living room to scare the crap out of me. Could it be a coincidence that it showed up just before the girl fell, right where I'd see it? Right where *Naomi* would see it?

I grabbed my phone and dialed Uncle Coby, nearly tossing it when the call went to voice mail.

There was only one other person I could call.

The phone rang seven and a half times before Mama answered, so I knew she was still upset with me.

"Hey, Mama. How are you doing? How's the new house?"

"Is that you, Kyle?" she said.

I fought real hard not to curse at her. Who else was it gonna be but me? I sat back on my bed, my head resting against the plaster. The building was so old that even with the heating turned all the way up, the walls were always cool to touch, like they were connected to cold, dead things buried underground.

"Yeah, Mama. It's me. Didn't you get my messages?"

"Oh, I . . . I didn't think to check. Is everything okay?"

I hadn't expected her to call me back, but I'd hoped she'd listen to my damn messages.

"Yeah, Mama. Everything's good. It's nice to hear your voice, y'know?" There was no point telling her about Casey. It would only upset her.

She didn't answer, anyhow. So I asked her the thing I really needed to ask instead.

"Mama, there's a girl in my class, she's . . . Do you remember Naomi Steadman?"

"Naomi Steadman?" I knew right away she didn't recognize the name. Mama avoided the details of the murders from the start, and those she couldn't avoid she'd forgotten real quick, wiping them clean away.

"She's a girl in my class. It doesn't matter." I gave it one more try, just to settle it. "Mama, how come you chose this school? What made you want to move here, to Killdeer?"

"Your daddy was always saying to Uncle Coby how he'd like to come see Killdeer, so I thought we'd honor . . . "

I stopped listening. My stomach turned over at the thought of why my father might've wanted us to come here, and I sure as shit wasn't gonna *honor* him for it.

Naomi was the only one to see the Bonebreaker and get away. Had my folks talked about that the few times Mama visited him in jail? Did they hold hands, talking over how Naomi would feel when she found out she was sitting next to the son of a killer?

" . . . delivered the wrong kind of poppyseed for my poppyseed chicken, but then they told me that they don't sell our usual kind up here. What am I supposed to do without my usual kind?"

As if there was some comment I could possibly make about her damn poppyseed.

"What else did Dad say?"

"Pardon me?"

"About moving to Killdeer—what else did he say about it?" I said.

Mama spluttered. "He didn't say nothin', Kyle. Just that he wished he'd come here when he had the chance is all."

Had we really ended up in this town through some sick notion of my father's? Did Mama really have no other reason for choosing this place, this school?

"I'm looking forward to seeing the new house this weekend," I said at last. "I got signed out from Saturday morning to Sunday night."

Mama giggled. "You're gonna love your room, Kyle. I did it just the way you had it back in Whistler."

I bounced my head against the wall. "That's real sweet of you, Mama. I can't wait to see what you did to the place."

I hung up a couple minutes later, feeling like I'd just pulled rope out through my eye sockets.

CHAPTER THIRTEEN

BURTY SEES IN THE DAWN

Naomi

The first light filtered down through the entrance to the quad, the sun not yet high enough to vault the Academy roof. My bed was a crumpled mess next to me, but I hadn't slept in it. Hadn't slept at all, even after the murmurs of all the girls in North Wing had eventually faded to silence. With Casey gone, Mrs. Kendrick from Chemistry had been called in to keep an eye on the dorm, but she'd just left everyone to gossip and cry and do whatever they needed to, just as long as they did it quietly.

I kept seeing flashes of Casey's broken body when I closed my eyes, and even those split-second glimpses were too much like Mom. I couldn't deal with the dreams I knew were waiting for me if I gave in to sleep.

A draft whispered through the gap where the wooden window frame had warped with age. Down on the quad, there wasn't a whole lot to show that anything had happened there the night before. While we'd all been put on lockdown in our dorms, cops had stomped around on the roof and photographed the spot where Casey landed below. It had all been cleared and cleaned away within a few hours.

I'd heard someone in Casey's room again later, after all the officers on the quad had packed up and gone. Probably Kincaid double-checking for a suicide note, as a little careful spying told me the cops hadn't found one. It was all quiet by now, and the silence felt empty.

Something moved in the deep shadows still clinging to the corners of the quad.

Someone was down there.

I couldn't tear my gaze from the furtive movement, though my instincts told me to hide. Finally a figure stepped out into the open.

I recognized Fletcher's gray trench coat even before he started walking across the stones toward where the cops had gathered last night.

Fletch walked straight past the spot where Casey had landed, keeping his eyes fixed near his feet until he reached the opposite wall. Then he turned, moved a little to one side, and started walking back the same way he'd come. Again, he passed near the scrubbed-clean stones, but didn't stop until he'd reached the other side.

He walked back and forth across the quad until he'd covered the entire courtyard, always watching the ground. I would have opened the window and called down to him if it hadn't been so obvious he didn't want to be seen. It was barely dawn, and apart from the familiar shifting sounds of the building, I couldn't hear anyone else moving around. It was as if Fletcher and I were the only two people in the whole world, and we were hiding from each other.

But there really was one less person in my world now.

Maybe Fletch had been shaken up by what happened to Casey and couldn't sleep, either. Maybe having the police crawling all over the Academy had stirred up old memories for Fletch from when they busted the commune he grew up in. Or maybe he was just pacing because it helped him relax.

Half a minute later footsteps sounded out in the hall. My breath caught as they halted outside my door, then quickly moved on again.

I unlocked my door quietly and opened it a crack. The hallway was gloomy, the windows still hidden behind the curtains. There was nobody out there now, but I couldn't shake the feeling that someone *had* been. I was about to close the door when something rattled at the other end of the hallway. A pause, then it started up again.

What *was* that? I crept out, pressing myself close to the wall.

"Fletch!" I hissed. The door leading to the roof staircase had been locked after the cops left, but now Fletcher was doing something to the lock. He looked up.

"What are you doing?" I said.

He slipped whatever he'd been using on the lock into his coat pocket. "Couldn't sleep. Thought I'd take a look around while it's quiet."

"What are you looking for?"

"Nothing in particular. Just trying to wrap my head around what happened last night."

"By picking the lock to the roof? Why?"

"Don't worry about it," Fletch said. He squeezed my shoulder as he walked past me, back out through the door to the staff staircase.

This was odd, even for Fletcher—even after what had happened to Casey. But if Fletch wanted to talk, he'd come find me when he was ready.

The water pipes at the other end of the wing began to clang as the early risers cranked on the showers. North Wing was waking up, finally.

~~~~~~~~

Sux what happened 2 Casey. R U OK?

I frowned at Jackson's text, keeping my phone hidden under my desk. What happened to Casey didn't *suck*, it was horrific. Everyone was talking about it, saying stupid things like she'd killed herself because she had gambling debts or because she was pregnant. The younger kids were all convinced the ghost of Crazy

Jake—Killdeer Academy's very own urban legend—had pushed Casey off the roof. Whatever the truth was, Casey had died right outside my window, and there'd been nothing I could do.

Jackson was down in the yard, still doing something with his phone. I watched him through the classroom window, ignoring whatever the teacher was saying about iambic pentameters. Jackson had stacked a load of recycling in the recess where all the garbage was piled up for collection. Now he leaned against a crate, sneaking a smoke.

Maybe I was being too hard on him. The text message had been sweet, if badly worded. Thoughtful, in a Jackson kind of way.

One of the younger teachers walked over to him in the yard, and I saw how he leaned into her, the way she stifled a laugh behind her hand. He could be charming when he wanted to be.

Kyle sat two rows in front of me, his head stiffly facing forward, shoulders bunched. He'd been so sure that it was Jackson who'd put the owl in my room. It didn't make a damn bit of difference now, but it was weird how that had happened right before Casey fell.

"Are you trying to decide who's hotter?" Kit said next to me. "Because I can see why you're struggling. I think you should make them take off their shirts so you can make a more informed decision. Like, for science and shit." I slugged him in the shoulder, and he grinned, hands up.

I looked from Kyle to Jackson and back again. Jackson's hair looked like he'd dragged his hands through it too many times, maybe wondering why I didn't answer his text?

He was actually fun to hang out with when he wasn't being a complete tool. He'd been the one to suggest cutting my hair when I told him about Grandpa getting me mixed up with my mom, which led to his pretty awesome—if embarrassed—confession that he was saving up to study hairstyling at community college. When he was all *trust me, I'm being honest and sincere and I rescue little puppies from burning buildings on my time off*, he was *kinda* cute. But the idea of dating someone who worked at my school was just cringe-making.

I was busy staring at Kyle when he glanced at me, so quick it was like being touched. Then Kyle turned away, his buzzed hair revealing a purple mess of bruises behind his ear.

"What do you think of Kyle?" I said to Kit.

"I like him." Kit frowned. "But he seems wary, like he doesn't trust our innate coolness."

I hadn't told Kit or any of the others about the stuffed owl in my room. That awful dead weight hit me in my stomach every time I pictured Casey outside my window, her face all twisted and wrong. I never thought I'd see that look on anyone's face again. Not after Mom.

"He asked me if you were okay, you know, after Kincaid finally let you out of her office," Kit said.

I'd been thoroughly grilled about what I'd seen, but Kincaid had mostly been concerned about making sure it was understood that *"Killdeer Academy is not where people come to commit suicide, Naomi. What happened was a tragic accident—nothing more, nothing less."*

The other girls were the ones speculating and making up stories, not me. Most of the girls didn't even know that the nice lunch lady who gave them extra fries was Casey's mom. They hadn't seen her face as she left Casey's room clutching a box of her daughter's things. They didn't seem to notice that she'd been missing from the cafeteria since Casey fell. They just grumbled about the stingy servings of fries from the substitute lunch lady.

Kit nudged me with his bony elbow.

"I got the feeling there was more to it than just Casey. Should I be worried about you, kiddo?"

I drew a smiley face on his forearm. "Nah. I'm a trouble-free zone these days, McCarthy."

Kit snorted, then tried to style it into a cough when Ms. Calhoun pointed at him with her marker pen.

When I glanced back out at the yard, Jackson was staring up through the window, his eyes trying to send me a message I just wasn't getting.

CHAPTER FOURTEEN

BURTY ON THE HIGH BEAM

Kyle

It'd taken a while to get used to the almost constant sounds of people around me, shuffling around in their rooms or running down the corridor or flushing the toilet at four a.m. The old building let out creaks and groans of its own, too, like it wanted to remind everyone inside it'd been around a long time, and already had a history that we had no part of. But as I put some clothes into a bag on Friday night, I heard a different sound. It scraped above my head like something being dragged, but that made no sense—my room was on the top floor.

God, not again.

But it didn't sound like it was on the roof, more like it was coming from inside it.

I tracked the shuffling sound moving across my ceiling toward the square attic hatch. I'd already taken a look around up there on my first day, and I'd discovered a pitch-black space that wasn't high enough for me to do more than crawl a couple feet inside.

It sounded way too heavy to be a rat. I eyed the baseball bat leaning against the desk next to me and waited. A second later, the hatch cracked open, and a pair of eyes fixed on me before it slid all the way back.

"Jesus, Kit!" Kit's blond hair looked gray with dust and stuck out in all directions over the black band of a headlamp. He tossed a spare one down to me.

"Put that on. It's fricking dark up here." He checked out my clothing. "Have you got any shittier jeans than those?"

"Not really."

Kit made a clicking noise in his mouth. "Yeah, they are pretty shitty. Okay, come on."

"Where are we going?" I reached up and pulled myself through the hatch, ignoring his offered hand. Not to be rude or nothing, but he'd stretch like grilled cheese if he tried to haul me up.

"You'll see," he said.

"This better be good."

It took ten minutes or so to crawl the length of South Wing, balancing on wide wooden beams and whacking my head on low-hanging eaves when I didn't watch where I was going. It was hard to see with only the light from the headlamp, and there wasn't much to look at anyhow apart from Kit's butt.

"Be careful not to fall off the beam," Kit whispered over his shoulder, "or you'll go right through the ceiling."

A spiderweb glued itself to my head, and I almost knocked the headlamp clean off dealing with it. Something sparkled in the wavering beam of light, then vanished.

"What the hell was that?"

Kit's light ran a half circle as he looked at me over his shoulder. "What was what?"

I angled my headlamp to where I'd seen them. Beady black eyes fixed on me from a rigid face. The rabbit's fur was thick with dust, missing in some places and diseased looking.

"A flea-bitten rabbit, apparently," I said.

"Oh, Mr. Bunnykins? He lives up here with all his friends. See?" Kit panned his headlamp along the eaves. There must've been hundreds of them—all kinds of animals, all stuffed and in various stages of decay. Next to the rabbit was a blue jay, a possum, and a raccoon that, for some reason, was sitting on a miniature tricycle.

"They *your* friends, Kit?"

He laughed for real then, and started choking on the dust. "Dude, don't do that! They're leftover junk that Kincaid shoved up here out of the way. I'm pretty sure she'd do that with all of us if she could get away with it."

"Yeah, Naomi told me the old inmates made them," I said.

"Don't you think it's strange how it's just the predators that got left out in the hallways? All the other animals got put up here." Kit faced me, blinding me for a second with his flashlight. "Like Kincaid's hiding all the victims."

He shuffled on again until we came to a vertical grate. It was still dark on the other side of it, but there was enough light to show a window or something nearby. A board lay next to it, so I crawled over for a better look.

I almost spilled clean off it when Naomi's face appeared on the other side of the grate. The light hit her square in the eyes, and I tried to angle my head away.

"What took you two so long?" Her voice echoed. The grate disappeared, and Naomi ducked out of sight.

Kit nudged me with his shoulder. "After you. Be careful on the ladder." He stopped me as I swung around to face him. "Oh, and turn your lamp off. We don't want anyone to see it through the window."

My foot found the rung of the ladder, and I eased down. As I neared the bottom I felt someone behind me, then a hand on my shoulder.

"It's just me," Naomi said. I almost knocked the ladder over trying not to fall on her. She touched my arm, steadying me, then moved to hold the ladder again for Kit.

"I was starting to think you two had forgotten I was up there," he said as he climbed down.

Wherever we were, even our whispers echoed, like the ceiling was real high above us. Specks of light cut through the old stone walls every few feet, windows shaped like arrow slits going down on a spiral—it was a circular stairwell.

"How come you're not up there already?"

I couldn't see who Kit was talking to, but assumed it wasn't me.

"Got in late after visiting Gram and Grandpa, so I only just got here," Naomi said.

"How *did* you get here?" I asked. I was starting to get a better idea of my surroundings. This was one of the turrets at the corners of the building—the northeastern tower, if I hadn't gotten completely turned around. If Kit and I had to crawl in through the attic space, it couldn't be as easy as just climbing the stairs from the ground level.

"Over the roof."

Like that explained everything. I looked at the window nearest to us. It was roughly covered over with some kind of blackout material, but stood open. Beyond it a narrow, flat section of roof ran out into the night, the tiles sloping away from the catwalk into a killing drop.

"Don't you . . . I mean, after Casey, aren't you worried about going up on the roof?" I said. It had rained earlier, and the roof tiles were still slick with it, casting their own reflected light through the open window.

"I've walked across that roof like a million times. But let's not talk about Casey tonight." Naomi's light tone didn't quite hit the spot. "It's Friday night, and wallowing isn't doing anybody any good."

We climbed the stairs in single file. I traced the wall with my fingertips, feeling the paint flake away underneath. As we neared the top, I heard pounding bass coming from somewhere nearby. I damn near walked into Kit when he stopped in front of me, and then light and music flooded out through a doorway as it was flung open. Naomi strode in ahead, and I saw she was wearing a bright blue sweater and tight jeans, a red scarf tied around her hair. She looked so different to how she normally did in her blazer, like an updated version of Snow White.

Kit turned to me with a look that was all trouble.

"What happens in the tower stays in the tower. Okay?" he said.

I nodded, and followed him inside.

CHAPTER FIFTEEN

BURTY HAS ONE DRINK TOO MANY

Naomi

The catwalk was so high up the night air burned your lungs when you breathed in. It was like being on top of a mountain, and not just the roof of a school. Maybe that was what Casey had felt, before she slipped. Or maybe not slipped, but I just couldn't think about it any other way.

Taking the catwalk beat crawling under the eaves, anyway. Kyle was covered in dust from his trip through the attic, but he didn't seem to care too much. He hovered by the door until Kit waved him over to a sofa on the far side of the room, and I climbed over the assorted bodies and beanbags littering the floor to join them.

"Breaker!" Kit shouted over the noise. For the first time, Kyle's neutral expression faltered.

"*Breaker?*" I said as Kit squeezed me in a bone-crushing hug, like we hadn't seen each other thirty seconds ago. "Are you seriously running with that nickname?"

"Don't you think it suits him?"

Kit swooped at Kyle like he was going to man-hug him. Kyle looked like he'd been Tased, all his muscles seizing at once.

"Leave Kyle alone, Kit. And tell Fletcher to stop—"

"Tell me to stop what?"

The music seemed to fade, like it wouldn't dare compete with Fletcher when he spoke.

"To stop calling Kyle *Breaker*," I said. "He's not your henchman, Fletch." He gave me a look that said not to push it. I let it go—for the moment. "I'm going to get a drink. Any of you want one?"

By the looks of things, the Friday Nighter had been going on for an hour or so already. The air was thick with weed smoke.

Addison was dancing with a few of her outer-circle friends near the speakers, their grinding motions a little wobbly already. Addy waved me over, but I mimed getting a drink and caught her rolling her eyes as she turned away.

I could hear snatches of conversations when the music dipped. Most of them were talking about Casey. She hadn't been a regular at Fletch's Friday Nighters since she became a proctor, but her name drifted from every corner of the room. Maybe it was because Kincaid had drilled it into me, but I didn't want to talk about it. Didn't want to keep seeing her every time I blinked, lying twisted in the dark flashes.

I went into what passed for a kitchen in the tower, which was actually a large closet with a window we'd blacked out like all the others. Kit followed me.

"Not having fun?" he said.

"I only just got here. Why?"

"I caught a glare-vibe between you and Addy just now. You should really work out whatever is going on with you two. Preferably in the Jell-O wrestling arena. Especially when she's obviously making plans to steal Breaker right from under your nose."

I almost choked on my beer. "Kyle isn't mine to steal. Besides, why is Addison interested? Isn't she dating that college guy . . . Brett? Brad? Something."

"They broke up a couple months ago. He got clingy, apparently."

"Oh. Well, Addison can do whatever she wants." I finished my beer and reached for a fresh one. "And you should stop calling him Breaker. You can tell he hates it."

Kyle was sitting next to Fletcher on the sofa. He looked up and caught me staring so I gave him a beer-wave.

"Can't go against Fletch Almighty," Kit said, "and he has decreed it to be his name. So mote it be."

"Fletch is a controlling mofo, and we let him get away with it far too much," I said.

Kit was smirking when I looked at him, and I realized I'd been staring at Kyle again.

"You really like him, huh?" he said.

"Eeew. I like a boy." I made pukey noises.

"Oh yeah, you should totally give him that face. Guys dig the barf look."

Addison's fake-flirty laugh drifted in from the next room. She'd squeezed herself in between Fletch and Kyle on the sofa, practically sitting on Kyle.

"Speaking of barf," I said, "I need to hit these beers a little harder if I'm gonna make it through tonight without shoving Addy through a window. . . . Sorry, bad choice of words."

Kit nodded. "Yeah. But I know what you mean."

CHAPTER SIXTEEN

BURTY ON THE BELL ROPE

Kyle

I had to hand it to Fletcher, the tower was pretty sweet. I figured he'd been the one to turn it into their Friday night hangout, including the "dropout," a hole in the floor set up with a rope pulley to bring in beer and lower down the partiers who were too wasted to crawl back through the attic. All the windows in the tower were covered with black garbage bags and duct tape, and Kit waved a headlamp in each hand as he showed me their lair.

"The hole used to be for a bell rope. The bell got disconnected like twenty years ago or something when they started to convert the towers into extra dorms. They never got around to finishing this one."

It looked like the contractors had up and left on a whim, leaving a bunch of bolts and other junk lying around.

Kit leaned in close to me. His breath smelled like beer and smoke. I stepped away, trying to look casual about it.

"Kincaid doesn't want to spend the money on the school. She's siphoning it into her own pocket," Kit said. Fletch stared at him and he shut up. It didn't last long. "Ooh, this you have to see!"

Beyond the dropout, the room was sectioned off with roughly nailed boards and a curtain hanging where there should have been a door. Kit pulled back the curtain to show a cot made up on the floor with some raggedy blankets.

"If you're ever too trashed to make it back to the dorm," Fletcher said, "you crash here. If you hurt yourself or get caught, you'll be bringing down a world of trouble on the rest of us. Just make sure you're back in your room before anyone notices."

"And check nobody's in there before you bust in," Kit added. "Fletch likes to use this as his personal wankorium."

"*Kit.*" Fletcher spoke between clenched teeth.

"What? Oh, sorry, I forgot—he prefers to call it his *masturbatoire.*"

Fletcher sighed and walked back upstairs. From all the laughing and creaking floorboards above our heads, it sounded like half the school was up there.

I followed them back up to the tower and headed to find something to drink. The kitchen was so small it felt cramped with only me in it. I leaned into the refrigerator to see what was left.

"Hey, Kyle."

I bashed my head on a shelf as a warm body pressed against my back. When I turned, I thought it was her for a moment—

Naomi—but this girl only looked like her a little. I didn't even know her. Then I recognized her as the one who'd wedged herself next to me on the sofa before I escaped, pink lips all shiny and smudged at one corner.

"It's Addison, silly. We haven't really met properly, but we bumped into each other the other day." She waited, still smiling. My palms got sweaty and I wracked my brain, trying to place her. The smile melted like hot wax. "Monday, in the cafeteria?"

Monday.

I'd seen Naomi sitting with all her friends. I'd tried so hard not to stare at her, and then someone had tripped and torn the arms right off my blazer.

"You're the one who fell over." I meant it in an *it happens to everyone* kind of way, but I guessed from the rising color in her cheeks that I'd said something wrong. "I mean, I didn't even remember you until just now."

"You did *not* just say that."

"I didn't mean—"

"And I did *not* fall over. I can't believe I made the effort to even *talk* to you, some hick who moved here from bumfuck *nowhere* and thinks he can act—"

"Hey, Kyle, I got you a soda."

At the sound of Naomi's voice, I slid away from between

the angry girl and the refrigerator. Naomi handed me a slightly warm can.

"Thanks for keeping Kyle company, Addy."

Some look passed between the two girls that didn't feel friendly. Addison screwed up her pink mouth.

"Oh, I get it now. Have fun with your new *project*."

Naomi shrugged, which somehow made the other girl even angrier. Then Naomi slid her hand into mine, her fingers filling the spaces between my own. She was touching me. I hoped to God my hands weren't as sweaty as I thought they were. Addison stormed out of the kitchen.

I was in a whole mess of trouble. "I didn't mean to upset her."

Naomi shook her head and let go of my hand.

"Addison's all right. Don't worry about it." Naomi grabbed my drink and took a mouthful before giving it back, her hand lingering on mine again.

Don't even think it.

"What all just happened? With that girl, I mean? We've never spoken before tonight. I don't think we have, anyhow." Though I couldn't say for certain I hadn't knocked the memory of her clean out of my head.

Naomi moved closer, lowering her voice. She smelled nice, like some kind of fruity shampoo. "She'll have decided you must be gay or something, you realize."

I shrugged. "I'm not."

She closed the space between us another inch. "Duly noted." We'd somehow ended up too damn close, me leaning back against the counter, Naomi's thighs warm against mine even through my jeans.

She didn't say anything, just stayed there, eyes darting to my mouth every couple seconds. I cleared my throat. "I think I'm about ready to head back to the dorm."

She pulled away. "Oh God, do I have beer breath or something?" I looked down at the can in my hand, then at my watch. Anywhere but her face. "Did I do something wrong, Kyle? I thought maybe you liked me."

"Yeah, well, I don't. I mean, not like that. You're not my type." Even as the words jagged out of my mouth, I knew I sounded like an ass.

"Oh, right. Sorry." She stepped away, with a look on her face that made me feel like the biggest shit ever. Naomi shook her head, already halfway out the door. "I'll see you around, I guess."

I didn't leave the party. I didn't want to be *that guy who's a complete jerk to girls*. I didn't want Naomi to think that. So I sat next to Kit, trying to figure out how to fix it, while Naomi had fun with her friends like a normal person.

You've got a fresh start now. Nobody knows who you are. If you stop acting like a jackass, there's no reason for anyone to think you are one.

I needed to stop whining. Be normal.

Naomi's laugh drifted across the room. I should have stuck to my plan to stay away from her, even if she seemed to be everywhere, inside my head even when I tried to think of *anything* but her.

If I hadn't said what I did in the kitchen, it would've passed, settled into a habit of just saying *hi* when we saw one another in homeroom and nothing more. Now it'd grown to be something else, and I needed to fix it. I needed to tell her *something*. Just something, so that she wouldn't think I was a tool.

But not tonight. I couldn't think straight looking at her laughing at something some guy said. Some guy who wasn't a complete screw-up. Some guy I had the urge to smack in the mouth.

People were starting to swerve toward the edges of the room, some in pairs, some alone. I went back into the kitchen for a break, and found Addison in there leaning against the taped-up window, making a point of ignoring me. It wouldn't be hard to change her mood, if I wanted to. I'd seen other guys act a certain way, how it could draw out a smile from a girl if he looked at her right, moved just right. Maybe I could be *that* guy, if I wanted to. It sure wouldn't hurt to try.

I rolled my walk until I got way up close to her, stopping once her crossed legs were bracketed between mine. This was a move I'd never have tried back in Whistler, leaving my junk in the line of fire like that.

"Hey," I said.

She still had a real face on her, but there was a crinkle next to one corner of her mouth that told me she'd smile if I only said the right thing. That she'd do more than smile, if I handled it right.

And that would settle any crazy ideas about Naomi once and for all, if you hooked up with her friend. Her friend who looks just enough like her that if you squint . . .

"I always say the dumbest things to the prettiest girls," I said. I knew it wasn't smooth, but I threw in an apologetic smile, and she already had her hand on my arm.

"So maybe you should stop talking."

I leaned in, tried to focus on kissing her. Addison's lips were greasy, and tasted like some awful fruit flavor that hadn't been anywhere near an actual fruit.

Her hands moved down my arms, squeezing. I felt her tongue sliding around the back of my teeth like she was checking for cavities, and I tried to angle my head so I could breathe.

What the hell is wrong with me?

Addison wasn't really that bad a kisser. But it was making me feel sick to my stomach, touching her, tasting her nasty lip gloss in my mouth. I started to wind it down, pull away, but she grabbed my butt and pulled me toward her. My muscles bunched up. She mistook the tension for something else and started working on the top button of my jeans.

"Don't . . . "

She latched onto my neck with her mouth, working one hand down the front of my jeans, forgetting all about the damn button.

"Get off of me!"

I shoved her away, feeling sick and angry and weird. Addison looked at me like I was touched in the head.

"Are you for real?"

I tried to calm down, to stop acting crazy, but I was so damn angry with her. Not just her, either. I hadn't wanted to kiss Addison, much less have her hands all over me. But I had a point to prove, didn't I? Some stupid point I had to make to Naomi. To everyone. Or maybe just to myself.

It was exactly what it'd been like back in Whistler, where any girl who gave me the time of day made me feel normal for a minute, right up until I figured out what kind of point *she* was trying to make by being with me. That wasn't what I wanted, not in Killdeer. That wasn't who I wanted Kyle Henry to be.

"I need to get out of here." I wasn't talking to Addison, not really. I scanned the tangle of heads and bodies through the kitchen doorway.

"You're looking for Naomi, aren't you?" she asked. I hoped like hell Naomi hadn't seen me with Addison, though that had kinda been the point at the start. "You think you can come on to me and then ditch me when she crosses your mind again? Screw. You."

"No. I mean, I thought . . . " I didn't know what I thought, only that Naomi had taken up all the empty space in my head, which seemed to be a lot of space just lately.

"You know she's messed up, don't you?" Addison leaned in, like she was whispering a secret. "She saw her mommy get murdered years ago. It, like, *scarred* her or something. Mentally."

"Whoa, I thought you two were friends?" I said. She looked sorry for a moment, but it passed real quick. "That's a shitty thing to use against her."

I barged past Addison, not giving a crap that she damn near fell over.

"Careful with your little doll, Breaker," she yelled after me. "She's already damaged!"

CHAPTER SEVENTEEN

BURTY'S FIRST CAR

Naomi

Varaday Maxwell's pupils were wide like black canyons. Varaday—a senior I only knew because she hung out with Addison sometimes—was slumped in the crash-cot Fletch had set up on the far side of the dropout.

"Hey, Naomi," she said, slurring my name so that it sounded like *Gnomy*.

"Where's the new guy? I thought you two were hanging out."

"Not really."

"Sure, sure," she said. It was hard to read her expression when she was so obviously feeling the effects of whatever she'd taken. Varaday had some bad habits. "If it's Addison you're worried about, don't be. She's not really into him."

"What do you mean?" I'd seen Addy looking pretty *into him* a few minutes ago.

Varaday squinted, trying to focus. "She's got some secret thing going on with this older guy."

"God, seriously?" My trouble with Addy had all started with an *older guy*.

For months she told us all about this secret new boyfriend. It was only when Addy came back from summer vacation that she finally admitted there was no boyfriend. She'd made it all up because of some stupid crush, except Paolo had noticed her flirting. She told me how he'd started coming on to her when her mom wasn't around, and cornered her behind the summerhouse. The gardener had seen and told her mom how Paolo had groped her, but Paolo blamed it all on Addison.

"I told Mom it wasn't like that, that he'd totally predatored me. She said it was my fault for leading him on." I'd hugged Addison until her tears soaked through my shirt, feeling *so* mad at her mom. I was pissed that Addy had lied about Paolo being her boyfriend in the first place, but that didn't excuse what Paolo had done to her.

Maybe I shouldn't have called Addy's mom. Maybe I shouldn't have said the things I did, but after Mrs. Mendez-Bianchi had yelled back at me for ten minutes, Addison's sister, Alana, came on the line.

"You really shouldn't listen to her, Naomi. It's just like when she told Mom how Martin, that guy I was seeing last year, was supposedly *ogling* her when he stayed with us over Christmas break. It was all a lie so she could swap bedrooms away from the guest rooms to the new penthouse extension."

Addy had been so excited to get the best room following the renovations, but surely she wouldn't have done something so cold and calculated to get it?

"I mean, I never believed her, but Mom did," Alana continued, "and then she totally gloated about it afterward, said she didn't care about my boyfriend being barred from the house. That was so the reason Martin broke up with me, FYI."

"Even if that's true," I said, hoping it wasn't, "that doesn't mean she's lying about Paolo."

Except I *knew* she was lying about at least some part of it. She'd been calling him her boyfriend for months.

"Oh, sure. And it's totally a coincidence that Mom said Addy couldn't have the new car she's been dying for because it won't fit in the garage with Paolo's Hummer, and suddenly Paolo groped her." Alana tutted. "She wants him and his car gone, and only a yellow Ferrari will make her feel better. She's such a weasel."

I'd felt sick when I hung up the phone.

A yellow Ferrari. She'd been talking about wanting one ever since she saw one in some old action flick, giving me that Addy-look and tapping the side of her nose when I asked how in hell she thought she could convince her mom to buy her one when she was still angry about the last car Addy wrecked.

But it seemed like Addy had a plan all along. When I confronted

Addy about it, she'd stuck to her story—for a while. Then she laughed it off, like lying about stuff like that was no big deal.

"You're so oblivious sometimes, Nai," she'd said. "It's all just a big joke. I mean, it couldn't *possibly* be true, could it?"

At first I hadn't been sure what to say, and Addison acted so normal with the others, telling them she'd dumped her boyfriend over the summer because she didn't want to limit her options in senior year. She was so plausible, so *Addison*, that I started to wonder if I'd remembered the whole thing wrong. She never mentioned it to me again, and every time I tried to bring it up, she changed the subject.

The way Addison acted around me after that felt like some kind of test, like she wanted to see how far she could push me before I spilled her secret. But that wasn't how the four of us worked—me, Kit, Fletcher, and Addy. There were secrets we told each other, and secrets we didn't.

"The Breaker thing is just to piss you off," Varaday said. She bit her lip, like she wanted to stop the words tripping out.

"No big deal. Thanks for the heads-up, anyway."

Varaday staggered to her feet, veering off toward the main room. She bumped into Fletch as he walked in, and giggled.

"You took your sweet time," I said when she'd gone.

Fletch did his nonsmile. "I could always push you down the

hole. That would be quicker." His eyes flickered to mine and held, gauging my reaction. "I didn't mean that how it sounded."

"I know. It's fine."

"About Casey." Fletch shifted his weight. "I can't help feeling like I . . . "

I waited, but he didn't continue. "Fletch, we all feel bad about Casey. But it wasn't anyone's fault. You didn't make her go up on the roof." But then I remembered something else: Fletcher, pacing the quad the morning after Casey died, staring intently at the ground as he walked like he was looking for something. Maybe something Casey might have dropped when she fell? What could he be interested in that she might've . . .

Drugs.

That was the only link between Fletch and Casey that I knew about. I nudged him with my elbow. "She made her own choices, and whether or not she chose to do what she did, that's not on you. Okay?"

His expression cleared. "Do you want me to help you get down or not?"

I laughed. "Yeah, I do, asshole."

I gripped the bell rope while he used the pulley to lower me down, the safety clip making my jeans wedge right up into my butt crack.

Fletch peered down at me from the top of the tower, a circle of light haloing him.

At some point during the unfinished renovations—presumably when the scaffolding was in place—someone had sneaked in and graffitied a bunch of screaming skulls running the full height of the tower in glow-in-the-dark paint. The paint dripped down from some of them so it looked like they were crying or bleeding from those empty eye sockets, weeping in the dark where nobody was meant to see. I tightened my grip on the rope. I wanted to shut my eyes. It would've been easier to pretend they weren't there, but I was never very good at pretending. I spun in a slow spiral, watching the skulls howl. They watched me right back.

I unhooked myself at the bottom, then signaled all clear. The circle went dark as Fletch lowered the trapdoor over the hole, locking it in case some idiot took a drunken tumble down the four-story drop.

The air smelled fresh when I opened the door to the tower. The place used to be locked up tight by Principal Kincaid, and the old brass doorknob was missing from the outside. It was one of the reasons we couldn't get in from ground level. That, and who could be bothered climbing a rope? But Fletch had worked his magic on the lock, so we could at least open the door from the inside.

I hooked my finger into the hole where the door handle had

been, pulled it closed behind me. Didn't need to invite anyone to come and see why it was open. I wasn't a complete idiot.

Bet Kyle thinks you are.

I followed the gravel path around the school building. Maybe I *was* an idiot—at least where Kyle was concerned. I'd thought . . . well, I'd thought he was hot, and that my pathetic attempt at flirting might actually be working, until I made an idiot of myself. He looked so horrified by Addison's particular brand of attention, too, although I'd obviously totally misread that.

Damn. No matter how I replayed it, Kyle had been clear as hell when he said he didn't like me.

Keeping close to the wall of the school, I walked back to North Wing. Although we weren't allowed to be out of our dorms after dark unless we had a pass, the proctors tended to go a little easier on us as long as we didn't push it too far.

I checked the time on my phone. It was a little before midnight. The temperature had dropped as the night wore on, the damp air like an icy lick in the dark. I kicked at a loose stone on the path, and it pinged against a metal rain barrel.

The light was on in the proctor's room. I wasn't sure who was on duty tonight, but it felt wrong that Kincaid had handed over Casey's role to someone new already. It hadn't been nearly long enough.

I focused on sobering up as I rounded the corner, not wanting to clatter my way into the quad. My breath came out in clouds in front of me, the fresh air clearing my head a little.

When I slowed my steps, I heard the crunch of gravel behind me. It was the sound of someone moving quickly, and trying to be quiet about it.

I rounded the corner and tucked myself into a recess where the ivy hung in a thick curtain. I couldn't see the path, and didn't dare move. My chest was so tight I couldn't have breathed even if I'd wanted to, so I kept still and quiet, and waited. The footsteps continued for a second, then stopped.

I was a part of the ivy and the bricks at my back. The breeze trickled through the woods across the soccer field, and some night bird hooted in the distance. My heartbeat thundered inside my head. Everything else was dead quiet.

Had I imagined the sound? I'd almost convinced myself I was being paranoid when something shuffled on the path, just out of my range of vision. If they took a few more steps toward me, we'd be looking right at each other.

I counted off the seconds in my head. There were no more noises, but I knew someone was there.

Then I heard it, just once. Whoever was on the other side of the wall took a step, then . . . nothing. No lights came on in the main building, either.

Dammit.

If it was Jackson following me around campus at night, then that was creepy. If he was hiding until I let my guard down—that was just psycho. And what if he got rough? I was smaller than him, so unless he was completely wasted, I probably wouldn't have much chance of fighting him off. I knew if I screamed, someone would hear me and be out to help in less than a minute. But bad things could happen in a minute—I knew that from experience.

Or it might be someone else. Whoever it was, I couldn't hide in the ivy all night. I tried to be logical or rational or something that wasn't scared. It was only a feeling in the air, maybe a twist of the shadows. I adjusted my footing, getting ready to run, and almost turned my ankle on a loose stone. I'd already made the ivy rustle, so I stooped to pick up the stone without caring too much about being heard.

"Jackson? Is that you?"

I waited with the stone in my hand. I felt better with the weight of it there, small enough that I could wrap my fingers around the edges, but big enough to crack over someone's head if they came near me. I gripped it so tight, my fingertips started to go numb.

There was no answer. Just the sound of a footstep, then another.

Shhh.

I heard the word, even though nobody said it.

A crunch of footsteps running over gravel, and then a light passed over me.

"Who's there?"

I didn't wait for an answer this time, and hurled the stone as hard as I could at the light. There was a satisfying crack as it went out, and I took off down the path for the quad.

Noises followed me—footsteps, maybe more than one set, and someone cursing. I hurried on, grateful for the shadow of the building hanging over me. My eyes were adjusting to the dark, adrenaline draining away any residue of the alcohol I'd had earlier.

"Hey!"

Was that Jackson's voice? I bit my tongue as a low tendril of ivy swept across my cheek, but I didn't scream. I knew better than to scream. They always found you if you screamed.

"*Shhh.*"

It was a hissed curse, and not far behind me.

"*Naomi, wait!*"

I stopped, almost stumbling in the dark. I knew his voice, and it wasn't Jackson.

"Kyle?"

CHAPTER EIGHTEEN

BURTY GETS INTO A SCRAPE

Kyle

Idiot.

I switched on the headlamp I'd borrowed from Kit.

"Shit!"

Something flew at me in the dark, smashing the damn thing in my hand.

I couldn't tell which footsteps were Naomi's and which weren't, so I called for her to wait up. Naomi turned, said my name, and I tripped trying not to crash into her. I landed hard, sharp stones digging into my hands. When I pushed back into a crouch and wiped my gritty palms on my jeans, one of them felt tacky. I guessed I'd bloodied it up some.

She moved closer. Then she started hitting me.

"Hey! What the hell—"

My teeth snapped together as something—a knee, or maybe an elbow—connected with my chin. The world rocked back on its heels and I grabbed hold of whatever limb she'd thrown my way and yanked her down with me. Her breath *oof*ed out of her, and then she was at it again, smacking me with her fists.

"Naomi, stop." She straddled me. I shoved her off. "Hey, come on now! Please, stop."

"Why did you . . . why were you chasing me?" she said, breathing hard.

"I saw someone tailing you and ran to catch up, but they took off. I guess you didn't hear me hollering."

Time stretched, her breathing the only sound between us.

"It wasn't you." She said it like she was just realizing it for herself. "It wasn't you."

"No. It wasn't me."

And then her hands were on me again, except she was done hitting me.

"God, I'm so sorry, Kyle! Are you hurt?" She kept on running her hands over my chest and arms, checking for who knew what in the dark.

"What are you doing?"

My voice sounded strange in my ears. Her hand slid into mine, but I pulled away.

"Kyle, I'm trying to help you up—"

"Yeah, I know. My hand is bleeding."

"Oh!"

She slid her hand up to my arm instead, leaving it there even after I was back on my feet.

"Come up to my room," she said as we walked into the quad. "I'll clean your hand."

There were only a couple of lights on in the upstairs hallway, but they made it bright enough to see Naomi rolling her eyes when I hesitated. She hauled me along with her to the staff door.

"You have the code to get in, right? They keep the doors locked at night," she said. I shook my head, then regretted it when my vision went tilt-a-whirl for a minute. "Four, six, five, nine, B. Got it?"

I repeated the code.

"Good. They change it every month, but Kit always manages to get hold of it somehow," she said.

The door opened real quiet, and I followed her into the dark stairwell.

You shouldn't go up there.

I knew it, but short of yanking my arm from her grip and making a run for it back across the quad, I couldn't get out of it without acting like a complete ass, and I was pretty sure I'd done enough of that for one night.

At the top of the stairs, she checked along the hallway before pointing up at two of the stuffed animals sitting high on the shelf above our heads.

"*Cameras*," she whispered. I peered up at them—one was a fox, the other some kind of weasel. Predators, just like Kit had said, and each had a red dot glowing in one eye.

Naomi stayed close to the wall and signaled me to follow her. She locked the door once we were inside her room, leaving me in total darkness until she lit a lamp on her windowsill. I looked across the quad to my own darkened bedroom window, then she closed the curtains.

Her room looked a lot like mine—same small bed, small desk, small closet with a small sink next to it—but every surface was covered in crap. Clothes, magazines, tubes of hair stuff that looked like a Reddi-wip fortress on her desk.

"I know. It's kind of a mess in here," she said, nudging a pile of clothes to one corner with her foot. Then Naomi looked down at my hand, which I held away to avoid messing up my T-shirt. Mama would notice if there were big red stains all over it when I took it home to wash.

Home. It didn't feel right to think of a place I had never been as *home*.

The graze on my left hand wasn't too bad. Both my hands were filthy, which made it look worse. Naomi didn't seem like she was about to throw up or anything, but she was staring at the blood. I cleared my throat.

"Are we gonna talk about the guy who was following you?"

Naomi shrugged. "What is there to talk about? It was probably someone who left the tower after me, too out of it to realize they were being freaky. Take a seat."

I sat at the end of her bed while she rummaged in a cabinet over the sink. The springs groaned under me when I shifted my weight.

"It's not like I have a stalker or anything," she said, without looking up.

"Jackson was lurking outside your window the first night I got here. And he probably left that dead owl in your room. Doesn't that count as stalking?"

Naomi glanced at me real quick, then turned away. In the mirror's reflection, I saw her touch her fingers to her throat. She caught me staring and dropped her hand.

"It might not have been Jackson outside just now," she said. "I don't know *who* that was. And the owl was probably some lower-classman punk."

A plastic jar fell out of the cabinet and bounced in the sink. Naomi grabbed it, like she could take back the sound. We both stayed quiet, listening for some sign we'd been caught.

"I don't know, Kyle," she whispered. "I don't really care right now, either. Can we focus on getting your hands cleaned up?"

Naomi took my hands in hers, turning them over to take a closer look.

"Aren't you worried that creep might be dangerous?" I said. Maybe the asshole didn't know how messed up it was to play tricks on Naomi after what had happened right in front of her. What had happened *again* just a couple days ago. Or maybe that was why he was doing it, for some kind of sick thrill.

"No. They're pranks, that's all. Just some loser's idea of fun. Nothing to get worked up about." She ran some water in the sink, tipped in a capful of antiseptic. "And even if it is Jackson, he's not exactly dangerous."

"*Do* you think it's Jackson?"

When she looked up at me, she seemed paler than before. "No. Maybe. Look, I can't believe I'd be stupid enough to date someone who'd do that. It'd mean I have the worst judgment ever. You know?"

"Yeah," I said, my head pounding again. I'd lived with a serial killer for seven years and not known it. "But it's not always easy to see."

"Or to admit. I'm tired of talking about this. Let's talk about something else."

She soaked a cloth in the warm mixture, her movements quick and precise—like she'd done this before a dozen times. Naomi held the cloth against my skin, and it felt good, despite the raw meat sting of the antiseptic doing its job.

"You moved here from North Carolina, right?"

I didn't like where this was headed. "Yeah."

"Is it just you and your mom?"

The clipped way she said it told me she'd somehow taken a dislike to Mama.

"Just the two of us, yeah."

"What about your dad?" I jerked my hand out of hers. "Sorry, did I hurt you?"

I shook my head and she went back to cleaning my graze.

"My dad died last year," I said at last. "Mama doesn't do so well on her own. I worry about her." Naomi looked up from my hand. "She was in a car accident when I was a little kid. Hurt her head real bad. *Traumatic brain injury*, the doctors call it. Mama can seem a little strange to other people when they don't know her."

"I'm sorry. My dad got into a really bad car crash, too. He— well, he died. I was only a baby, though, so I never really knew him." Naomi shot me a look of sympathy I had no right to. "So why did you move here?" Her fingers traced over my palm, and my teeth clicked shut. "Sorry, did I do it again?"

My dad got a kick out of sending us here, hoping you'd know who I was. He wanted to taunt you with what he'd done, what he's still doing, even now.

I curled my hands closed and Naomi covered them with her

own, gently peeling back my fingers. She traced a few of the old lines on my knuckles.

"How did you get these?"

Nobody had ever asked that back in Whistler. Nobody cared, I guessed.

"We moved here because I was about to get kicked out of my old school," I said, ignoring the other question.

"Why were they going to kick you out?"

"Got into a scrape or two. My own damn fault."

I hoped she'd leave it at that, and she did.

"I'm really sorry, you know, for beating you up and stuff," she said.

Her voice had gone all soft. She had no idea how much I deserved the beating she'd given me, and plenty more besides.

"Don't worry about it."

She looked at me like I was a dumbass. "Don't worry about it?"

"You thought I was chasing you. I'd have smacked me around some, too. But seriously, you call those punches? I've had worse mosquito bites." I wanted her to laugh, or at least lighten up.

"Kyle, it's not okay for anyone to hit you. Not a girl. Not . . . Not anyone, okay?"

I shrugged. "All right. Next time I'll hit you back." I curled my good hand into a fist and popped her on the shoulder in slow motion, like she'd done that day in the woods. She laughed finally.

"Earlier tonight, why did you . . . Is Addison *your type*, then? I saw you two together."

She studied the cloth in her hands a little too hard.

"No, she's not my type. That won't be happening again."

Naomi nodded, dabbed some more of the disinfectant on my hand. It didn't hurt now.

"I shouldn't have lied about you not being my type," I said, and bit my tongue so hard I tasted blood. But when Naomi looked me in the eye, it felt like I'd said the right thing for once.

Oh shit.

~~~~~~~~

I knew which house was ours as soon as I turned onto our new street. There were only three to choose from, all spaced far apart like neighboring didn't mean much to the folks who lived there. That'd suit Mama, all right. She didn't like being on her own too well, but she liked making nice with strangers even less.

Our house was painted white. White door, white walls, white picket fence. Paint so crisp it would hurt to look at it on a sunny day. Just like we'd had back in Whistler, except the white there had gotten patchy where I kept having to paint over the ugly words.

I stepped onto the front porch and knocked. I heard the locks unsnapping on the inside, and then Mama's eye appeared in a crack above the security chain. Old habits.

"Hey, Mama."

"Oh. You're here."

She disappeared again, unsliding the chain to let me in.

Mama walked back inside without telling me where anything was, but she didn't need to. The inside was just like the outside, everything clean and neat and in its right place. The same sideboard in the hallway with the pottery kittens Mama collected. Same framed photos of me, Mama, and Dad, how we used to be before he was arrested.

Through a doorway, I spotted the high-back armchair that nobody would ever sit in again. Mama just couldn't bear to get rid of it.

I kept my bag slung over my shoulder, not wanting to make a mess and upset her, and followed Mama into the living room. Tiny black eyes caught mine, and I stopped.

The owl was poised over the fireplace with its wings stretched out real wide, the mouse clutched in its claw like always. Mama walked into the kitchen, so I stepped over to look at it up close.

My daddy had loved to spook me with the owl, telling me it'd come get me at night if I was bad. That it was watching me whenever I left the house. Owls could see a person's soul, he said, and they'd tear it right out of you with those big old claws if you didn't behave yourself.

For all the fear he put in me, it wasn't the owl that scared me most, it was the mouse—frozen in the worst moment of its tiny life, never escaping, never put out of its misery. The mouse was a reminder that life could be a cruel sonofabitch, and it didn't matter if you were minding your own damn business and being a good person, someone bigger and stronger than you could swoop in and destroy you in a heartbeat.

I told Uncle Coby all that a couple months after they locked Dad away. We were tossing a baseball between us in the park at the time, and I felt like a jackass spilling my guts to him, worried he'd call me a sissy. Uncle Coby just nodded and walked over to sit next to me in the grass.

"We could take it away, if you wanted," he said, setting the catcher's mitt down on the ground between us. "Get rid of it. You'd never have to look at it again."

"Mama won't let me."

"We won't ask," he said, winking down at me. "There's not much she can say once it's gone."

But then I thought about Mama being all sad, and I told him I'd just suck it up.

"It's only a stupid mouse."

It was the right answer, because Uncle Coby took me for ice cream on the way home, even though it was almost time for dinner.

"Kyle? Come through a minute, would you?"

I left the owl and mouse and followed the sound of Mama's voice to the kitchen, where her favorite Disney soundtrack was playing from her old CD player next to the refrigerator.

Mama held out a jacket in front of her. A man's leather jacket. I could tell just from her eyes peeking over the top of it that she was smiling. I was about to ask her where she got it when it hit me: that smell of leather and cigarettes. He couldn't have worn it in years, but it still smelled like my father.

"I found this when I was unpacking the last of the boxes, and I reckon it'll fit you now that you filled out. What do you think?" she said.

"Is that *his*?" I could barely unclench my jaw to speak.

"Your daddy always looked so handsome when he wore it. Like a movie star or something."

The waver in her voice stopped me snapping at her, but I still had to dig deep to work up a smile. "Thanks, Mama, but it's not really my style."

"Aw, hush. A leather coat never goes outta style. And you need a good heavy jacket with this weather setting in," she said.

I stared at it, then at Mama's smiling eyes. I'd never be cold enough to wear that bastard's clothes.

"Go on, try it on."

I put up my hands, not to take it, but to keep it away from me, and Mama yanked it back when she saw the mess I'd made of my palm. I'd taken the bandage off, thinking the scrape wouldn't stand out so much, but I guess she was used to looking for the marks.

"Are you in trouble again?" she asked, setting the jacket aside and forgetting about it, just like that.

"I tripped outside school last night. Landed on my hands." I flexed my fingers like that would somehow make it look better. "You know how clumsy I am."

"You're not clumsy."

"I am when it's dark and I can't see where I'm planting my big ol' feet."

"Mm-hmm." Mama didn't look like she believed me. "I'm making your favorite for dinner."

"Aw, Mama, you're the best."

"My favorite" meant poppyseed chicken, which I liked well enough, but it was really Dad's favorite. She'd never moved past the need to please him, even after he was gone. Some things never get unlearnt, I guess.

~~~~~~~~

I woke early the next morning, used the trimmers to take care of the fuzz starting to take over my scalp, and went to knock on Mama's door. Her room was at the back of the house where she could look out on the rose garden. Taking care of the yard had been one of my chores back in Whistler, so I'd need to see to it before going back to school.

Maybe if I let it go wild, she'll be forced to go out there and take care of it.

It was a dumb idea, but I'd run out of good ones. From the lack of fresh food in the refrigerator, it didn't seem like Mama was leaving the house at all. The pantry was packed with desserts and processed crud that the doctors said she shouldn't be eating.

There was no answer, so I knocked again. "Mama? I'm fixing breakfast. Would you like eggs this morning or cereal?"

Still no answer. I knew she had to be awake, though. I'd never known her to sleep past six.

"MAMA?"

I banged on the door.

"I'm in here."

Her voice came from behind me, sounding real small through the door of her bathroom across the hall.

"Can I get you something for breakfast, Mama?"

A long silence followed, and I knew something wasn't right.

"Are you okay in there?"

"I'm fine." Her voice was muffled. I leaned my ear up against the door, and heard the shower hissing away on the other side.

"What's going on? Are you sick?"

She was outright sobbing now.

"You go on with your breakfast, Kyle," she said. "And you should head on back to the Academy, make sure you're not late now, ya hear?"

"Mama, you got me worryin'. I'm coming in there."

"No!"

The door was locked. She babbled something, her voice pitched real high, but I couldn't make out what she was saying. All I knew was that she was in there, crying, alone. And I was not going to just eat my breakfast and head back across town.

"Mama, please open the door. I need to know you're all right."

She didn't answer. I tried the door again, rattling the handle until she wailed at me to stop. "I can't open it. I'm stuck."

I stopped the rattling. "Stuck where?"

"I-In . . . the . . . tub."

Shit.

"Mama, stay back from the door." It was a dumb thing to say, what with her already telling me she was stuck. "I'm coming in."

I was vaguely aware of her screeching at me not to look at her as I stepped back, and gave the door two good kicks near the handle. The wood splintered, shattered, and the door flew open.

I felt for her bathrobe hanging on the hook and stepped over to the bath to cover her with it.

Her eyes were swollen from crying, but I couldn't see right away why she hadn't been able to get out of the tub. The overhead shower was still on, streaming water down on her. I reached up and turned it off.

Mama clutched the bathrobe to her with only one hand.

"Did you hurt your arm, Mama?"

She shook her head, not looking me in the eye.

"I'll lift you out," I said, "but tell me if you're hurt anywhere first. I don't wanna make anything worse."

"I'm fine," she sniffled. "Don't look at me!"

I only nodded and leaned down.

"It was so slippery when I stepped in, I keeled right over and tried to catch myself, but I got my arm wedged up under me," Mama said as she wrapped her free arm around my neck. "It was a stupid thing to do, a stupid, stupid thing."

This shouldn't have happened. I shouldn't have let her get to this point.

"Shhh, Mama, it's okay. Please don't cry now."

I need to take better care of her than this.

I reached behind her back on one side, over her shoulder on the other. It was awkward, made harder when she kept trying to pull the bathrobe up where it slipped down between us.

"What would your daddy have said about all this? He woulda been so mad!" The mention of my father had me gritting my teeth. He knew Mama couldn't help the way she was, but he'd still yelled at her for any little thing she did wrong. I would never be that way with her. Not ever.

"I'm so sorry, Kyle," she whispered.

"Nothing to be sorry for."

I lifted her, trying real hard not to show how close I was to bursting a blood vessel with the effort. Just as I got her to her feet, the pressure in my head released like a mule kick, and dark spots moved in front of my eyes. When they cleared, Mama was still weeping and clinging to me, but I was leaning on her more than the other way around. It seemed that crack to my head was going to keep biting me in the ass a little while yet.

I blinked hard to shake off the dizziness, and stepped back to give Mama some space. I looked away while she pulled her robe around her, covering herself from neck to ankles. Then I looked at her for real, saw the misery and shame on her face.

"You okay? You hurting anywhere?" I said.

She shook her head, still not looking me in the eye.

"All right then. I'll leave you to get dressed while I get us both some breakfast." I took one step toward the door. I'd need to fix it right away or Mama would be reminded of what had happened every time she saw it. A busted lock was easy to fix. "We're gonna make sure this doesn't happen again, okay, Mama? Just you and me, all right?"

She didn't say anything, but I knew she'd heard me. I went and made her cereal.

[Note from Social Services case file for Burt Steadman]

Mr. Steadman's condition continues to deteriorate, with more frequent episodes where he is unable to distinguish between current events and those from his past. Attempts at memory-enhancing exercises only confuse him, and have led to angry and sometimes violent outbursts.

Increasing his medication has proven similarly ineffective. He has begun hallucinating in particular about someone named Jake. It seems Mr. Steadman has received no visitors by that name and that "Jake" is no recent acquaintance of Mr. Steadman. My conclusion is that this person either does not exist or is someone from Mr. Steadman's distant past. Either way, this new development is worrying.

Mrs. Steadman has confirmed that the granddaughter is no longer residing in the marital home, and insists that she is able to manage Mr. Steadman's increasing needs. I remain concerned, however, at Mrs. Steadman's refusal of all domiciliary care and support. She currently maintains a part-time position as a caterer at her granddaughter's school, and although their home is on school property, my view is that it is unsafe for Mr. Steadman to be left unsupervised at home for any length of time.

If the situation remains the same at the time of our next visit, I will again strongly urge Mrs. Steadman to agree to a more suitable residential setting for her husband. While forced intervention is not my preferred option, I am extremely concerned about the safety of both Mr. and Mrs. Steadman if no proper solution can be agreed upon very soon.

CHAPTER NINETEEN

BURTY BACK IN THE BARRACKS

Naomi

It was crazy to read too much into what Kyle said right before sneaking out of my dorm room Friday night, but I'd had the whole weekend to stew over it.

Maybe he was just grateful that I'd cleaned up the cuts on his hand, and telling me that I *was* his type was only his way of making up for hurt feelings or whatever. But the way he looked at me, the way he'd been looking at me since that day in the woods, made me think I wasn't completely off base. I thought about him while I showered, the way his hands had felt so rough and warm as I cleaned them. It was easy to imagine that touch, how it would feel in other places.

After the water turned cool, I dressed and walked across the little kids' playing field over to the staff cottages, the last of the morning mist curling up from the grass.

I let myself in, calling out to my grandparents as I went down the hall to the kitchen. It didn't feel right. No—it didn't *smell* right.

I moved quietly through the house with a gut feeling that I was walking into a scene. A place didn't become a *scene* until something bad happened there. I knew that. I felt it.

There was no scent of bacon or fried bread cooking, and as I stopped in the doorway to the kitchen, I saw why. The kitchen was empty. No skillet of bacon hissing on the stove. No Grandpa at the breakfast table with a newspaper he never bothered reading anymore. No Gram bustling between the counter and the stove, muttering to herself like the whole production would fall apart if she missed a step.

"Gram? Grandpa?" My voice sounded small. I moved into the family room, where the TV was dark and silent, the curtains still drawn. My heart beat out a warning against my ribs, and I forced my feet to keep moving as I headed upstairs.

Something's wrong.

There were three doors on the second floor. The bathroom, my grandparents' bedroom, and the bedroom that had been mine. The bathroom door was open, so I skipped it. I had my hand on the door handle to my grandparents' room when the phone started ringing downstairs. I jumped, a nervous laugh breaking loose before I could stop it.

I raced back down to where the phone sat on the wall of the kitchen, the plastic receiver warm from the morning sun blazing through the window.

"Hello?" I gasped.

"Oh, good, I caught you."

"Gram?"

"Naomi, we're at the hospital. Grandpa was having some trouble catching his breath yesterday evening. I left in such a hurry that I forgot my pocketbook, so I didn't have your phone number to call and let you know, and it was so late I didn't want to wake Principal Kincaid—"

"Is Grandpa all right?" I couldn't stop myself from shouting. There was some pressure behind my ears, like my head might explode any second.

"Well, he's breathing better, yes." I could tell Gram would have given me *the look* for interrupting her if we'd been in the same room. "The doctors think he has an infection, so they're keeping him here another day."

"I'll come over to the hospital right now," I said. "What would you like me to bring? A change of clothes each?"

"Stay where you are, child. I'll come back to the house in a few hours to pick up some things, and then I'll spend the night here with Grandpa in case he wakes up and panics," Gram said.

"I can—"

"You don't have a car, Naomi, and it would take you at least an hour on the bus. Besides, there's no need for you to come all the way down here to hang around us old people."

"But—"

"Hush, now. Don't worry. Your Grandpa will be back to his old self in no time. And stop grinding your teeth! I can hear it down the wire."

I unclenched them with difficulty. "Sorry, Gram."

She sighed, and I could hear how tired she was.

"Can you grab a pen to take down my number, in case you change your mind and want me to bring you anything?" I said.

"I already have a pen and paper here, dear. I'm waiting for the numbers."

I recited my cell for her, listening for the metal click of the clasp closing on her purse as she tucked it safely away. After making her promise to call me if anything changed, I hung up and turned to leave the house.

The skin at the back of my neck prickled.

The door was unlocked.

Gram might have grown up in a house where the doors were never locked, but after what happened to Mom she'd made sure all the doors and windows were locked up tight at night, and had drilled it into me to do the same.

Maybe she was in a hurry to get to the hospital, and forgot to lock up.

Then I saw them.

Five framed photos lined the hallway from the kitchen to the backdoor, pictures of me in various stages of gangly growth. Except now the frames on the walls didn't have me in them. Every photo had a blank space where I'd been, neat edges showing where someone had carefully trimmed me from the photo before replacing it in the frame and rehanging it on the wall.

I took the pictures down, clasping them to my chest until I had my arms full. They shouldn't be on the wall like that. Gram *couldn't* see them like that.

I shoved them in a bag and bolted for the door, running all the way back to the Academy. As soon as I was in my room I locked the door behind me, scanning the familiar space for any sign of an intruder.

Nobody has been in here. They would have been seen by the proctor.

Casey's fall had happened right after Kyle spotted someone in my room. Had she seen someone coming out? Could they have gone up onto the roof and . . . what? She'd gone up there after them, and whoever it was pushed her? Or maybe she'd just heard someone up there like before, and thought it was kids sneaking off for a smoke.

I swallowed, listening to the drumbeat pounding inside my skull.

"Shhh, don't make a sound."

It was his voice, the Bonebreaker's voice. That was impossible, had been impossible since they injected that monster full of poison a year ago. I still heard him. He was in my blood, *my* poison, whispering through me like he belonged there. He'd clawed his way into every memory I had of my mother, infecting that part of my life until I just couldn't bear to think about it. Couldn't think about *her* without seeing the monster standing in the shadows behind her.

I stopped breathing. The pounding only got louder.

"*Shhh.*"

I breathed. In, out. Again.

I carefully laid the frames down on my unmade bed and sat next to them, my hands shaking so badly I had to clasp them together in front of me.

"Need to call the police," I said, feeling both better and stupider for breaking the silence. I reached out for the handle of the door just as someone started turning it from the other side.

"Why is this door locked, Naomi?"

If anyone had a right to be pissed, it should have been me—especially after I had the crap scared out of me. Kincaid seemed to think otherwise.

"Uh, because *privacy*?" I said as I opened it.

The principal tutted. "Don't get smart with me. I'm here about your grandfather. Have you spoken with your grandmother yet?"

"Yeah. Not long ago. Gram said he's doing much better."

Kincaid nodded, mentally checking me off her to-do list. "Good. Well, I'd better be getting on."

"Wait—there's something else. I think someone broke into the cottage. There were these photos on the wall and someone cut me out of them."

I picked one of the frames up off the bed and showed her where I'd been neatly trimmed from the shot.

She looked at me like I was an idiot. "This happened around the time your grandfather had a bad turn?" Kincaid paused while I stared back at her. "This seems less like something a burglar would do and more like the confused action of a man with progressive dementia, don't you think?"

I gritted my teeth. "My grandpa didn't do this. I'm going to call the police, get them to come and check it out."

"You will not," Kincaid said. "I cannot have the authorities trampling all over this campus again, Naomi. Not after that unfortunate business with Casey last week. We have the Academy's reputation to think about, and I'm sure your grandparents don't need the added worry of having to deal with the police."

She turned and left without saying anything else. I stood there in the doorway, not quite believing what an asshole she was. Then I closed my door again, locking it to spite her.

*[Extract from hospital report re: patient
Olive Bluchevsky, dated August 20, 2003—
George Whistler Memorial Hospital, West Whistler]*

BACKGROUND: Mrs. Bluchevsky suffered a traumatic
brain injury following a car accident. According to Mrs.
Bluchevsky, she has no memory of the collision itself,
but had been experiencing blackout periods prior to it.
Scans showed a preexisting fracture to her skull, and
she claims not to know how the injury was sustained.

ONGOING SYMPTOMS INCLUDE: Impaired peripheral
vision (though improved since last visit); emotional
outbursts (becoming more frequent); loss of emotional
connection with spouse and young son.

FURTHER TREATMENT: Continue with psychotherapy
indefinitely. Ongoing course of medication per
attached script.

RECOMMENDATIONS: Patient should refrain from driving
until reassessment shows judgment and vision are
sufficiently restored.

NOTES: Mrs. Bluchevsky appears in better spirits since
her last visit, but admits she is nervous about getting
into a car since the accident. The patient's spouse
continues to support her in terms of physical care
and in caring for their young son, who was also in the
vehicle at the time of the crash.

CHAPTER TWENTY

BURTY AT THE ENTRANCE TO JAKE'S CAVERN

Kyle

I hung up as Mama's phone went to voice mail. That made five calls she'd ignored now. I knew she was embarrassed about the whole thing with the bathtub, but she didn't need to take it out on me.

I almost hurled the damn phone at the wall, but a knock at my door interrupted me. I threw it open.

"What?"

"Well, funny you should ask," Naomi said, completely unfazed. "Years and years ago, there was a student here called Crazy Jake who got totally obsessed with a girl in the grade above, only she had this really hot jock-type boyfriend, and didn't even know the kid existed. He started throwing these epic tantrums, but everyone thought he was just goofing around and didn't get how seriously deranged the kid was, until one day Crazy Jake sneaked up behind the boyfriend and shoved him right out of a window on the top floor of the school. The guy fell and landed on the big clock over the main entrance. You've seen the one, with the hands that don't move? Yeah, that one. Anyway, he got impaled on the minute hand, and bled to death before they could cut him down. Gross, huh?"

The girl was nuts, but I kinda liked that about her.

"What happened to Crazy Jake?" I said.

Naomi gave me a look full of trouble. "I'll tell you on the way."

"On the way where?"

"An adventure. Just a small one, so we'll be back by curfew."

We took the back staircase and left the Academy. Outside, the sky hung dull and gray, so flat it could've been painted on. I followed her across the back field and into the woods, my boots crunching against the half-frozen ground. Naomi's footsteps were lighter as she led the way through the trees.

I was driving myself crazy over her. Yeah, it'd be wrong to be anything more than a friend from homeroom. But I could be that. Kyle Henry could be the safe guy someone like Naomi would be happy to call a friend, and wouldn't see as any kind of threat. Wouldn't see me as anything but an *okay guy*. And she'd never need to know I was anything else, because she'd never *want* to know.

Except I didn't want to be that Kyle Henry. Not really. Not if it meant she only ever saw me as an *okay guy*.

"Fine, I'll tell you what happened," she said. "The story goes that Crazy Jake was possessed by the ghost of one of the inmates from back when the Academy was a madhouse, and that's why he turned psycho and shoved the boyfriend out a window. That's BS, of course. Not that the rest isn't, but you have to draw the line at ghosts, right?"

"Of course."

Naomi disappeared under an overhang of branches. I followed her, sweeping them aside, and stepped out onto the muddy bank of a narrow stream.

"Think you can jump it?" she said, not waiting for me to answer before she backed up, took a run at it, and barely made it over to the far side. She turned, waiting for me to follow.

"I'm not really built for flying," I said, but I went for it. My boot hit the far bank, then the mud slid under my foot. I windmilled my arms for a half second before Naomi grabbed my hand and yanked me toward her.

"There you go," she said. "I wouldn't let you fall, would I?"

"Thanks." My face burned, and she laughed before trudging into the woods.

When the trees thinned out and the steep rise of a hill faced us, she stopped. It was only maybe three stories at the highest point, but the way it rose straight up out of the ground in a sheer rocky wall made it look taller.

"Remember I told you about the photos I take to recreate my grandpa's old scrapbook?" Naomi said. "Well, I wanted to do this one where he's standing at the entrance to a cave. He used to tell me it was where they found Crazy Jake hiding out after he killed the girl's boyfriend. It wasn't until I came walking out here a couple of weeks ago that I found it. It's right there, do you see it?"

I looked up to where she pointed. There was a dark recess in the rock, maybe ten feet up the sheer side and set back a ways so that it was impossible to see inside.

Naomi took off toward the rock face, hopping over the loose stones at the base. I saw why a ladder wouldn't work, anyhow.

"Little help, big guy?" She held her arms straight up, like a little kid waiting to get picked up.

"I shoulda known you only wanted me for my height."

She sized me up. "Nah, Kit's taller. I just figured I'd drag you away from all that brooding in your room you seem to like doing so much."

I didn't answer. Instead I hoisted her up around the tops of her legs and held her within grabbing distance of the ledge.

"Higher!" Naomi said.

"Grab it, and I'll push you up."

After some shimmying and shuffling, I finally looked up as her feet disappeared. Naomi peered down at me a moment later, the gray light making a hazy halo around her head.

"Can you pass my camera up here?"

I swung her canvas bag up and she caught it. She held her hand out to me, and I stared at it, confused.

"Aren't you coming up?" she said.

I shook my head. "There's no way you'd be able to pull me on up there."

"You're such a chauvinist, Kyle." She was teasing, but I didn't like her thinking of me that way.

"Unless you want to end up with one arm longer than the other, I'll stay right where I am," I said.

Naomi laughed. "Fine. I won't be long."

I heard the click of the camera going off a bunch of times, and Naomi moving around on the ledge above me. After a minute or so, it all went quiet.

"Naomi?"

Silence.

"Hey! You all right up there?"

She answered finally, her voice echoing from inside the cave. "Two secs, I think I found something."

Naomi's flushed face reappeared, and she handed the camera down to me.

"Is everything okay? What did you find?"

"Oh, it was nothing. I got the shot I needed. Catch me?"

"Sure. Or if I miss, at least I'll break your fall."

"You see?" she said. "Kit would've been useless as a crash mat."

She wriggled her butt to the edge and slid off, no hesitation. I caught her, lowering her feet to the ground between mine. Then we stood there, not a breath of air between us.

She looked up at me, eyes wide.

"Thanks, Kyle," she said, and headed back toward the stream. My heart thumped like it was trying to chase after her, and I wanted to punch it right back into my chest.

CHAPTER TWENTY-ONE

BURTY'S BEST GIRL

Naomi

JW and AS. Those were the initials I'd found carved into the rock inside the tiny cavern, barely visible in the half light, dulled where the rain had poured in through a crack in the cavern wall. It was probably a coincidence that AS were Mom's initials, and that the cave was one my grandpa had photographed when he was barely older than me. But was there a chance Mom had seen Grandpa's scrapbook and gone looking for the cave, like I did? Had she taken a boy there with her, made it their own secret place? And could JW be Crazy Jake, the boy from the story?

It felt strange, like I'd caught a glimpse of a life I had no business seeing.

"Hey!" Two tanned, perfectly manicured fingers snap-snapped in front of my face. "I said, did you finish your English Lit assignment?"

I leaned over to lace my shoe after gym class, taking too long about it for Addison's liking. "Assignment?"

"Where is your head lately?" She frowned. "I should have known it was pointless asking you. I'll see if Kit will lend me his."

"Oh, uh, I guess I've been kind of distracted." Addy was turning away, but I caught her hand. "Hey, can I ask you something?"

Addy didn't move, which I took as an *okay*. That was fine. Small steps.

"You know the story about Crazy Jake and the death clock, and how he ran away and hid in a cave after he killed that boy?" I said. "Do you think that story could be true?"

Addy gave me a raised eyebrow. "What, like he was possessed by a ghost?"

I shook my head. "I don't mean that part. But the rest of it could have happened, couldn't it? I went into the woods with Kyle—"

Addison jerked away from me like I'd burned her. "If you say one word about that Neanderthal, I will cut you."

"You mean Kyle? No, I—"

"You know he was all over me at the tower after you left, don't you? Couldn't keep his hands off me, the perv."

"Why do you keep saying this stuff? Do you seriously expect me to believe you after Paolo?" I said.

Her eyes darted around the locker room, but everyone else had already left. It was just the two of us. "I *knew* you were dying to bring that up again! Poor little Naomi, who everyone treats like a special snowflake but doesn't actually give a shit about anyone but herself. Jesus!"

Addy pinched her lips like an angry cat's butt and stormed out, her black ponytail swinging behind her.

I was alone. I stuffed my things back into my gym bag and slammed the door on my way out.

Jackson walked out of the guys' locker room across the hall. He jumped when he heard me, and all my angry hissed out in a sigh. This was the first time I'd been alone with him in weeks, and as many times as I'd rehearsed my *are you the psycho who stole photos from my grandparents' house and left an owl in my room* speech, now that I stood across the hall from him while he leapt out of his skin at the sound of a door slamming, I couldn't picture it.

"Hey," I said. I could see him debating whether to ignore me as he scanned up and down the corridor in case any of the faculty caught us together. At least, I hoped that was what he was doing.

"Hey yourself." Jackson shifted his weight from one foot to the other. "I figured you weren't talking to me after what happened with that new kid last week."

I shrugged, my gym bag slipping off my shoulder so I had to shove it back up into place. "Beating on Kyle in the bathroom was kind of a dick move. You could have really hurt him." *Had* really hurt him, from the look of the ugly marks on the side of Kyle's head.

Jackson frowned. "He shouldn't have tried to get between us."

"Jackson, there is no *us*. Not anymore."

His face fell. "You don't mean that. You wouldn't lead me on this whole time for nothing."

"Lead you on? I didn't . . . that's not even the point. Us dating was never a good idea. You know that."

"Oh, I know that, do I?" His face was all hard angles under the harsh lights in the corridor.

He took a step toward me, and I jerked away from him.

"You're so smart, aren't you, Naomi? Telling me what I know, what I want, just because you go to this fancy school. Do you know what I want right now?"

"I don't care what you want," I said, taking a step back and trying to look nonchalant, not scared. My neck was hot and itchy, a blush rising that had nothing to do with being embarrassed. "I don't want anything to do with you. Not anymore."

"Look, I get that you've got guy issues after that Bonebreaker dude and your mom—"

"That has nothing to do with it!"

I could see he knew he'd gone too far. Not enough to actually be sorry, though.

"Stay away from me, Jackson. I mean it. I'll call the police if you don't leave me alone."

I held his gaze, knowing I couldn't back down—not if I wanted to finish this.

"The police? Are you crazy?" he said. "Like I'd want anything to do with you anyway, you goddamn dyke. Who would even look at you? You look like a *guy*."

I took a deep breath, and another, fingernails stinging my palms.

"Thank you," I said, "for clarifying what an asshole you really are." Then I walked away.

CHAPTER TWENTY-TWO

BURTY'S RAIN DANCE

Kyle

"That performance on Friday was pathetic! We had a shot at an interstate invitational right here, in our own backyard, and we screwed up. Big time."

The coach paced up and down in front of the bench, jabbing his clipboard at the team.

"I know you can do better. I know you can *win*. And Friday was a setback, but now is the time to turn that around! Shape up, guys! You don't always get a second chance."

Coach's eyes locked on mine for a second up in the bleachers before he moved on. He kept drilling his team, and I got lost thinking about all the things I was getting to do here. I could be whatever I wanted, *whoever* I wanted. I could be part of a team, a group of friends. There wasn't anything stopping me. Just as long as nobody found out.

"Breaker—you're up. Good luck, dude."

Kit was sitting next to me on the bench, and elbowed me in

the ribs. The coach waved me over, his whistle hovering near his lips in case I needed another blast to get my butt up.

I jogged over to where a bored-looking center was defending the key. He tossed me the ball then turned back to the coach, not even bothering to size me up.

This guy's cocky.

The coach blew his whistle, and I stepped one-two around the center and planted the ball in the net.

"Nice shot, Henry," the coach said.

The defender snorted. "Lucky shot, more like it."

I took my spot again, waited for the whistle, and put the ball back in the net like it had no other place to be. The center was paying attention now, and so was the coach. I figured I was about to get a tough time.

The coach pointed at the guy facing me.

"At least make it look like you're trying to block him this time, Lowell."

Coach blew the whistle, and sure enough the center—Lowell—made more of an effort to block me. I sidestepped, waited for him to shadow, then spun around him and sank the ball a third time.

"All right, Henry." Coach took the ball from me, shaking his head. "Come to practice next week. We'll see how you play with the rest of the team."

A huge grin broke out across my face and there was nothing I could do about it. Kit slapped me on the shoulder.

"Don't let it go to your head just yet, Henry," Lowell said, but it didn't sound unfriendly. "This doesn't mean you're on the team, you're only getting to try out against the rest of the guys." Lowell held out his hand and I stared at it until Kit nudged me again. I took Lowell's hand and shook it.

"Formality, dude," Kit said. "Welcome to the team."

The rest of the team had all trickled away in a sweaty haze, so I was the last to leave after getting cleaned up. I stepped outside the gym, still buzzing from my victory.

Big puddles dotted the pavement from an earlier rain, making me watch my step as I made my way around back of the school, my breath making trails of mist in front of me. Maybe that was why I didn't notice her right away.

Naomi sat on the wall behind the gym, near where some of the kids who weren't boarders left their bikes chained up during the day. The rack was empty now.

I'd seen Naomi in the special assembly that morning, sitting at the back of the hall. Fletcher, Kit, and I were the last ones in, so we'd loitered up against the back wall while the principal talked about Casey dying, and how it was a real tragedy, but we all had to move on.

I played it over and over in my head while Kincaid's words echoed around the hall: Naomi's expression when she looked out her window, how Casey's eyes had been so wide, like the whole thing had surprised her. But I hadn't known the girl, didn't feel sad about her dying the way others did. Grief brought them together, but not me. I was intruding here. An outsider.

I cleared my throat in case Naomi hadn't heard me leaving the gym, then walked around in front of her. The wall was high enough that her knees were on my eye level, almost like she was waiting to take a ride on my shoulders.

"Naomi?" She looked up. Her hair was soaking wet and stuck to her head. "How long have you been sitting there?"

"I dunno. A while, I guess."

"Are you okay? Is this about Casey?"

She shook her head.

"No. I'm fine, really. You're a nice guy, Kyle."

I studied the pavement instead of looking at Naomi. "Not sure what I said to deserve that, but thanks."

I held up my hands to her. The grazed one was a little sore again after playing basketball, but it was healing. "Want a hand down?"

She scooted forward until I could catch her hips to ease her down, just like I had at the rock face in the woods. My pulse thudded at my fingertips where I touched her. The last dregs of adrenaline from the game, probably.

We started walking around the Academy building, heading for the dorms. We were almost at the turn onto the quad when she spoke at last. "Could we walk a little while longer? It isn't dark yet, so we're not breaking curfew. Do you mind?"

Naomi looked out at the woods across the parking lot. I didn't want to go there, didn't want to be alone with her in the woods again when it made me feel things, *think* things I shouldn't. Still, I couldn't let her go by herself if that jerk was still giving her a hard time. And if she wasn't upset over Casey, it was probably something jerk-related. Besides, I was *nice guy Kyle*. This was what nice guys did.

"Sure," I said.

We walked into the woods, past where she'd taken the picture with the squirrel, and came onto a trail leading deeper into the trees. It wound away from the Academy, getting narrower until it was just a strip of mossy ground that wasn't as wild as the rest of the woods. It smelled peaty, but fresh—not like the sun-rotted stink of dead leaves back home.

Trees hung low over us, blacking out the sky and making it seem a whole lot later than it was. Naomi stared straight ahead, eyes red like she was trying not to cry. Or had been crying already, maybe. I wasn't sure what to do, so I kept going until the path ended in a tangle of weeds and brambles growing around a fallen tree. Naomi went and sat on it, not bothered about the dirt or the rain soaking into her uniform shorts. I sat down next to her.

"I ran into Jackson," she said. Naomi looked completely calm, except her knuckles glowed white where she gripped the tree trunk.

"What happened? Did he do something to you?"

A tight shake of her head. "No. We just talked. I still don't really think he's the one who stole those pictures from my grand-parents' house, or left that thing in my room." She looked up at me. "Someone broke into the house while my grandpa was in hospital. Cut a bunch of pictures of me out of their frames and hung them back on the wall."

"That's . . . " I'd been about to say *psychotic*, but I'd never felt right chunking that word around.

"I don't actually know if it is him. I mean, I don't see what he'd stand to gain from it. But at least he can't possibly think there's anything going on between me and him now." She swung her legs so that her heels knocked against the wood. "I can't trust my gut with things like this. I don't understand these kinds of games."

I imagined smashing the guy's face in with my fists. How it would feel, the sound it would make.

"I'm sorry," she said, "I shouldn't be laying all this on you. I just feel really weirded out, and I know my other friends would make a big deal out of everything if I told them the whole story. I can't deal with that right now."

"What about the police?"

"Kincaid said I wasn't allowed to call them."

A part of me was glad she hadn't involved the cops. If they started looking at Naomi's classmates and neighbors for possible stalkers, it would take them all of five seconds to turn my way.

"Do your grandparents know what's been happening?"

Naomi shook her head. I held her hand, mostly to stop her squeezing her knuckles so hard. Her skin was cold and a little damp from the tree trunk.

"I think Grandpa's getting worse. I can't tell Gram about all this right now."

I understood. How many times had I kept things from Mama because I knew how much she'd worry?

This wasn't right, none of it. Naomi'd already had more than her share of horror to deal with. And the fact that she was sitting with me, telling *me* all about it because she thought I was her friend? Someone she could trust? It was messed up.

But I couldn't tell her she was wrong to trust me, even if that made me a coward.

I slid my hand from hers, real casual.

Naomi stood and started pacing. At first I thought she was mad at me, that I'd done the wrong damn thing again, but she wasn't focused on me at all.

"It makes me so angry, you know? Like my grandparents, Casey—there are really awful things happening right now, and Jackson, or whoever is doing all this sketchy stuff, is playing childish games. But he knows he can keep screwing with me because there isn't a thing I can do about it!"

Her voice had risen almost to a yell, her footsteps like bullets hitting the ground.

"What'd you like to do about it?"

She looked at me for a second. "What?"

"What would you wanna do about it, if you could?"

Naomi quit pacing. "I'd kick the shit out of him."

"I thought you said you weren't sure he was the one who left the owl for you and took your pictures," I said.

"Yeah." Her hand was on her hip now. "But you should have heard the things he said to me! He was an asshole, Kyle. He deserves to have his ass kicked just for that."

I breathed out long and hard through my nose. "I'll do it for you."

Her eyes narrowed like I'd played some kind of trick on her. "I don't *want* you to."

"You said—"

"I said *I* want to kick his ass. In a completely theoretical, not going to do it kind of way. I'm just venting, making myself feel better. I'm not going to send you after him like some kind of hired hitman. Wait, is that why you thought I was telling you all this? Because Fletch has decided you're our *Breaker*?"

I shrugged. Naomi stepped closer, then again. "What are you doing?" I said.

"Do you think I could? Fight someone, I mean?" Closer again, and she had her fists clenched. Bark bit into my palms, but I didn't move. "What do you think?"

She held her arms straight out to the sides, then curled them up to show off her guns.

"Are you afraid, Kyle?"

I burst out laughing. "I've seen more muscle on a string bean."

Naomi flexed a few more times, then we were both laughing. I stood, and mirrored her pose.

"Show-off," she said, smiling up at me. Something shifted then. Whatever had been pushing us apart turned on a dime.

I let my arms circle her waist, feeling her shiver under her soggy uniform. We stayed like that, listening to new rain starting to fall onto the tree canopy above us. It hadn't found us out yet. Her skin warmed as she rested against me, and I could see each of the dark lashes framing her eyes.

"Kyle, do I look like a boy to you?" she said.

I almost choked on my tongue. "Uh, no. Why?"

"Never mind."

I wanted to kiss her. Knowing that it was the worst thing I could do in the entire world didn't make me want it any less. I drew in a breath, reaching for words that fled the moment she brushed her thumb over my bottom lip. Back and forth, her eyes never leaving my mouth.

I kissed her. Naomi's lips moved with mine. I pulled her close, my hand smoothing up her back, accidentally slipping under her blouse. I made to pull away when she shivered against me, but Naomi caught my hand and put it right back. I kissed her deeper, harder, until her heart beat as crazily as mine.

"You're really good at that," Naomi said after we broke apart, like she needed to explain her shaky breathing. "Like, *really*."

I grinned, and she kissed me again.

"Say you like kissing me, too, Kyle." And again. "Say it." And again.

"All right!" I choked out. "I like kissing you, too!"

Satisfied, she stole one more kiss, then pulled away. The rain was getting heavier, breaking through the tree cover.

"We should head back," she said, holding out her hand to me.

I took it.

~~~~~~~~~

Was that a really bad thing to do?

I knew it was, but I didn't want to believe it. Last week I'd been horrified to recognize Naomi sitting in my homeroom. I'd promised to stay away from her, to follow my perfect plan to live a life free of what Dad had done.

That plan had just been shot to shit, and right at that moment I couldn't have been happier.

Calm down, hoss. She only kissed you.

Naomi had already gone inside, but I took a minute to watch the rain peter out to occasional fat spatters, each one lighting up like a spark as it fell past the windows. It'd gotten true dark, way past curfew by now. I shoved off the dorm wall to head back inside, but a clattering sound stopped me. It came from outside the quad.

I followed it back around the side of the Academy building. I didn't go far, the single security light up ahead cutting deep shadows that made the path hard to see. The wall of the main building was set back a ways behind a tool shed, nothing but a black line to my eyes.

I went over to the shed. The thin light hit the brass padlock on the door. I tested it. It was locked, so the sound probably hadn't come from inside.

All I could hear was the dull thud of raindrops hitting the shed roof and scattering over the gravel path behind me. One fat droplet hit the back of my neck, crawling past the collar of my shirt and down my spine.

The sound came again—closer, now, but quieter. More a shuffle of grit than the clanging I'd heard before.

"Hello?"

No answer, just another shuffle, but I tracked it to the dark mouth of the recess into the main building.

"Is anyone—"

A fist came out of the shadows and glanced off my shoulder, not hard enough to hurt, but forcing me back a step. I didn't get a chance to see who it was before he lunged at me, his full weight almost taking me down. The stink of piss and liquor coming off him was so strong I retched.

"Sonofabitch!" I shoved him, catching just a glimpse of his face as he tripped back into the shadows with a grunt. *"Jackson?"*

The asshole scrabbled to right himself against the wall of the building. "Can't find me . . . gonna kill me . . . " His words came out like chewed marbles, and I could barely make sense of what he said.

"Quit it, man. I don't care if the principal catches you—it'll serve you right."

Jackson clawed at me again, trying to grab on to my sleeve.

But his hand caught on air, as though he was seeing two of me.

"Hey! I don't wanna whup your sorry ass when you're drunk, but I will," I said.

He didn't answer.

"All right. Sleep it off, asshole."

I left him to stew in his own piss while I headed back to the quad. Seconds later, I was back in my room, the door slamming hard enough to splinter. Sure enough, when I turned on the light, there was a crack all up one side of the wood. Dammit.

At the sink, I threw cold water on my face, trying to claw back that feeling I'd had before Jackson made an ass of himself. A deep breath, more water, and my temper simmered down some. Leaning against the porcelain edge, I looked at my reflection in the circle of mirror, and frowned at the strange marks smeared on my shoulders. They looked like two smudged, bloody handprints against the soggy white cotton of my shirt. But if it was blood, it sure wasn't mine.

Jackson's blood, then? I'd taken him for drunk, but maybe he'd been hurt somehow, and I shoved him away like garbage. Then again, he might've been drinking and gotten into a scuffle with someone, got bloodied up that way.

But there was only one way to find out.

~~~~~~~

Kit gave me a once-over and a raised eyebrow.

"Can I borrow your other headlamp?" I said before he had a chance to speak. I dangled the broken one from my fist with an apologetic shrug. "Sorry, this one kinda died."

He opened his door wider and stood back to let me in. I was glad to find him alone.

"Yes," he said, taking it from me and frowning at the smashed lamp. "I can see that." Kit grabbed the other lamp from among the crap piled high on his desk and tossed it to me. "What are you up to?"

He was studying the jacket I'd thrown on to hide the bloody shirt. I tugged at the collar, hoping he didn't see the rain-wet cotton underneath.

"Dropped something on my way back to the dorm," I said. "I'll bring the lamp right back."

I didn't give him time to ask any more questions, just turned and slipped back out onto the quad. The rain had stopped for the moment, but it was just a breath held between showers. Lamp on in my hand, I swept it left and right over the path as I ran, not stopping until I was at the spot where I'd left Jackson.

But he wasn't there anymore.

I searched farther into the recess, then around back of the main building, scanning the path for blood tracks or any sign he'd fallen. But there was just rain-slicked gravel mussed up from hundreds of feet passing over it during the day.

CHAPTER TWENTY-THREE

BURTY'S BATTLE CRY

Naomi

I woke to a faint flashing red light in the dark. I rolled over to grab my phone, blinking as it lit up to show I had five new messages. I opened them to see if any were from Kyle.

They weren't. All the messages were from Jackson.

Baby, are you awake? I need to see you.

What the hell? It was past four a.m., and that message had been sent an hour ago. And "*baby*"? Jesus. The next one:

Come meet me, PLEASE.

Then:

Don't ignore me. I need to see you.

ANSWER ME BITCH

YOU'LL BE SORRY YOU EVER SCREWED WITH ME

"Okay, what?"

I set my phone down, then felt around for the switch of my reading lamp. The glow flooded my room, and I picked the phone up again, sure I'd misread Jackson's messages in my half-asleep fuzziness. But no, they were the same words, the same five messages the asshole had felt compelled to send me at three in the freaking morning.

I typed a message in reply calling him every ugly name I could think of, then deleted it before I could send it. I needed to do something, *hit* something, but responding to stuff like this only opened the floodgates.

I stuffed my pillow over my face and screamed into it, vile things I hoped wouldn't carry to Gina in the next room, and finally just wordless yelling until I ran out of breath.

I shoved my pillow aside and lay there panting until I fell into a sweaty sleep, dreaming about ripping off a certain part of Jackson's anatomy and beating him with it.

~~~~~~~

Kit's eyes were almost as wide as his grin when I finished telling him. "Seriously? You full-on made out with the new guy in the woods?" he said.

Ms. Calhoun continued writing on the whiteboard, only the occasional whisper from one of our classmates interrupting the squeak of her marker pen.

I bit my lip. My predawn rage at Jackson's asshole-ness had faded to background noise when I saw Kyle in homeroom.

"What was he like?"

I felt embarrassed talking about Kyle like this, even with Kit, but it beat telling him about the text messages. I rested my chin casually in my hands.

"He's that good, huh?" Kit laughed.

Fletcher half turned toward us. "If you're talking about Breaker, I haven't finished checking him out yet."

There were a lot of things Fletcher took for granted. Mostly because he got away with stuff. He assumed that someone he brought into his circle of friends should expect to be scrutinized—or Googled the crap out of, at least. Or that I'd wait for his *all clear* before I hooked up with Kyle.

"Fletch, I appreciate you being all Big Brother and everything, but I don't need you to look out for me—not with Kyle. He's a good guy, I know it."

His eyes became half-lidded. "What do you know about Breaker, then?" He wasn't even fake-copying the notes in his notebook now, but when Ms. Calhoun dropped her marker pen and glanced his way as she retrieved it, she pretended not to notice he wasn't working.

"His dad passed away last year," I said, moving on before Fletch could ask how he'd died. "He reads a lot." Okay, so anyone who spied through bedroom windows as much as I did would have seen the stack he kept on the desk in his room.

"Probably all porn," Kit whispered, and I elbowed him in the ribs.

Then a tidbit resurfaced in my brain, and I blurted it out without thinking. "He got into a lot of fights at his old school. Almost got kicked out because of it."

Fletcher tapped his pen against his desk. "Hmm. He moved from somewhere in North Carolina, didn't he? Do you know where?" I shook my head. "I'll dig around some more, see if I can find anything out about his last school."

"Please, Fletch," I said, "back off on this one, okay? You like him, too, I know you do."

"Not until I know what he's about. Don't get too involved with him, Naomi. I mean it."

I almost smacked him. "You *mean it*? You're not my dad, Fletcher. You don't get to order me around."

"You're right," he said, but that tic was still pinching at his cheek. "I can't tell you what to do. But the same goes for you. I'll back off when I'm certain I know everything I need to know about him."

"Oh, for God's sake!" But there was no way I'd get Fletch to come around until he was satisfied Kyle wasn't some kind of ax murderer. "Just don't dig around too much, okay? We both know what it feels like to be caught in someone's crosshairs."

After class, Kit caught up with me. "Jeez, what was all that about?" I let him pull me to one side while the other students filtered past, ducking into an empty classroom so we wouldn't have to fight to be heard. "Don't tell me you've had a bust-up with Fletch now, too? I mean, he's acting kind of weird about you and Breaker hooking up."

I shook my head. "You know Fletch. He's just super cautious. He's probably worried Kyle will turn out to be an asshole, and I'll get hurt."

"Fletch *does* prefer to be chief asshole," Kit said. I turned for the door, but he stopped me. "Speaking of assholes, I haven't noticed Jackson lurking around you lately."

"Looks like I'm off the hook," I said with a shrug.

"Hmm . . . is that the fragrant aroma of bullshit I smell?" He sniffed the air around me, and I slapped him away. "Yes, definitely a bovine tang. Spill it, Steadman."

"Firstly, you're gross. Secondly, I had a few weird texts from Jackson last night, but I really think he's given up now."

Kit gave me one final petulant sniff. "*Sure*-sure?"

I shoulder-nudged him. "Sure-sure. And please don't mention any of this to Addy or Fletch, okay?"

"Of course. I know things aren't cool between you and Addy at the moment—which you totally need to work out, by the way, because the two of you hissing at each other is driving me nuts. And Fletch, well, he's being even more Fletchery than usual."

"Is he still worried about the whole Casey thing?"

Kit frowned. "What Casey thing?"

"It's probably nothing. It just seemed like he had something on his mind after she . . . after that night. Is he worried the cops are going to bust him? And is that why he has such a stick up his ass lately?"

Kit's frown lifted. "Oh, no. At least, I don't think so. Casey's habit was getting out of hand, so Fletch cut her off. But she just went somewhere else for her stuff. If there'd been anything on Casey, it wouldn't have led back to him."

"I didn't know he'd stopped selling to her." I said. "Casey made it sound like he'd just run out when she asked. How do you know she was getting it from someone else?"

"Fletch told me. Apparently it's someone else in this school."

I nodded slowly, following Kit back out into the now empty hallway. Despite his breezy reply, he had to know Fletch would never let anyone else deal at the Academy. The only reason *he* did it was so he could control it.

What exactly had Fletch said the last time he'd spoken to Casey?

CHAPTER TWENTY-FOUR

BURTY'S BACKFLIP

Kyle

"I'm a magnificent tumbler, Breaker," Kit informed me, wearing a very serious expression. "I've been told it's like watching a spider in a vacuum cleaner."

Kit being almost the same height as me, and maybe half my weight, I could imagine it real easy.

The gym teacher—I hadn't caught his name when he first said it, so I was stuck calling him "sir"—showed us how to flip each other on an island of rubber gym mats.

"That wasn't meant as a compliment." Fletcher stood on Kit's other side, shaking his head.

"You *wound* me, Fletcher. *Wound* me."

The teacher blew his whistle, waving at everyone to come closer. "You need to partner up. Groups of three, and as close in height as you can get. Go!"

He clapped his hands together, and I expected all the guys around me to start bunching into groups. Aside from a few who shuffled around, there was no movement whatsoever. The teacher rolled his eyes.

"Right, I'll do it." Everyone groaned. "Kit McCarthy, get over here! You're with Darryl and Keith. Gavin, Trayvon, and Craig. Fletcher . . . " He kept reeling off names, putting the groups together and sending them off to their own chunk of the gym island. The number of students around me had dwindled when he reached me, and I already knew who I'd be grouped with. There were only two other guys even close to my height, and they were both shooting dirty looks my way.

"Taylor, Dominic and . . . new kid. Sorry, forgot your name." I went and stood next to Taylor and Dominic on the gym mats.

I did my best not to nail them with a flying kick the one time they managed to flip me, until the teacher blew his whistle and waved us over. From the look on his face, it wasn't to congratulate me on my tumbling.

"Not you two—go back to your spot." He waved Taylor and Dominic away and turned to me. "Principal Kincaid wants to see you in her office. Get changed and go straight over there."

"Yes, sir."

I'd avoided the principal's office since my first day at the Academy, so I had to check my orientation map to find it again. I trailed the hallways lined with portraits covered in clear Plexiglas, the cracked floor tiles patched with spackle, quarter-circle scuff marks showing where doors had been hung crooked and never set right. The place had once been *ritzy*, as Naomi said. Now it looked tired and shabby.

The principal couldn't be calling me in for anything to do with Jackson, seeing as the guy would be in as much trouble as me if he said he'd been outside the school when he wasn't meant to be. I hadn't seen him around the Academy that morning, but I was curious to see what kind of state he'd be in when I did.

I passed a small, arched window, looking out over the woods where Naomi had been attacked by the squirrel. Where she'd kissed me.

If I'm kicked out, we'll probably have to move. And I'll never see her again.

I didn't like that idea one little bit. Although if I left now, she'd never know who I really was. She'd never know I'd lied to her.

I knocked on the door to the principal's office. It opened a few seconds later, and I found Principal Kincaid looking up at me over the rims of her glasses.

"You wanted to see me, ma'am?" But she wasn't alone. "Uncle Coby!" My voice broke, and I would've been embarrassed as hell if I hadn't been so glad to see him.

"Kyle, your uncle has something he needs to speak to you about," Principal Kincaid said.

Something in her tone held me in place when I would've gone over to him. "Has something happened to Mama?"

"Your mama's just fine." Uncle Coby shot Principal Kincaid a smile so sweet it should've rotted his teeth. "Can you give us a minute, Loretta, sweetheart?"

Principal Kincaid looked like she was going to argue, probably not appreciating being dismissed from her own office, but Uncle Coby squinted up his eyes until you couldn't be sure whether or not he was winking, and she sighed.

"Of course," she said. I waited while the sound of her heels clicked down the stairs.

"You know her, then? Principal Kincaid?" I said.

"Oh, we've talked some. Had to grease the wheels to get you in here, didn't I?" He laughed. "That woman gets real friendly when she smells hard cash."

"Why are you here? I mean, it's great to see you, but is everything all right?" There had to be some reason for him to have come all the way up from North Carolina.

"Quit worrying so much, boy. I caught a flight up yesterday so I could spend a few days with your mama, see if I couldn't cheer her up some."

"Cheer her up? Why?"

He took a seat behind Principal Kincaid's desk, just like it was his own office. "She called me all in a tizz because she says you're not letting her eat."

"She *what?*" I might've suggested cutting back on all the junk food she'd stuffed into the pantry, but I hadn't said it in a mean way. At least, I didn't think I had.

Uncle Coby sighed, but it seemed like there was some current running through him. "You know what your mama's like, Kyle. You have to treat her real careful-like, make sure she don't do nothing stupid that'll get you taken away from her. I understand you wanting to keep an eye on what she eats—heck, she sure let herself go after your dumbass father got himself arrested—but if she starts kicking up a stink saying you're starving her, that ain't gonna work, is it? You gotta be smart about this. You don't want the cops or social services or whoever coming in with their questions, getting all up in your business, now, do you? You'd have to come back to Whistler where I can keep an eye on you both." He didn't seem angry or upset, or even like he was busting my chops, really. But I figured he had to be.

"Did she tell you about what happened last weekend? About getting stuck in the tub?" I said.

I could tell from the look in Uncle Coby's eye that he knew.

Mama would have told him everything before he came all the way up here.

"She's gonna hurt herself if she keeps on eating like she does. I want her to get healthy is all," I said.

Uncle Coby looked at his watch.

"Telling her you were going to take her to see some doctor was only ever gonna put her in a funk," he said.

"Okay, so I might've suggested she go see a nutritionist. But I only wanna make sure—"

Uncle Coby held up his hand. "I didn't come all the way up here to argue with you, Kyle. It's time to step up. A real man don't need no one else fixing his problems, does he?"

"No, sir," I said, blood burning under my skin.

"I knew you'd understand. You always were a smart kid." He rose to his feet, bouncing back on his heels a couple times. "I haven't got to be back in the office for a few days, so we can have a real catch-up at your Mama's over the weekend, 'kay?"

I hugged him goodbye, glad to know I'd be seeing him again real soon, and he finished by scruffing his hand over my head.

"I like the buzz cut," he said. "Real neat."

Uncle Coby left, and the low growl of a car sounded out on the driveway a short while later. Principal Kincaid came back in and sat at her desk without speaking, chewing the inside of her cheek like she was thinking big thoughts. She looked up a minute later, seeming irritated to find me still there.

"You can go back to class now, Kyle," she said.

"Yes, ma'am."

By the time I left her office, she was already staring out the window again, following the fresh tire tracks along the gravel driveway.

CHAPTER TWENTY-FIVE

BEDTIME FOR BURTY

Naomi

Saturday was one of Grandpa's bad days, where he kept calling Gram and me horrible names—worse than *Burty*—and eventually started throwing dinner at the wall. Gram kept her eyes on me, kept her smile fixed in place, but she startled every time Grandpa moved. I hated him then for a little while, and then I hated myself for it.

Eventually he wore himself out and fell into a kind of trance. This was almost worse, because it was too easy to see him as a corpse that just hadn't stopped breathing yet. The disease was taking him apart, piece by piece, until there was nothing left of him. And then he'd die, just a shell, and Gram and I would have to really try not to remember.

It was always that way, whether a person died quickly or not. The people left behind only remembered the end. It had been that way with Mom, too, until I'd realized it was easier not to remember her at all. Maybe that was how Grandpa had felt. Maybe that was how the disease had crept into his mind in the first place.

"I'll help you get him to bed," I said.

"He's my husband, child." Gram smiled at me even more tightly. As hard as it was to see her struggle, we both knew what Grandpa had been like before his mind went fruit loops. He'd have hated knowing this was waiting for him.

"Just to the top of the stairs," I insisted, and she gave in. We took an arm each and half walked, half dragged him up the stairs to the landing outside their room. I left Gram to it then, ducking inside the door to my old bedroom to listen in case she needed help getting him into bed.

I stood in the dark, the only light coming in through the window and reflecting from the mirror on the dresser.

My old room was half a junk room now since the flooded basement was unsafe for Gram's more precious stuff. Apart from that, it hadn't changed much since it had been my mom's room. It had the same worn carpet, the same dresser with old nail polish stains on it. And her photograph in a corner in front of the vanity mirror so I could see exactly how much I looked like the face staring up at me. I couldn't see the photo now, but I could picture it exactly. Same eyes as me, nose straight like a pencil. We even had that same slightly crooked top canine. But I didn't actually remember the face in the photo. She was just a created memory, a story I'd been told over and over until it almost felt real.

The only real memory I had of my mom was of her screaming, twisted in agony. Then she was still, very still.

Something caught the light as I turned for the door. Mom's sunflower necklace was still draped over the corner of the mirror where I'd left it when I stopped wearing it a few months earlier. Gram hadn't moved it, either. It was like my mom might skip through the door at any moment and grab her forgotten necklace. Like I'd never worn it, never lived here at all.

"Naomi? What are you doing there in the dark?"

I stifled a yelp at Gram's voice coming from the doorway behind me.

"Nothing," I said. "Come on, I'll make you some tea before I go."

I passed by the newly printed pictures in the downstairs hallway as I left the house a little while later. There was nothing to show that they were fakes, nothing my grandparents would ever detect, but I knew. I told myself it didn't matter. All photographs were fakes, really.

The ones in my grandparents' hallway had been taken on days they'd wanted to capture and hold precious—my first day of school, when I'd received a ribbon in eighth grade for my science project, me riding a horse for the first time back when Grandpa had still kept a couple at the Academy stables. All these moments of my life were now forgeries, paper-covered cracks we'd never talk about, even as the cracks got deeper and deeper.

CHAPTER TWENTY-SIX

BACKWOODS BURTY

Kyle

I caught an afternoon bus to the new house and got there just as Mama was setting the table for dinner. Uncle Coby was in some funny kind of mood, chattering away nonstop and whisking Mama into the lounge to dance when one of her favorite Disney tunes started playing on TV. She shrieked and giggled as he spun her around the room, Mama blowing kisses at me as she twirled past, all the things that'd been waxing sour between us forgotten in the space of a few bars of *The Lion King*.

My muscles unbunched in places I didn't even know could bunch. It was like being back home in Whistler again, only better. Here there'd be no bricks tossed though our windows, no ugly words scratched onto our car in the night.

"Olive," Uncle Coby said, catching my eye. "I reckon Kyle and I could use some guy time. You don't mind if we head out for a couple hours after dinner do you, sweetheart?"

Mama beamed at him. "Of course not, Coby."

~~~~~~~~~

The temperature had dropped real low, and I jogged around the front of Uncle Coby's rental to the passenger side, thinking to dive in out of the cold. I almost tripped over the front fender on my way past—it was bent so far out it looked set to fall off.

"What happened here?" I said, pushing it back into place as best I could.

"Oh, some jackass ran into me," he said. "Thank God for insurance, huh?"

"Yeah, I guess."

Uncle Coby snorted. "I don't think the rental place'll be too happy when I drop it back tonight, though."

"Tonight? Aren't you staying the whole weekend?"

He shook his head as he took a right turn onto what looked like a backroad to nowhere. "Naw, turns out I can't. Got things I need to catch up on in the office. As much as I like spending time with you and your mama, Big Blue won't run itself."

"Oh, yeah. Of course." I did my best not to sound too disappointed.

I cranked up the heater as soon as we hit the road. He hadn't said where we were headed, but seemed happy enough without the GPS that I didn't pay any mind to the roads rushing into the glow of our headlights.

A few minutes later, Uncle Coby turned off into the lot of a bar that looked out of place outside of a swamp, let alone on the edge of a money town like Killdeer. More a shack than a bar, the few rusty trucks and dust-beat hogs parked up next to Uncle Coby's rental clued me in on the kind of people we'd likely find inside.

"Would you look at this place? Looks like a good sneeze'd take it down, don't it?" He got out of the car and hustled over to the door.

The only light came from a single bulb flickering above the bar sign, the edges of the building sucked into the blackness of the backroad. There was nobody at the door to ask for ID, so I walked straight into a hot waft of beer and sweat and other bodily fluids. As the door swung shut at my back, I counted only five other men in the place, then followed Uncle Coby to a seat at the bar.

The guy standing behind the bar was an ape with a dishrag thrown over one shoulder, and a face like tenderized beefsteak.

"What'll it be?"

"Two beers," Uncle Coby said, and the barman tossed me a smirk.

"And what's the kid gonna drink?"

"One of those beers," Uncle Coby said. "Take one for yourself, of course." He held his hand over the bar just long enough to slip the barman some cash. Uncle Coby took the beers and handed me one as the ape wandered off to serve a squirrely-looking guy at the other end of the bar.

"I know this is meant to be a father-son type of thing, but being as I'm the closest you got, I figured it was about time I bought you your first beer. After all, we're celebrating," he said.

"Celebrating what?" I took a sip, trying to hide how much I hated it. It wasn't my first taste of alcohol by any stretch, but beer had a particular aftertaste that reminded me of the smell of a guys' locker room.

Uncle Coby threw up his empty hand. "Your new start! New home, new town, all of that. It only seems right that you get to drink a couple beers with your old Uncle Coby to mark the occasion."

I didn't quite understand the need to celebrate—especially not quite so loudly, as I could see a couple of the other patrons looking over at us—but I downed another mouthful anyway. I wasn't gonna be the one to knock his good mood.

"So come on—tell me about this new school you're at. You getting on all right with your schoolwork?"

"Ha, yeah. I'm doing okay, and I made a couple friends, I guess. There's an empty tower room in the school where they have these *Friday Nighters*, as they call them, and I got invited. It's kind of a secret thing. None of the teachers know."

"Oh yeah?" Uncle Coby said. "Sounds like fun."

"Did I tell you I'm trying out for the basketball team? Had a one-on-one this week, and Coach asked me to come try out with the rest of the team at the next practice."

"Hey, no shit? That's awesome, kiddo."

"And there's this girl." I raised the bottle to my lips, thinking of jamming the thing right in there to stop the words from getting loose. I couldn't tell Uncle Coby about Naomi—couldn't risk him recognizing her name. I knew exactly what he'd do: tell me to keep away from her, and quietly arrange with Mama to send me to another school. It was the smart thing to do, the thing I'd wanted so bad when I first started at Killdeer Academy. But not now.

"A girl, huh?" His eyes crinkled at the corners. "About time, too. Hope she's not like those tramps you fooled around with back home."

I choked on my beer. I'd inhaled the poisonous crap but good, and kept sputtering while Uncle Coby gave me a good clap on the back.

"Whoa there, you're meant to drink it, not breathe it in," he said.

I thumped my chest, like it'd help clear it, and managed to knock my bottle over with my elbow. I grabbed for it, but it'd already rolled off the edge of the bar, and it smashed in a mess at the feet of a guy standing behind me.

"Hey! Watch it, asshole!" The dude was wide enough that I couldn't see the other guy with him until he took a step closer.

A scrape of wood, and Uncle Coby was on his feet. "The boy

didn't mean no harm. Here, let me get you and your buddy a beer, call it bygones."

The guy snarled like Uncle Coby had insulted his mother, and I knew it was time to leave. I slid off the bar stool, a good head taller than the pissed guy.

"He got beer all over my boots." He pointed a blunt finger at Uncle Coby. "You gonna pay for them, too?"

"Come on, let's just go," I said, turning my back on them. Then a heavy hand fell on my shoulder.

"I *said*, are you gonna pay—"

My fist connected with his face before I even got it in my head to move, and the guy went down like a blimp after the big game.

"Hey!" The barman yelled over. "Take it outside, all of you!"

But the man at my feet was out cold, and his buddy had backed off a step. Uncle Coby grabbed my arm and dragged me outside, where the night air was like a wet slap on my skin. He didn't say a word as he shoved me in the car, or as he took off with a screech of rubber out of the lot. It was only when we hit the main road that he started laughing.

"It's not funny, Uncle Coby."

That only made him crease up even harder, until there were tears running down his face.

"You'll crash your car again," I said, but he acted like he didn't even hear.

"Did you see—HA!—did you see that sack of shit hit the deck? Oh my Lord, that was something!"

I allowed a small smirk to escape.

"There ya are. No sulking, boy. Wait—I can't call you that no more, can I? Drinking beer and laying out losers makes you a man, I reckon. HA!"

The smirk fell from my face, but Uncle Coby carried on. Popping some asshole in a bar didn't make me a man. If it did, it sure wasn't the kind I wanted to be.

CHAPTER TWENTY-SEVEN

BURTY GETS DOWN TO BUSINESS

Naomi

Principal Kincaid's words echoed around the hall like a blanket of sound, unintelligible and easy to ignore once you stopped trying to decipher them. The weekly school assembly had never really served the purpose she had intended. Half the time I had no clue what she was talking about, and the other half I could guess from her stabby hand gestures and the way she scowled over her glasses.

Kyle was sitting at the far side of the gymnasium that doubled as our assembly hall, having come in late. It only took Fletcher a couple of tries before he located the perfect spot for our group to congregate for assembly—near the back and off to one side, where the echo wasn't so bad, and our own conversations wouldn't carry.

Fletch made a point of sitting next to me, his long, brown fingers laced in front of him.

"What's with the business hands?" I said.

He looked down, gracefully unlaced them. "I don't get much past you, do I?"

I shrugged. I was on edge. Because I'd spent the weekend at my grandparents' house, I hadn't seen a whole lot of Kyle since that afternoon in the woods, aside from in homeroom. I didn't even know if Kyle had gone to Fletcher's Friday Nighter, and whether Addison had been there throwing smoldering looks his way.

So what if he made out with Addison first? That doesn't mean what happened between you and him wasn't different.

I wished Kyle would come over and be normal with me so I'd stop feeling like such a tool.

"Kit hasn't been able to find anything on Breaker," Fletcher said, pausing like he was waiting for some shocked reaction.

"So?"

He stared at me. "I mean *nothing*. He's not on Twitter, Facebook, any social network Kit can find. He doesn't blog, isn't mentioned on any of the feeds of students from any of the high schools I searched in North Carolina. He has no Google footprint."

Again, he gave me the *dun-dun-duuuun* stare.

"I guess he's not the social media type," I said.

"*I'm* not the social media type," Fletcher pointed out, "but I still have a couple of accounts. I'm traceable. He has *nothing*. It's like he didn't exist before he came here."

"Did Kit search his mother as well?"

"Of course." The *duh* was implied. "He ran the plates of her car. All he found was that she didn't buy it—it was first registered to a *J. Wickes*. Has he ever mentioned anyone called Wickes?"

"I think you need to leave it there, Fletch. I know you're looking out for me, but he's a good guy. He's kind of sweet, and I'd feel really bad if he found out about it."

Fletcher said nothing, and I knew he had no intention of backing off.

"Fletch, is everything okay with you?" I lowered my voice to a whisper, and leaned in. "I mean, if that whole *Aseycay uyingbay omfray anotherway ealerday* thing is still on your mind . . . "

"It's not. Do me a favor and forget you know anything about that, okay? It's over."

I sighed. "Sure, Fletch. Whatever."

After lunch, I had Geography and the whole class went down to Van Sciver Lake to study land erosion or something. Addison and I went to stake out a good spot for avoiding doing any work while the rest of the geeks splashed around in the freezing water at the edge of the lake.

A bridge ran over Van Sciver about a half mile from where we sat, the cars crossing it almost invisible. The hazy gray light made it look a million miles away.

"Miller's got egg salad again." Addy's nose was wrinkled like she could smell something nasty. Then I smelled it, too—the funk of boiled eggs drifting from the other side of the bluff, presumably where Mr. Miller had crept off to eat his packed lunch.

"Gross," I said. I elbowed Addy gently, remembering my promise to Kit that I'd try harder to get things back to normal with Addy. "Smells better than those disgusting chili dogs they had in the cafeteria. What the hell was in those?"

She snorted. "I don't even want to know. Anyway. I've been thinking about inviting the new custodian over to the tower this Friday."

There was a note of challenge I couldn't miss, and I studied her face. Did she know about me and Jackson?

"Why would you want to do that?" I said.

She waved the question away. "He seems like a cool guy, don't you think? And just because he's *staff* doesn't mean he's not worth our time. Right?"

Addy gave me a pointed look. My friends were all at Killdeer Academy because their parents were wealthy. I was there because my grandparents had worked there their whole lives. None of them had ever made a big deal about that, not even Addy—until now.

"Aren't you worried he'll tell the principal about the tower?" I hedged.

Varaday had said Addison was seeing some older guy. Was that Jackson? It made sense, except if Jackson was seeing

Addison, then he couldn't really still be hung up on me. And his messages from a few nights ago seemed to indicate he wasn't exactly feeling the Addy-love.

Then there was the stuffed owl in my room, and the vandalized photos in my grandparents' hallway. Before the weird texts, I hadn't thought Jackson would really do those things. But the fact that he was being a dick to me didn't mean he wasn't also messing around with Addy.

"Nah. He seems like someone who's more interested in having a good time than keeping on Kincaid's good side," Addy said.

"I had no idea you knew him. Been keeping that quiet, huh?" I kept a neutral tone.

"I guess."

I knew I should tell her what an ass he'd been to me the week before, but that would mean confessing something really had happened between me and Jackson, and we weren't anywhere near being back at a place where I could confide in her.

"If you want Jackson to come on Friday, you'll have to clear it with Fletcher, not me," I said. I'd gotten my fingers burned the last time I got involved in Addy's mess. I knew better than to interfere this time.

Addison smoothed a hand over her ponytail and checked her nails. "I wasn't asking, but whatever."

CHAPTER TWENTY-EIGHT

BURTY WEARS A SHINER

Kyle

Naomi passed the door to the gym, a flash of her smile and her short, wild hair. My fingers felt strange, like the feel of her skin was imprinted on them. Wanting to touch her again.

And now every time I sat next to her in homeroom, every time she said hi, I couldn't think of anything except wanting to slide my chair closer so I could touch her.

I turned away from the door as the last of the players left the locker room and headed back to the dorms. The game was over. It'd been over even before the final whistle.

"Heads up!" Kit yelled as the basketball beaned me in the side of the head. It bounced once, twice, the sound ringing longer and louder than it really should have. My head still felt funny, and the fact that assholes kept knocking it didn't help any.

"Shit. Didn't mean to do that, Breaker."

I picked up the ball, and chunked it back at Kit. His face was red and his hair was plastered with sweat from the game.

Although I'd already known Kit was on the varsity team, I'd been surprised by how good he was.

"I came back to tell you that Coach announced it just now— we're officially teammates. I think he's cursing the fact that you weren't here for the interstate qualifier."

I fell into step with him as we headed through the door to the locker room. "I made the team?"

"As if there was ever any doubt," he said.

The room was empty, and had a real thick funk about it. I'd hung back after the game so I wouldn't have to shower with the others. I hadn't counted on Kit waiting for me.

I turned away as he started stripping off, and made ready to hit the shower myself. As soon as the water turned from ice to lava, Kit's head popped over the divider between his stall and mine. "We have a friendly against Mayfair next week. After that we'll be into the tri-counties, so you're probably gonna want to clear your after-school schedule for the next few months."

"Sure." I turned under the spray of water to hide my junk.

"How'd you get all those scars?" he said.

For the first time, I'd forgotten about the white zigzags covering my arms and chest. I stood there with my back to Kit and what I suspected were two tightly clenched butt cheeks.

"I heard you'd been in some fights in your old school. Are

those your battle scars?"

"Something like that." Some of them were. Not all, but some.

Kit made a noise in the back of his throat. I turned around and grabbed my towel, wishing I had another one to throw around my shoulders.

"It's no big deal. I'd prefer you didn't turn it into one," I said, holding Kit's eye. He nodded slowly.

"Sure, man. We've all got our secrets."

He was gone by the time I got out of the shower, and I was grateful not to have to answer any more questions or have him look at me like I was someone to feel sorry for.

I grabbed my clothes out of my locker, a screwed-up pile that I was sure I hadn't left like that, and something clattered to the floor.

A set of brass knuckles. They lay there looking right back at me as I crouched over them, my hand hovering in midair.

I'd once asked my dad if he had a paw-shaped cookie cutter on his nightstand. That was what the brass knuckles had looked like to my little kid eyes, until he showed me what they were really for. He'd kept his all shiny and new looking. These were bashed-up and scratched, and there were brown, crusty patches on them. I knew what the patches were. What they meant.

I ran to the bathroom and grabbed wads of the crunchy paper towels, then hurried back to my locker. I covered the knuckles with the paper, making sure I never once touched them with my skin as I wrapped them in more of the paper towel.

What was I meant to do with them? Maybe they hadn't been used, and the blood on them was just paint. I still couldn't dump them in the trash, where someone might find them.

I wadded them into my gym bag and walked out through the back door, listening to the faint rustle of the trees behind the Academy. They were just fuzzy black shapes against the evening sky now, like those woods weren't the same ones where I'd kissed Naomi Steadman.

I could hide the brass knuckles, sure. Maybe bury them in the woods or toss them in a river or something. But someone at Killdeer Academy knew my secret, and I doubted they'd let me keep it hidden long.

I rounded the corner into the quad, punching in the access code to South Wing three times before I got it right.

Those bloody handprints Jackson left on my shirt—had it been Jackson's blood, or somebody else's?

And how come I hadn't seen him once since that night?

~~~~~~~

The sweet, tangy smell of weed was obvious as soon as I closed Kit's door. Kit was leaning out through the window, curtains pulled around him like a smoke barrier so all I saw was his bony ass sticking out the middle. I ducked under the curtain and leaned out next to him.

Kit's room was in one of the renovated towers, higher than all the other windows facing down into the courtyard. It all looked smaller from so high up.

Kit made a choking sound as he offered me the joint, and I shook my head no. "Helps me chill out," he said, like the look I'd given him had called for an explanation. "So, what's up? You heading up to the tower?"

"Yeah, later. Hey, did you leave something behind in the locker room after the tryouts?" I hedged.

"I dunno. Like what?"

Kit looked at me, too sharp for a guy who should have been feeling pretty high.

"Look," I said. "If you heard something about me, some rumor, I'd appreciate it if you'd keep it to yourself." Kit didn't say a damn thing for once. "I swear, no matter what you're thinking, I'm not a bad guy. I'm not here to cause trouble, okay?"

"Okaaaaaay. What kind of rumors?"

I switched tactics. "That Jackson guy . . . have you heard any-thing about him getting canned?"

Something tensed in Kit's posture. "He's not been hassling Naomi again, has he? After those texts, I thought he'd finally realized he had no chance with her." Kit looked up at my face. "Ah, right. Forget I said anything. What was the question again?"

"What are you talking about, Kit? What texts?"

Kit held up his hands, nearly catching the curtains with the lit end of his joint. "Look, I'm not supposed to say anything. He drunk-texted Naomi last week, and she was kind of upset about it. That's all."

"When was this?"

"Last . . . oh, you mean exactly. Uh, it was . . . yes, it was Monday night. Well, early Tuesday morning, technically—"

If Jackson texted Naomi after I saw him that night, then he wasn't lying in a ditch somewhere. And maybe he'd just fallen and skinned his hands when he messed up my shirt. Hell, I knew firsthand it could happen.

But maybe he *had* been the one to put the brass knuckles in my locker—which would mean he knew who I was.

"Anyway, it's nothing." Kit pulled hard on his joint. "She isn't seeing him anymore, if that's what you're worried about. And yes, she's into you. Did that save you some time?"

He didn't look at all worried about me showing interest in Naomi. That *had* to mean he didn't know who I really was.

"Yeah, it did. Thanks."

"So you're *sweet on 'er*, huh?" His accent was lousy, but it wasn't hard to guess he was mimicking mine.

"Yeah, I guess I am." There was no way I could flat-out deny it now.

"Just . . . " Kit seemed to search for the right words. I waited for him to threaten me—to give me the *if you hurt her, I'll mash your balls into pink paste* speech.

"I think I'm a good judge of character," he said finally. "And you seem to be an okay guy. So don't worry about Jackson, or any stupid rumors. She won't. And don't go making a big deal about her past, either. You know what I'm talking about?"

"Yeah."

"She never talks about it. Thinks what happened makes her a freak."

"Why?" I said.

"She got hassled about it a lot when she first moved here. Press hanging around outside the school, and she got a few letters from admirers of that Bonebreaker psycho. And kids can be real assholes, too."

"I know all about that." Sour spit built in my mouth.

"Yeah," Kit said, "I thought you might."

He stubbed out the last little pinch of his joint and tucked it into a metal pencil box on the windowsill.

"So, here's a random question," I said. "You know the cameras around the school? The ones in the stuffed animals?"

"Oh, the TaxiCams?" Kit said, looking pleased with himself for the name he'd given them.

"Yeah. Do you know where the feed goes? Where the footage is stored?"

He gave me a look I was starting to recognize as him thinking I was an idiot. "If you're planning on messing with it, you're on your own. Kincaid will turn your ballbag into a new purse."

CHAPTER TWENTY-NINE

BURTY GETS BUSTED

Naomi

"Of course I said no. You think I'd let someone like *him* up here?"

Fletcher was so scathing that I wasn't surprised to see Addy slink away to a bunch of girls on the other side of the tower. Fletch seemed really pissed about it. But after steeling myself to face Jackson again at the Friday Nighter, I almost did a victory dance on my way to the kitchen after Fletch nixed Addy's plan.

Kyle and Kit had basketball practice again after school, so I'd gone to the tower without waiting for them. It wouldn't be safe to cross the roof for much longer since the frost would make it too risky, so I was making the most of it while I could.

Still, I'd shuddered when I passed the spot from where Casey must have fallen. Kincaid would probably have blocked access to the roof altogether if putting new locks and railings up there wouldn't have meant spending money.

Kit was sitting on the lumpy sofa when I went back through to the main room of the tower, and he moved over for me. I looked at all the faces surrounding him. Kyle wasn't there yet.

"Hey, don't I even get a hello these days?" Kit pouted, so I punched him in the arm.

"Hello."

"I need an adult! Somebody! I'm being abused!"

"You're such an idiot," I said. "Isn't Kyle with you?"

"Nope." Kit leaned back and sighed. "I'm worried about that guy."

"Why? What has he done?"

He shook his head. "It sounds like he had a pretty tough time of it before he moved here." Kit's face brightened. "Maybe he'll talk to you? He likes you. A lot."

"You think so?"

"I know so. He checks you out a hundred times a day. But I guess he's too shy to make a move on you or something." Kit leaned in again. "He might still have his V card."

I almost choked on my beer. From the way he kissed, it hadn't even crossed my mind that Kyle might be a virgin.

"So where is he?" I said. "Didn't you have basketball practice with him earlier?"

Kit side-eyed me as he finished off his beer. "Yup."

I headlocked him.

"Okay, okay! I'll tell you where he is!" I let Kit go, and he sank back against the ratty couch, his hair a crazy tangle. "But you're not going to like it."

I edged inside Kincaid's office a few minutes later, careful not to trip in the dark. It had been years since Fletcher had shown me the panic room behind the principal's office—Principal Turner, then—and we'd found the stash of booze and porno mags. Even then, Fletcher was too smart to take enough of anything to get caught.

I could hear Kyle inside the panic room. He'd left the door open, and the flickering light of the security monitors bled out through the crack.

"Kyle," I whispered, and the sounds stopped. "Kyle, it's me."

The crack widened, and his surprised face appeared. I pushed him back inside.

"What are you doing here?" he said. The room was narrow, with a bank of monitors taking up most of one wall, a bench seat, and not much space for anything else. Which suited me, as it meant I was smooshed up tight against Kyle's chest.

"Kit told me you were in here looking for something," I said.

"Dammit, I told him not to—"

"Don't get mad at Kit, I *literally* twisted his arm. What are you looking for?"

He got that cagey look Kit had earlier. "Someone put something in my gym locker as a joke. I wanted to find out who it was, is all."

"And did you?"

I tilted my head up to look at him, and Kyle swallowed hard. "Uh, no. There's chunks of footage missing. And the cameras don't record in the locker room, anyhow."

"I see."

"Then I thought maybe it would show who went into your room that day when Casey fell, but there's nothing. Just whole sections of the video gone."

"Bummer. It was a smart idea, though." I pulled the door closed next to us. It was completely silent in the small space now, with only the dim flicker from the TV monitors casting any light. "You don't mind the door being closed, do you?"

I was about to reach for the handle when Kyle's fingers closed around my wrist. "I don't mind," he said.

His hand felt hot, and his fingers lingered. He'd been quiet since the afternoon we went into the woods. If Kit was right, and he was just shy, I had to work out how to make Kyle relax around me—especially after all the bizarre things that had happened lately.

"Are you humming?" Kyle said, his chest moving against mine.

I stopped humming. "I read somewhere that the vibrations are meant to calm you down, like a cat purring."

"Uh-huh. And which one of us would you be trying to calm down?" He didn't wait for an answer. "Crazy girl."

Kyle leaned in and kissed me, slow and deep, like there was

nothing more important than kissing me so thoroughly.

I forgot how to breathe. How to think. I leaned back against the bench seat, drawing Kyle with me, his arms around me, his legs between mine.

The muscles in his back flexed when I pulled him closer. I kissed him, running my hands up over his shoulders until my fingers tingled at the feel of his short-cropped hair. I let them drift down over his biceps, his chest, lower. My breathing was loud, but so was his. Kyle changed the angle of his body, and my lips brushed against his jaw.

"I can feel your heart beating," he said.

I felt it, too. Only I felt something else with it, less tangible than a heartbeat, but just as real.

"Naomi, I . . . we shouldn't be doing this."

"Why?" I half turned away, giving him an out, but he held me with one arm around my waist, my back pressed against him, his bare arm against that strip of skin above my jeans where my sweater had ridden up. I felt his stubble against my ear, the heat of his body behind me. His clean guy-smell was all around me, and it was so, so *good*.

And then his arm tightened, like all the muscles had seized.

"God, I'm sorry, I didn't mean to grab you like that, I—"

"You didn't . . . "

"Please don't think I was gonna make you do anything, I'd never—" His voice was sharp and quick at my ear.

"Really, it's fine."

"It's not, I—"

"Kyle, please shut up." I put my hand over his. He took a shaky breath, his chest rising against my back like we were connected. "Are you okay now? Or should I start humming again?"

He made a choked sound that was almost a laugh, so I stayed quiet until his breathing evened out. I splayed his fingers with my own against my stomach, moving them in slow circles against my skin.

"I like how your hands feel on me," I said. His breathing quickened again, but it was different this time. It matched my own.

"What all are we doing here?" he said finally, and his low voice made me shiver. I thought about my answer. I *really* thought about it, even though it was hard to think at all.

"Just touching, for now. But I want to touch you, too."

He nodded against my ear, and I turned so we were pressed front to front. A *click* made me freeze, like someone had hit Pause on the remote.

Footsteps. On the other side of the door, heading toward the closet. Moving slowly, like whoever it was—and it was either a member of the night staff, or Kincaid—was happy to take their time busting us.

"We should hide," I whispered. Kyle shook his head. If the door opened, there'd be nowhere we could hide. Like he'd guessed what I was thinking, Kyle reached up with one hand— so, so slowly—and slid one of the bolts across the door.

We waited, silent, while the footsteps seemed to circle the office. There was a sound of papers being shuffled, drawers opening and closing, before we heard Kincaid's voice.

"Right, I have the spare set. I'll put them through the door when I . . . " It sounded like she was on the phone, and someone had interrupted her. My heart pounded so hard I even wondered for a second if she'd heard it. But then she spoke again, and I allowed myself to exhale. "Of course I respect your right to privacy, and I have no need to hold the spare keys. But in exchange I expect—"

I heard her suck in a sharp breath. I'd never heard anyone interrupt the principal before. Whoever was on the other end of that phone was about to feel the wrath. "I . . . apologize. I meant no disrespect. You'll have them shortly."

I looked up at Kyle, and saw he was wearing exactly the same *WTF* expression I was. There was a jangle of metal—probably the keys Kincaid had mentioned—before her heels clack-clacked away, and her office door closed sharply.

"I think she's gone," he said, and stepped back. My hands fell from where they'd been frozen halfway underneath his shirt.

"Uh . . . okay."

He moved, swatted my leg, then muttered an apology. I pushed back against the bench to try to stand, almost falling when my hand caught on something hard, and the wall of monitors went dark.

"Damn . . . hang on a sec." I felt around until I found the switch again. The screens flashed back on one by one until the whole wall showed a storyboard of the Academy, with the recording moving at quadruple speed. One of the younger kids zipped along a hallway in his bathrobe. A proctor with headphones on painted her toenails at record speed on her desk. Kit had a three-second convo with one of his film club friends in the media lab. Just people, life, happening silently in the hallways around us. "Maybe we should head back."

But he wasn't listening. Kyle stepped around me, eyes fixed on something as he knelt to inspect one of the screens.

"What is it? What have you seen?" I said.

I crouched next to him to get a better look. The camera was positioned somewhere near Fletcher's bedroom window, looking diagonally down over the quad, where a figure was carrying something across the cobbles and into the recess where the recycling was kept, back and forth, over and over again. Kyle hit a switch under the monitor and the timing slowed right down, until the figure barely moved.

"Oh my God, that's Grandpa."

"Your granddaddy? I thought he was sick?"

I kept my eyes fixed on the screen so I wouldn't have to look at Kyle. "Yeah, but he can still get around okay. He has Alzheimer's." *Yeah, no big deal.*

"What's he doing?"

"He's feeding the horses," I said. "That's where the stables used to be."

The footage showed Grandpa carrying a bucket full of water into the recess. He set it down in front of a stack of recycling crates and stood there talking to them for a while. Just out having a nice conversation with the trash.

Kyle's hand slid into mine. He said nothing, and it was exactly what I needed. I flipped the switch, squeezing Kyle's hand when the bank of monitors went dark.

"Let's get out of here before Kincaid sends her flying monkeys after us."

CHAPTER THIRTY

BURTY'S NEW DIGS

Kyle

I'd felt like crap plenty of times in my life, but the mix of excitement at what had happened with Naomi in that fancy closet, and beating myself up over getting so caught up I hadn't even thought about who she was—who she'd *been*—sure was new.

I couldn't lie to myself that I'd forgotten all about Dad and Whistler and the goddamn Bluchevsky legacy, either, because I'd been in that closet looking for a clue to who'd figured it all out, and what, if anything, Jackson had to do with those brass knuckles.

I'd taken some bleach earlier that morning from a cleaner's pushcart and dealt with the blood—or sauce, or paint, or whatever the hell it was—left on the brass knuckles. They were now double-bagged in the side pocket of my backpack, and I held it tight in my lap as the bus rattled along to the next place where I'd have to change.

I got off at the stop where I'd seen a sign for boat trips out on the Delaware River, and headed down to the jetty. It was still early, too early for most folks to brave a cold morning out on a riverboat, so the jetty was good and quiet. I pulled my hood up high, walked not-too-slowly to the end of the boardwalk.

The boats docked farther along the harbor were big so the water had to be deep. If I'd had more time, maybe I'd have gone out on the tour boat, waited for a point in the middle of the river where the current was strong, but I didn't want to hang around. I tore the plastic, careful not to touch the metal even with my glove, and let it drop down into the dark water.

Deep water could keep secrets.

〰〰〰〰

I woke in my own bed the next morning, and thought at first I was having another fuzzy spell. The window was six inches to the left of where it should have been, and nothing looked quite the way it ought to. Then I remembered. Not Whistler. Killdeer.

I was surprised I'd slept at all. I couldn't stop going over what had happened, was happening, between me and Naomi. How good it felt to be so close to someone, even when that someone was the one person I should stay the hell away from.

It would hurt her more to know who I am.

It was an easy lie, but I couldn't make myself believe it. And even if I could, there was someone else out there who knew who I was, and a set of brass knuckles wasn't going to be the last I'd hear about it. Had it been a warning, or a threat? Were they meant to screw with my head, or to force me to come clean?

I checked the time on my phone and saw I'd missed a call from Kit the night before. It was only seven a.m., so I put my phone back on the nightstand. I'd see him back at school in a few hours.

There was a knock at my door.

"Yes, Mama?" The door opened, and it wasn't Mama standing there at all. "Uncle Coby!" A surprise visit probably meant I'd done something wrong again. But he was here, and no amount of ball-busting was going to put me in a funk. "What are you doing here?"

He grinned back at me. "Seems like I can't keep away."

CHAPTER THIRTY-ONE

BURTY'S SECRET HIDING PLACE

Naomi

Cleaning sucked ass, but at least it was *something* I could do to help Gram out. I scrubbed harder at the wooden baseboard on the first landing.

I nearly fell on my butt when a footstep sounded behind me. I knew Gram was downstairs, and I'd thought Grandpa was napping.

When I looked up, Grandpa was staring at a photo on the wall. It was one all three of us had posed for one summer when we'd gone camping up at Bear Mountain.

"Hey, Grandpa. Did you have a good nap?"

He didn't answer, just kept staring at the photo.

"Grandpa?"

He raised one wrinkled finger and pointed at the photo, muttering to himself too low for me to make out his words. He seemed very adamant about whatever he was saying, jabbing repeatedly at the picture until the glass was covered in finger smears. I went over to him, touched him gently on the shoulder.

"She's not meant to be there," he said.

I followed the line of his finger, saw he was pointing at me. I was perched on top of a trash can for the photo, Grandpa on one side and Gram looking disapprovingly at me on the other.

"Yeah." I laughed. "I fell off right after the camera flashed."

He shook his head, still pointing. "She tells lies."

I caught my breath, even though I knew he didn't mean it. "I'm not a liar, Grandpa."

He looked at me then, like he was noticing I was there for the first time. "Jake told me. You've been lying to me."

"Lying? Oh, you mean the pictures?" I stopped. *Jake?* "Are you talking about the kid from the story? The one who hid in the cave?"

He didn't say anything.

"Grandpa, I wasn't lying, I was trying to help you—"

"A liar and a manipulator, that's what he said. And I told him no, not my girl, but I'm beginning to wonder if he wasn't right about you, Annabel."

"*What?*" Grandpa hadn't confused me with Mom in months. *She's dead, Grandpa. She's dead.*

"You're always running off with that boy. You think I don't know, think he doesn't gloat about it when he sees me at the stables . . . "

His focus had shifted again. I'd never heard Grandpa talk this way, not even at his worst. I guessed this was a new worst.

He reached up, took the picture frame down from its hook and starting prying the stays away at the back with his fingernail. The back came loose, and he slid the photo out of the frame before squeezing it back into place and replacing it on the wall.

I gaped at him. "Did you take the pictures from the downstairs hallway, too?"

Grandpa shuffled to the top of the staircase and knelt down, tugging a loose corner of the carpet from by the wall, then sliding the photo down into a gap between the floorboards and the baseboard.

"Hey! Grandpa, what the—"

I tried to grab the photo back before it disappeared into the gap. Grandpa shoved me away, and I fell back onto my butt. He kept right on stuffing the photo into the floor.

"Can't keep things straight with all the lies."

I hadn't moved—couldn't, somehow—but I felt the hot trails of tears dripping down onto my neck. I wiped them away, rubbing at my throat.

"I didn't mean to lie, Grandpa. I—"

"Naomi? What's going on up there?"

Gram's voice broke whatever spell Grandpa had fallen under, and he jerked to his feet. But the sudden movement was too quick, and he teetered a little, trying to shuffle his feet to counter it. I lunged for him, my arm burning against the carpet, my fingers closing on nothing.

He slipped, one foot angled wrong on the top step. It was almost impossibly slow how he crumpled, disappearing from my view as he fell, arms and legs limp like he wasn't even trying to stop himself.

I screamed, and Gram's hands flew up to her face on the landing below.

I scrambled down the steps, nearly slipping twice before I reached the bottom. I climbed over Grandpa's legs, and felt Gram shaking as she clutched my arm. Grandpa stared up at me, filmy eyes fixed on my face.

"Grandpa, can you hear me?"

He groaned. I turned to find Gram already with the cordless phone in her hand.

"Grandpa, please be all right," I whispered. He blinked when one of my tears hit his cheek. "I promise to do better. Just please be all right."

~~~~~~

Gram went with Grandpa, leaving me to wait in the chemical-smelling room down the hall in the hospital with three other families, all looking pale and shaky. It had been an hour already, and she'd only come back once to let me know the doctors thought he'd suffered a stroke.

I sat on one of the plastic chairs, staring at the door with my elbows on my knees, shifting every few minutes when the carpet burn on my elbow started to sting against my jeans. I avoided looking at anyone directly. I'd learned my lesson after the first three well-meaning people had come over, telling me empty things about him being in the best place to get help and how the doctors would do their very best to make him better.

"Sweetie, isn't there anyone I can call to come sit with you?"

My hunching had failed. I looked up and found the receptionist peering at me.

"No, thanks."

It was getting pretty late now. It had been dark for hours, but it was hard to tell properly under the stark fluorescent lighting of the hospital.

"How about a ride home? I could call you a cab, save you waiting here all by yourself. You should get some rest—you look exhausted. And we can always call you to come back if there's any change."

I tried not to show how much she was pissing me off. Really, I did.

"No. Thank you."

"Naomi!" Gram pushed through the door from the mysterious corridor where they'd taken Grandpa. She looked so frail and old suddenly. Her eyes were red, and her hair had come loose from the twist she normally wore.

"What? Is Grandpa . . . is he . . . " My voice cracked.

Gram shook her head and pulled me into a hug. "No, child, he's still with us. The doctors have him hooked up to all kinds of machines, and they tell me he's stable for now." She leaned back and looked at me, hands still on my shoulders. "I'll stay here tonight. You should go back home and get some rest. Or to the school, so that you're not alone."

"I don't want to go, Gram."

"Now listen to me," she said, and I could tell she was being as sweet as her frayed nerves would allow. "He's not going any-where, and I don't want to be worrying about you sitting here all by yourself all night. Just do as I say, *please*."

I didn't like it. I really didn't like it. But I knew better than to argue.

"Is he awake? Can I at least say goodnight before I leave?"

Gram shook her head. "He hasn't woken up yet. If he does, I'll be sure to tell him goodnight for you."

"You promise you'll call me right away if anything changes, right? I'll be back first thing in the morning. Let me know if you want me to bring you anything."

Gram's face unpinched, and I knew I'd finally done some-thing right.

[Letter from the Warden, North Carolina Central Prison]

Dear Mrs. Bluchevsky,

Please find enclosed the personal effects of your late husband, Robert Kyle Bluchevsky.

Inventory:

›Blue shirt (one), brown leather boots (pair), denim jeans (pair)

›Pencil sketches (eighteen)

›Photographs (two: one of son—Kyle Henry Bluchevsky, one of spouse—Olive Henry Bluchevsky)

›Letters (two, scanned and unopened; addressed to

[Remainder of letter missing]

CHAPTER THIRTY-TWO

BURTY GETS BACK TO HIS ROOTS

Kyle

I heard about Naomi's granddaddy from Kit when I got back to the Academy Sunday night, so I was surprised as hell to see her in homeroom Monday morning.

"How's he doing?" I whispered, and she slid her hand into mine under the desk.

"Gram says he's going to be okay. The doctors are keeping an eye on him for a few days."

Naomi stayed at her grandparents' empty cottage that night, and I walked her there after our last class let out. I'd only seen the old staff cottages from a distance, and I'd kept well away from the kitchens where I knew Naomi's grandmother worked. These people were Annabel Steadman's parents, and my father had murdered their daughter. I didn't even want to guess how they'd react if they knew the son of that psychopath was now fooling around with their granddaughter.

"Do you want to come in?" she asked.

I glanced into the hallway behind her, saw the photographs of the three of them lining the wall. The kitchen was beyond it with lacy curtains over the sink. "I'd better not. Are you sure you wouldn't prefer to be in the dorm tonight?"

"I feel like I need to be here," she said. "I'll text you later, okay?"

She kissed me before I left, and I waited to hear the slide of the bolts hitting home before I turned away, down the path lined with rose bushes and out through an arch over the front gate.

Principal Kincaid's cottage looked no different, really, from Naomi's grandparents' place, except she didn't have a whole lot of flowers in her front yard.

The house in between the two looked dead, in that way that houses do when all the windows are dark and there's no sign of anyone living there. If it wasn't for the car sitting out front, I would have put money on it being empty.

Naomi didn't show up to class the next day, but she texted to say she was going to the hospital. I kept checking my phone about every five minutes, so I was glad when Kit reminded me we had a basketball game that afternoon.

" . . . up from someplace in North Carolina for the interstate invitational—which they *lost*, heh—and they're now trying to scrape together some pride by throwing us a pity game. Don't suppose you know these guys?"

I looked up from tying my tennis shoe. Todd—another guy from the team—leaned up against one of the lockers with Kit. They were both staring at me.

"Know who?"

Todd frowned. "The team we're playing this afternoon. Some big school in West Whistler. Is that anywhere near where you used to live?"

I studied Todd's face, looking for the smirk that'd tell me he was full of shit. No way could I be *that* unlucky. But there was no smirk. "What?"

"Is that your old school?" Kit asked. He seemed a little too interested in my reaction.

"Nah. I heard of it, though," I lied, pretty sure I looked like I'd just been pistol-whipped.

"So you know what their players are like?"

"Yeah. They're no great shakes."

Todd laughed. "Think we'll beat 'em?"

"No doubt." I threw my gym bag over my shoulder and walked out of the locker room, toward the gym. Then I kept walking straight out through the fire exit and into the parking lot.

The doors swung shut behind me, and I stayed real close to the school building as I made my way past the lot, back toward the front of the Academy and the way out. There, every last little bit of hope I'd been holding on to got shot to shit.

The West Whistler team bus was already parked, Coach Davis standing at the front giving a pep talk to the team before letting them off. It was getting dark, and the interior light of the bus showed every face inside. They were focused on Coach Davis, not looking my way, so I probably hadn't been spotted yet. I needed to get as far away from Killdeer Academy—and that busload of West Whistler basketball players—as I could. For the next few days, anyhow.

"Breaker!"

Dammit. I turned and waited as Kit came running over.

"Where are you going?"

I nodded at the gym bag slung over my shoulder. "I need to head off straight after the game, so I was gonna ditch my bag in the dorm. Why? What's up?"

He laughed. "Don't give me that bullshit. You're leaving."

The bus door hissed open across the lot, and Coach Davis led the players out in single file. "Fine. I need to leave before these assholes see me."

I turned to go, but Kit grabbed my arm. "Breaker, what's going on? Why don't you want them to see you? Has this got something to do with what you were talking about in my room the other day? Those rumors?"

I jerked away and started walking again, ignoring him as he called after me. At least the West Whistler players wouldn't recognize the nickname if they heard it.

Coach Davis's voice boomed across the lot. He was giving them a somewhat less peppy talk about *forgetting yesterday* and *moving on to make West Whistler proud* and some other BS. Then another voice answered him—Tyler Ross, captain of the West Whistler team, whom I'd left outside the grocery store in Whistler, groaning and rolling in a puddle of his own piss.

He climbed off the bus and walked right on over to me.

"Kyle Bluchevsky," he said. "I thought I saw you lurking out here, you sack of shit."

"What do you want, Tyler?"

He smirked. "Maybe I came over to say hi. Or maybe I came to show you what a pussy you are when you're not jumping someone from behind—teach you a lesson about screwing with a *real* West Whistler player."

"Whatever, Tyler. Just go back to your team and stay the hell away from me."

He made like he was scared, then laughed at me again. "Why should I do that? I bet you haven't told your new buddies all about daddy dearest, have you?" He glanced behind him, where the rest of the players were gathered around Coach Davis at the other side of the lot. Within shouting distance, if he needed them. When Tyler turned back, he almost bumped into Kit.

I knew when I was screwed, and this was that moment.

"What's going on, Breaker?"

"So you *have* told them, then?" Tyler turned on Kit. "You don't mind hanging around with a psycho who'll probably rape your sister?"

"Go to hell," I said, but there was no real strength to it. The women had never been raped, not one of them, but people always assumed. And there wasn't a damn thing I could say without it sounding like I was defending what my dad did.

Kit frowned, looking back and forth between us. "I don't know what you're talking about. Maybe you should go back to your team."

Tyler sneered, but Coach Davis was off the bus now, so his buddies were heading over to the open doors at the back of the gym. "Don't you even realize you're talking to Kyle Bluchevsky right here? Son of *Bobby* Bluchevsky?"

Kit stared at him.

"The *Bonebreaker*, Bobby Bluchevsky? The serial killing *psychopath*, Bobby Bluchevsky?" Tyler said.

I saw Kit make the connection. And then he made the next connection.

He knew who my dad was to Naomi.

Everything seemed to tilt on its side for a second, and this time it wasn't a dizzy spell. Kit would tell everyone at Killdeer Academy.

He'd tell *Naomi*.

Kit gave me a long look before turning back to Tyler. "You've made a mistake. This isn't Kyle Bluchevsky. His name's Henry." Kit steered Tyler back toward Coach Davis, who was now looking around for his missing player. He hadn't seen me yet.

"It's *him*!" Tyler spat. I couldn't hear what Kit said to him after that as Kit herded Tyler back to the other West Whistler players like it was no big deal. I sank to my knees, ignoring the hard bite of pavement against my skin. My lies had fallen apart right in front of me. It was over, all of it.

I couldn't seem to catch enough air, my throat getting tighter and tighter the harder I tried to breathe, just breathe.

Then the fire alarm went off.

CHAPTER THIRTY-THREE

BURTY SHIPS OUT

Naomi

The sunflower necklace hung from the corner of my mirror, just like I'd left it. Except I'd left it on the mirror in the cottage, not in my dorm room.

I picked it up, the thin chain tinkling against the porcelain edge of the sink. The sunflower sat in my palm. I could have described every petal, every notch in the silver, with my eyes closed. I'd been memorizing every facet of the sunflower necklace since I was a toddler, my chubby pink fingers tugging on it around my mom's neck as she laughed.

Her laugh. It was strange—I hadn't thought of the sound of Mom's laugh in such a long time, I'd thought it was lost.

I closed my hand around the sunflower. It was the same temperature as my skin now, and I could barely feel it.

"Weird," I said aloud around my toothbrush, which was probably another sign that I was overtired. How had I managed to forget bringing the necklace to my dorm? I must have picked it up from the cottage the last time I was there and not even realized. Or maybe I was just losing it.

My grandparents had both looked exhausted by the time the doctors allowed Grandpa home, and I'd left them earlier that morning with the mix of guilt and relief I'd gotten used to feeling whenever I closed the front door of the cottage.

Going back to class for the last day before Thanksgiving break seemed pointless, but I knew Gram would throw a major fit if she thought I was skipping school without a good reason. Moving on autopilot, I finished brushing my teeth, slipped on the pendant, and put on my Academy uniform ready for class.

One semiupside to being out of school the last few days was that Jackson—or whoever the hell it was—had left me alone all week. No dead critters in my room, no missing photos.

That meant I was looking forward to spending a fun night up at the tower with Kyle before he went home for the long weekend.

Lots of kids had already gone home, so the tower was much quieter than usual. Even Addy had bailed, and there'd been no sign of Kincaid all afternoon, so I guessed she'd gotten herself a ticket to Vegas or something.

Even if the room had been packed wall to wall with people, I'd have noticed him right away. Kyle walked in and came straight over to where I sat with Kit.

"Naomi, can I talk to you, please?"

It didn't really sound like a question so much as a command. Kit tensed up next to me. "Breaker, maybe you shouldn't do this now," he said.

Kyle looked confused for a second. "I need to clear this up."

I got up off the sofa and followed Kyle out of the main room. He didn't stop outside the door. He took the stairs down to the dropout, past the grubby little cot where Fletch ditched the pukers to sleep off the booze and whatever else they'd bought from him. Kyle stopped at the trapdoor.

"Oh, are we leaving? We'll need Fletch to come and—"

"Looks like he's already on it," Kyle said, and I turned and jumped when I saw Fletch standing right behind me.

"Jesus, Fletch! Way to creep up on me."

Fletcher didn't seem to be listening. He stared at Kyle over my head. "Leaving early?"

"There's something I need to talk to Naomi about."

"Help us down, Fletch?" I said.

Fletcher handed me the harness. His hand lingered on mine. "Is everything okay?" he said.

"Everything's fine." I smiled, and he let go of my hand.

Kyle held on to me as I went over the edge, into darkness. "I'll be right behind you."

Even without a flashlight, I could see from the glow-in-the-dark faces painted inside the tower when I was nearing the halfway point.

I strangled a screech when something touched my hand, but it was gone almost instantly. I'd either brushed against the hem of my own shirt, or high-fived a bat or something living in the empty tower shaft.

Thirty seconds later I came to a stop. I unhooked my clip and sent the harness back up the rope with a couple of tugs on it. It was pitch-black at the base of the tower, except for a vertical sliver of light showing the crack where the door stood slightly open. Someone must already have left the party, even though it was still early.

I could hear Kyle's and Fletcher's voices faintly at the top of the tower, followed by the clink of the metal clip reaching the top of the pulley. I took a step back toward the base of the rope, and walked right into something. It swayed, pushing back against me in the darkness, and I reached out with both hands. At first all I could feel was fabric over something not-quite-hard, like a punching bag or something.

"Hey, Kyle, can you bring a light with you?" I yelled up the echoing shaft. "There's something down here that—"

Then my hand closed around something soft and clammy, like putty. Something with fingers. I screamed, stumbling backward as it swayed toward me again. My teeth clattered together when my back hit the wall, and I shut up. I breathed hard through my nose, trying not to vomit.

I stared at it rocking back and forth on the rope, in and out of the slant of light coming from the trapdoor above.

In and out.

Back and forth.

Dead, dead, dead.

"What's going on? Naomi?" Kyle yelled.

I couldn't answer him. My fingers hurt where I'd been digging them in between the bricks behind me.

"Naomi? Are you okay? Dammit. I'm coming down!"

I still couldn't answer. Then the thing in front of me moved.

"Wait! Don't pull up the rope!" I yelled. The thing stopped moving. "There's . . . there's something on it."

"Hold on," Kyle said. "I'll shin down."

Seconds later, feet thudded behind me, and a light snapped on. Kyle dipped his head and the beam landed on the heavy bag. Only I already knew it wasn't a punching bag. Cold, dead eyes stared up at us, reflecting nothing in the unnatural light.

CHAPTER THIRTY-FOUR

BURTY'S NEW BOXING GLOVES

Kyle

Jackson's nose and mouth were ringed with dried blood, and his hands were totally messed up. His fingers were black and swollen, bent at angles bones didn't bend without breaking.

Naomi shot forward, wrapping her arms around his legs.

"Kyle, help me!"

I stepped forward and took his weight from her. There was no trace of heat in the guy's clothes, and the smell coming off the body was anything but fresh. "I got him. Can you cut him loose?"

Jackson's body finally buckled down over my shoulder. He'd been a lean guy, and should have felt hard and stiff, but he didn't. I laid Jackson down on the floor, and Naomi crouched next to him. She checked for a pulse, listening at his mouth for any signs of life, her actions as smooth and precise as when she'd fixed up my grazed hand.

"He's cold already," I said. I heard footsteps behind me, and saw Fletch had followed me down. "This hasn't just happened now."

"Is that Jackson?" he asked.

"Yeah." Naomi's voice was quiet. She should have been scream-ing. Instead she just stood there with this glassy look like she'd gone someplace else in her head. I put my hand on her shoulder and she jumped, making a harsh noise in back of her throat.

"What is Jackson doing here?" Fletcher said. He stood back against the wall, as far away as he could get, like being dead might spread. "Did he hang himself?"

I shook my head. "He didn't do this to himself. I'm pretty sure he's been dead awhile. I saw him a couple weeks ago, thought he was drunk and acting out, but he might've been hurt." He'd texted Naomi later that same night, though, hadn't he? If he'd been dead or dying then, surely he couldn't have sent her those messages. But I hadn't run into him since, and I was pretty sure someone at school would have mentioned seeing Jackson looking all beat-up.

"Why would anyone want to kill the custodian?" Fletcher said, looking anywhere but at Jackson's body.

I held the headlamp close to the body, lighting up the black bruising and swelling in his fingers. Those were the marks of the Bonebreaker. Even in the dark, I could feel Fletcher watching me. Kit might have been able to keep the rest of the Academy from finding out who I was, but I was sure he'd told Fletcher, even if he'd sworn he wouldn't.

I'd planned on coming clean with Naomi tonight. Maybe she'd hate me, or maybe it would shed some light on what the hell was going on with all the crazy shit piling up around us. I'd been set on doing my damnedest to convince her I wasn't some creep out to terrorize her. Now we stood over a dead body together.

Naomi's hand covered her mouth when she crouched down to take a closer look. I swung the light away before she could see.

"We need to call the police," she said.

I was about to agree when Fletcher said, "No police. Not yet, at least. You two need to get out of here first."

"What? Why?" I said. There was something about the way he kept staring at me. It made it even harder to think straight.

"You've had at least two altercations with him since you started here last month, and it sounds like you were the last one of us to see him alive. Naomi, you have a history with him, too, and I happen to know you've been arguing with him lately." No mention of what Fletcher knew about me. Could he really not know?

"Wait, you know about me and Jackson?" Naomi looked genuinely shocked. Fletcher nodded.

"And after the two of you moved the body and interfered with a crime scene, I bet you're covered in his DNA. Do either of you want the police poking around in your business?" He waited a beat. "No. I didn't think so. And I've got a shitload of drugs up in the tower that I need to get rid of before they start tearing through this place. I'll seal the trapdoor so nobody else comes down here, and call it in once I've found somewhere to move my stuff. You'll have to climb back up to the tower and go through the attic to your dorms to make sure nobody sees you. I'll sort things out here. Now get out of here, and hurry."

I couldn't tell whether he was working all this out as he talked, but it was the most I'd ever heard Fletcher say at once.

"Fletch, you can't be serious," Naomi said.

He turned those hard eyes on her, and she went quiet.

As much as I hated to admit it, he was right. The cops would figure out in two minutes who I was, and that Jackson was killed the exact same way my dad had killed those women ten years earlier. Even if they didn't find me with the body, I needed to get rid of everything I was wearing.

"All right," I said, laying my hand on Naomi's arm. "Naomi, can you climb back up?" She stood, staring at me. "Naomi?"

She nodded at last, and I waited for her to shin up the rope a few feet before I handed the headlamp to Fletcher and followed her.

CHAPTER THIRTY-FIVE

BURTY'S GREAT ESCAPE

Naomi

Only the narrowest strip of silvery light sliced through the gap where the window sat open overlooking the catwalk, not enough to chase away the feeling that there was something there, lurking in the shadows around us. All I saw was Jackson's face hanging there in the tower. His dead eyes.

"What are we doing?" I said.

"We're getting out of here." Kyle's voice was low, but still bounced off the inside walls. His hand was at the small of my back, warm from climbing up the rope after me. I had no idea how I'd managed the climb back up, must have just zoned out until Fletch shut the hatch.

"Wait!" I whispered, and Kyle grew still next to me. "Jackson is *dead*. There is a dead, *murdered* body right below us, and someone did that to him and left him hanging there! And instead of calling the police, we're sneaking off back to our dorms. How does that even make sense? We can't just leave him down there, alone. We can't."

Kyle hugged me to him, hushing me softly. I was cold, despite the heat pouring off Kyle, and my hands hung limp at my sides. *They felt like clay.*

"Fletcher's gonna call the police once he's cleared the tower," Kyle said, lowering his voice even more so it wouldn't echo.

"Why wait? The cops won't give a crap about a bunch of teens getting high when they've got a murdered body to deal with. Even Fletcher's not *that* paranoid." But why was he so intent on waiting before calling the cops? His face flashed through my head, his disgusted look as he'd stared at Jackson's body.

Kyle's shoulders were all bunched up in knots. "Who do you think the cops are going to look at when they start looking for a killer? Just because you know that bunch of kids aren't killers doesn't mean the cops will think that. And of all of them, don't you think they'll look hardest at Jackson's ex-girlfriend, and the guy he had a major problem with? And like Fletcher said, we're covered in his DNA. Won't that look kinda shady?" He leaned forward, his forehead resting against mine. "We'll do what Fletch said, and nobody will be looking at us, okay?"

I couldn't see his face in the dark, but there was a strained edge to his voice like he was struggling to hold it together, even more than I was.

"What's really going on here, Kyle?"

His hands smoothed up my arms and to my face.

"I don't know," he said.

"I should go to my grandparents' place, make sure everything's okay there."

"Naomi, whoever did that to Jackson, do you think it could have some connection to you? To what's been happening lately, Casey and the owl and the pictures."

Ever since things had gotten sketchy between me and Jackson and all the messed-up pranks had started happening around me, then Casey's accident and Grandpa and—

"Oh my God, do you think the same person who did that to Jackson hurt Casey? Maybe she saw whoever it was leaving my room, and they pushed her."

The image of Casey's broken body flashed in my head again. Her legs, bent at those inhuman angles. Her hands, bruised and swollen, broken like Mom's had been.

Jackson's, too. Kyle had tried to shield me from seeing it, but I'd caught a glimpse of Jackson's hands as he lay there, dead in the beam of the flashlight.

I clung to Kyle's shirt with hands curled into claws, and I couldn't let go.

"Kyle, the way they were hurt, their hands . . . " I swallowed hard to stop myself from retching.

"Try not to think about it. Just focus on little things, what we're going to do. Step by step."

I let my head fall against his chest for a second before I snapped myself out of it.

It wasn't the Bonebreaker doing this. That sicko was dead.

"I'll go and wait in my room until Fletcher's called the police," I said. "Just like we said."

"Good." Kyle touched my face with his fingertips before climbing up the ladder to the vent opening of the attic.

"I'm going over the roof," I said, as his head disappeared inside the rectangular hole.

"What? Why?"

"I'm claustrophobic," I lied.

"I'll come with you, then," he said, taking a step back down the ladder. I was already shaking my head. I knew he didn't like heights, or maybe it was just the catwalk. I didn't think my grandparents had even met Jackson, and I was probably just being paranoid, but I needed to run to the cottage and check on them. Whether it was connected to me or the Bonebreaker or something else altogether, I had to make sure they were all right.

It was easier just to go than to waste time arguing about it with Kyle.

"Can't get to South Wing that way, only through the attic."

"Then I'll wait with you in your room."

I hadn't expected him to suggest that, and I was thrown off a little. But not for long.

"Look, call me when you get back to your room, okay?" I said. "And then we can watch for the flashing blue lights down in the quad."

Kyle finally nodded and disappeared through the attic vent, and I climbed out onto the roof. I moved quickly toward the rear fire escape, knowing I didn't have much time before Kyle called me and found out I was already on my way to the far side of campus.

CHAPTER THIRTY-SIX

BURTY'S MAGIC TRICK

Kyle

Maybe I should have told her everything before I let her head over the roof by herself, but standing in a dark tower, above the broken body of her ex-boyfriend, really wasn't the right place to be talking about how my daddy was a psychopath. *But I'm not like him. Please believe that.*

I was screwed.

I crawled back through the dusty attic, specks of light beaming back at me from the eyes of dead creatures left to rot up there. Seeing Jackson's eyes, *real* dead eyes, was so much worse.

What would happen when the police arrived? It wasn't hard to imagine being dragged across the quad in handcuffs, every face of every student pressed right up against their bedroom windows. Maybe even Naomi's.

I could run. Could disappear from the Academy and be out of Killdeer—hell, out of the state—by the time the cops even thought to look for me. But I had no mind to run. The only thing I needed to do was tell Naomi the truth, and the rest of the world could go to hell.

When I reached her room, it was empty. Lord knew how long I'd wasted hauling ass back around the building in the attic crawlspace, only to find no sign that Naomi had been in her room since that afternoon.

I called her cell. Counting off the rings, I didn't think she was going to answer me, until it rang a seventh time and I heard her breathing.

"Kyle, I'm . . . I'm . . . " She was sobbing too hard for me to make out any more than that.

"Where are you?" *Please don't let him have her.* I didn't know who *he* was, or why he'd been screwing with us the whole time I'd been in Killdeer, but if anyone had hurt Naomi I would lose it.

"I'm at the cottage. It's my Grandpa, there's an ambulance here." She started to cry again, and I listened to her heart breaking. "I'm going with Gram to the hospital. I'll call you later."

~~~~~~~~

Fletcher paced the small space of my room, glaring at me when I slid down through the ceiling hatch. Kit was sprawled across my bed.

"What did you do with the body?" Fletcher said. "You moved it. Where?"

"What?" I said. He wasn't making sense. "I helped Naomi get it down from the rope. That's all."

Fletcher stopped pacing an uncomfortably short step away from me. Kit rolled to his feet, casually setting himself between us.

"I don't think Breaker moved the body, Fletch. Dude can't lie for shit," Kit said.

"He did this!" Fletch jabbed a finger at me. "You think you can screw with me? Get that dickhead to play dead so I call the cops and look like a tool? I know Jackson's the one who's been dealing on campus. I know he sold Casey something that messed with her head. He might as well have pushed her off that roof!" It was the first time I'd ever seen Fletcher shout, and I took a step back.

"Fletcher," I said, "I don't know anything about any drugs, but that guy was definitely dead. And I haven't been back to the tower since I saw you locking the dropout, so I couldn't have moved the body."

I glanced over at Kit, who was looking awful fidgety.

"Where's Naomi?" Fletcher said.

"I talked to her on the phone just now. Her grandpa's sick again, I think, and she's gone with him to the hospital."

Fletch nodded slowly. "She wouldn't have done this. She wouldn't have done this to me."

He wasn't talking to me or to Kit. In fact, Fletcher was looking more upset than when we'd first found the body.

"Fletcher, there's no way Jackson got up and walked out of there. He smelled like he'd been dead awhile," I said. Fletch went still, not looking at anything in particular. I cleared my throat. "So, someone moved the body?"

Fletcher jabbed a finger into my chest. "There was no body." And he walked out, leaving me and Kit gaping after him.

"Tell me you didn't have anything to do with this, Breaker," Kit said, hands on my shoulders until I shrugged him off.

"I didn't kill Jackson and string him up in the bell tower, if that's what you mean," I said.

I knew the moment he decided to believe me, saw the tension leaking out of him. "So, he's really dead, then?"

"Yup."

"Fletcher will calm down when he realizes nobody was messing with him." Kit didn't sound too sure about that. He didn't seem to find it strange that Fletcher was more worked up about someone playing a prank on him than about finding an actual dead body. Fletcher, I was learning, was an odd guy.

"You remember I asked you about Jackson the other night in your room? It was after I'd seen him all beat up around back of the school, only I'd taken him for drunk at the time. But then you said he'd texted Naomi later, and I thought . . . "

"You thought that meant he was all right," Kit finished.

"Yeah. Except nobody saw him after that, as far as I can tell. None of us did, and I didn't see him on any of the video footage from the principal's office. So now I'm wondering if he really sent Naomi those texts."

Kit stared at me with an odd look. "If you're suggesting Naomi lied about getting those messages, or had anything to do with his death, you're—"

I damn near choked on my tongue. "No! That wasn't what I was driving at. I meant that someone might've killed Jackson, finished him off after I saw him outside, and taken his phone. Maybe they sent those messages to Naomi to try to get to her." Because there was no denying the connection here. Naomi had been the one to find both bodies, with me a step behind.

Kit sank to the edge of the bed. I could tell my words were running laps inside his head.

"So what do we do now?" I said.

Kit shrugged. "Not a lot to do. No dead body, no problem, right?"

I stared at him.

"What do you suggest? Call the cops about a missing corpse? They'll think we're dicking around. And I'm betting you don't really want the cops here anyway, right, *Breaker*?"

"I had nothing to do with any of this, Kit. Naomi, she's . . . you know how I feel about her."

"Look, I'm getting the hell out of here. My mom's volunteering up at the hospital tonight, so I'll head over there to keep Naomi company. You can come, if you want," he said.

"I don't think I'm the best person for her to be around right now."

Kit rolled to his feet. "I covered for you when those assholes from Whistler were here, didn't I? I got rid of them before they could tell anyone else about you. But things are different now, Breaker. Naomi is one of my closest friends, and I won't keep hiding this from her—not with all that's going on. It'll hurt her when she finds out who you are, but you need to tell her. Naomi's tough. She's had to be. And I don't think she'll hate you for who you are, but she *will* hate you if you keep lying to her."

"I was going to tell her tonight. Then we found Jackson, and now her grandpa's sick, and it's Thanksgiving so I won't see her until next week."

Kit frowned. "Yeah. That's a full deck of excuses right there. Just don't wait too long, okay? Someone died tonight, and you and I both know it had something to do with you or her. Maybe both. And I was all right about keeping it a secret when I thought it was a case of you and her hooking up and then heading your separate ways at graduation, but if someone's going around killing people, you might not make it that far."

I knew Kit was right. And being chickenshit about it wasn't helping.

"I'll tell her," I said, shoving my hands deep into my pockets. "Just not tonight."

*There's a time in any man's life where he chooses.
Chooses what he's gonna be, how he's gonna live
his life. And if he's lucky, that's the same choice
God made for him, too. The truth is, I lived the
life that was meant for me. There's peace in that,
at least.*

*I know I left you with a good teacher, someone
who'll raise you to be a proper man. As much as
I loved your mama, she wasn't the one I knew
I could count on, who'd make sure everything
worked out the way it was meant to for you,
my boy. But I took care of it. And I know you
won't make the mistake of relying on no woman.
You're too smart for that.*

I ain't worried about you one bit.

CHAPTER THIRTY-SEVEN

BURTY'S BIG MOUTH

Naomi

Kit had been hugging me sporadically since he'd first showed up in the hospital waiting room.

"I'm so sorry to hear about your grandpa," he said in my ear, not letting up on the hug. I'd already been waiting there three hours, with little to no information from either Gram or the nurses on how Grandpa was doing. Once Kit arrived, he'd wrangled an update from his mom, who was volunteering in the cancer unit at the hospital.

On top of everything else, the doctors had confirmed Grandpa's stroke. A mild one, according to Kit's mom, but I knew that even if he recovered this time, Gram might not be allowed to take him home. With nothing else I could do, I let Gram know I'd be at Kit's house for the night, and would come back in the morning.

Kit's family owned an old colonial house just outside Bensalem, and I'd always loved it. The McCarthys had extended it over the years, building around the original stone part of the house as they had multiplied, and every room felt tousled and loved.

"Do you want to come watch some TV?" Kit said. I shook my head.

"Not right now."

Mr. McCarthy passed through the hallway behind Kit, and I waved. He raised his martini glass in a salute.

"I'm sure the old bugger will be all right," Kit said.

"Christopher!"

Kit looked up, genuinely baffled. "What?"

"Language, boy." Mr. McCarthy shook his head and wandered off to the kitchen, once again exasperated beyond words at his oldest son.

"Fletch called to see how you're doing," Kit said.

I rubbed at an ink stain on my jeans. The last time I'd seen Fletch, we'd been standing over Jackson's corpse.

"He was acting pretty sketchy last night, even for him," I said.

"Oh yeah?" Kit looked down into his drink.

"You know something, don't you? What's going on with him, Kit?"

"You already know about the Casey thing." He side-eyed me.

"Only that he stopped selling to her and thought she was getting her stuff from someone else in school."

Kit chewed his lip the whole time I was talking. "Yeah, that's part of it. He thought whoever was selling to her gave her something trippy. I dunno, LSD or sherm or something. The last time she tried to buy from Fletch, that was what she asked him for.

Anyway, Fletch got it into his head that was what happened—
that she was tripping or something when she fell off the roof.
Or jumped, I'm not sure. And he found out who she got it from."

I gripped my drink tighter. "Who was it?"

"Jackson."

Oh God. I pictured Fletch, the way he'd paced the quad the
morning after Casey's death, so calm and thorough, and his face
as he'd taken in Jackson's broken body in the tower. That swift
movement of his eyes giving away the fact that his thoughts
hadn't frozen in horror like mine had.

"You don't think Fletcher . . . "

Kit looked at me straight on. "Killed Jackson? Uh, *no.* Fletch
might be a stone-cold mofo, but he's no killer. You know how he
gets around blood." That was true. Fletcher had been so terrified
of blood after what happened at the commune that he passed
out when Kit had a nosebleed in fifth grade. He had it under
control now, in true Fletch-style, but the red stuff still made
him squirm.

"So he deals a little pot," Kit continued, "big freaking deal. If
he was really sure Jackson had something to do with Casey's
death, he'd have made certain the cops came to the same conclusion. I think it all just got to Fletch more than he'll admit. He
likes to make out he's an emotional robot, but a girl we knew

died, and he went into full-on guilt mode for cutting her off like he did. Of course it's going to affect him."

Fletcher was my oldest friend. Sure, he could be weird, but I was an asshole for thinking he could hurt someone the way Jackson had been hurt, even for a second. And while I'd been so focused on dealing with my own stirred-up traumas, I hadn't considered for one second that Fletch might be going through something similar.

"Kit, could I please use your phone? Mine's about to die, and I want to see if Fletch is okay. And I want to call Kyle, too."

Kit's face changed faster than he could cover. "Oh, uh, sure, I guess. But I'm not sure I've got Kyle's number saved in my phone. Let me check."

"Kit?"

"Damn, I think my battery's dead, too."

"Kit, I'm not in the mood! Give me the phone."

He stopped fumbling around with his phone. "Maybe you should wait until everything's settled down with your grandpa before you call him."

"Why?"

I tried to grab it from him, but he held it behind his back so we ended up wrestling over it on the hallway floor.

"For God's sake, Christopher!" Mr. McCarthy hissed, appearing again in the kitchen doorway. "The twins are asleep." He disappeared, leaving me to glare at Kit, still without the phone.

"Look, gimme a minute to explain, will you? Then if you still want to call Breaker, I won't stop you."

We went into the backyard and sat on the top step of the stoop. His dad had handed us a couple of cans of soda on our way through the kitchen, and we drank while I waited for Kit to explain what the hell the phone thing was about.

"I found out something about Breaker the other day. I really shouldn't be the one to tell you, especially not right now, and I know he's planning to tell you himself."

This was how people started conversations where they told you your boyfriend had cheated on you or given you crabs or something. "Will you spit it out?"

"Kyle Henry isn't his real name. I think it's his mother's maiden name. They only changed it recently."

"Kit!" I lost any shred of patience I'd had earlier.

He took a deep breath. "His real name is Kyle Bluchevsky."

"Bluchevsky?"

Kit nodded. My brain had obviously stopped working properly. I knew that name, of course I did. But I couldn't see how Kyle was connected to it. Bobby Bluchevsky was a monster. He'd been locked away for years and years, and now he was dead. So why would Kyle have that name? Kyle existed in a part of my life that was completely separate from the man who'd killed my mom. A good part. "I don't understand."

"He's Bobby Bluchevsky's son."

The soda can bounced along the path where I'd knocked it over. I grasped the stone steps, clinging to them while my insides splintered.

CHAPTER THIRTY-EIGHT

BURTY CARVES THE THANKSGIVING TURKEY

Kyle

All the kids who were heading home for Thanksgiving had gone already, and the last few who were stuck at the Academy had gone to sulk in their rooms. I'd even seen the principal heading out, hurrying across the field to her cottage like she couldn't wait to get the hell out of Killdeer.

I should've been gone myself, but I couldn't leave yet. Naomi's grandparents' cottage had stood still and dark when I walked by at daybreak. Same story around lunchtime. So I'd tried to do something useful instead.

By the time I'd downloaded the footage from Principal Kincaid's hidden video closet and started going through it on my computer, I was sure there would be something to find, some clue to who'd killed Jackson. This all had to be connected to my dad, or to Naomi's mom, or both.

The first time I'd checked the recordings, there'd been parts missing. That meant whoever it was had been inside the school without getting caught, and had sneaked into the principal's office and erased the footage without anyone seeing.

I scrolled through the videos, making sure I went over and over the time frames, but each time, the video had a gap cut—and the cuts weren't any kind of slick, neither. They hadn't tried to hide what they'd done, just erased whole chunks of time.

Wouldn't it have been easier to delete the whole damn video?

To be able to sneak in and out of Naomi's room, the principal's office, to hide the brass knuckles in my locker—that sure as hell made it seem like it was a student at Killdeer Academy. But the way Jackson had been brutalized, the broken shape of Casey's body lying against the cobblestones, spoke more of someone blunt and cruel—not the kind of someone to stay hidden for long.

How long would this go on before the killer showed himself? Before he came after Naomi or me—or both?

Fletcher had been wrong not to call the cops. And if anything happened to Naomi on account of me looking out for my own lying ass, I'd never forgive myself.

CHAPTER THIRTY-NINE

BURTY ON CLEAN-UP DUTY

Naomi

The morning drifted by at the hospital, marked by the beeping of monitors and the squeak of rubber shoes. I watched Grandpa's chest rise and fall just to make sure that it did. Gram dozed in the chair next to him, the fingers of one hand wrapped around Grandpa's. She wasn't letting him go anywhere, not even in her sleep.

If anyone saw me, they'd probably put the red eyes down to worry about Grandpa. Seeing how thin and frail he looked lying under the rough hospital blanket, it was hard to imagine Grandpa fighting off even a cold. I was worried about him, and about Gram. But that wasn't why my eyes were bloodshot.

I wanted to kill that lying asshole. Kyle was some kind of twisted psycho, getting close to me so he could, what? Screw with my head? Hurt me, finish off what his dad had started? Was I some kind of sick trophy to him?

He couldn't have moved to Killdeer and not known I was there, could he?

The tiny spark of hope fizzled out when I remembered the way he'd looked when I first introduced myself. Even if he hadn't known who I was before then, he sure had every day after that. Why would he have stayed at the Academy knowing who I was, if not to play some twisted game?

My hands started shaking again, and I balled them into fists. I wanted to hit something, smash it to pieces.

Yeah, just like someone did to Jackson.

It wasn't a huge leap to think Kyle could have done that to him. He'd even offered to beat up Jackson that day in the woods. And Kyle had been so insistent on talking to me last night in the tower, had even steered me to the dropout and let me go down first. Had he wanted me to see Jackson there?

Fear, real fear, was spreading through me, eating me up on the inside.

Wait—Kyle couldn't have murdered Jackson. Kit had been with him right before the tower. And if the same person killed Jackson *and* Casey, it couldn't be Kyle. He'd been with me the whole time.

I touched my throat, almost surprised to find the sunflower pendant there. Maybe the necklace really was bad luck. I still couldn't remember taking it from the cottage, but now it felt like some kind of omen. Maybe *I* was bad luck.

No. There was no such thing as bad luck, only bad people. And they all seemed to swarm around me like locusts.

Was Kyle a bad person? The idea just didn't seem to sit right. But I couldn't figure out Kyle's part in this, either. Maybe he wasn't a killer, but he was involved somehow. And he'd used me. Lied to me.

"Sweetie?"

I looked up at the sound of the nurse's voice.

"Why don't you go on home for a while? Your grandfather's doing okay, and you look like you could use some rest," she said.

"Thank you, Nurse. I'll see she gets home," Gram said, rousing and stretching her legs out in front of her. She'd been sleeping in one of those bendy plastic hospital chairs, and she stifled a wince when she sat upright.

The nurse left, and I glared after her.

"I'm not leaving, Gram."

She sighed, looking even older than she had last night.

"I won't make you go," Gram said, "but I wish you wouldn't stay. Your grandfather only needs to rest before they let him come home."

Grandpa's eyelids fluttered, and for a second I prayed he wouldn't open them just yet. I didn't want him to see me, didn't want him to see whatever he saw when he looked at me. Annabel, or Burty, or whoever else the disease conjured.

I kissed Grandpa and then Gram on my way out. I couldn't really bring myself to go anywhere, so I paced outside the hospital, feeling the stares of the smokers, all huffing away while they leaned on their IV poles.

My phone beeped a message. It was from Fletcher.

Heard about ur grandpa—hope ur OK. Sorry I'm not there with u. Call me when u can.

Should I call him? I knew he was probably home with his family by now. We hadn't talked about the Casey thing, but it could wait.

Thanks. I'm OK, will call when I have news. Have a happy Thanksgiving xoxo

I slid my phone back into my pocket. I felt alone. My only family were behind the hospital walls, and they didn't want me there.

I couldn't go back to Kit's. I was still pissed at him. Kit was *my* friend. He was supposed to be on *my* side, always. But he'd stood up for Kyle, making excuses for the lying turd.

I kicked at a loose stone on the path, flinching when it *pinged* off the alloy wheel of some fancy car in the lot.

Kit swore he hadn't known about it for long, and he didn't believe Kyle had lied to hurt me. It was pretty much the only reason

I hadn't lost my shit with him. Well, not completely. But at least Kit had told me when it really mattered. Not like Kyle. Asshole.

I could see that Kyle wasn't his father—of course I could. He'd only been a little kid when his father destroyed my life. My *mother's* life, and so many others. But I'd been lied to by everyone around me, by the boy I thought cared about me, by friends I'd known for years. I felt all the ugly things I hated feeling around the people I'd thought were safe. I almost wished I hadn't found out, that I'd continued oblivious, because I missed him.

How sick is that?

There was no way I was falling for him. No.

"Maybe what he feels for you isn't about all that stuff with his dad. You know? Maybe he didn't even realize who you were, at first." That was what Kit had said before I left, though I could tell he didn't believe that himself. That first day in homeroom, it was like I'd kicked Kyle in the guts when I told him my name.

I sat at the bus stop and followed the trickle of people onto the bus when it came. Only by chance, it was heading back toward the Academy. I rocked my head against the greasy window.

I checked my phone in case Gram was trying to reach me. The battery warning flashed at the same time it buzzed with a message.

I just heard what happened. R U OK?

I frowned. The message was from Addy. What had she heard—about Jackson, or about Grandpa?

Thx. Kinda rough.

Her reply came through less than a minute later.

Can I come see you at the cottage? Be like old times. XO

When I'd first started at the Academy as a day student, living with my grandparents on the far side of campus, vacations had been the times when Addy and I hung out by ourselves. Back then, Addy's parents had still been together. They'd traveled overseas a lot, always leaving her behind, even when they took Alana with them. Addy was one of only a handful of students who rattled around the Academy when everyone else had gone home. It was how we'd gotten close, really. We'd hung out, watched crappy movies together, played in the woods.

I wasn't sure what to make of Addy's sudden change of heart. Still, I wasn't going to be the one who slapped her hand away. I needed a friend. And I didn't want to be alone.

[Excerpt from a letter from Robert Bluchevsky
to Kyle Bluchevsky]

*They don't tell you how it feels, son. It's like
when you buy a new car—how you gonna know
what it's like to sit in her and push that gas
pedal to the floor until you do it? Same with that
metal shaped around your fist, like you grown
an iron shell and can't nobody break it. It's a
powerful thing, knowing you can break a person
and can't get broke yourself.*

CHAPTER FORTY

BURTY IN THE OLD BARN

Kyle

The dead mouse stared right at me over Uncle Coby's shoulder, so I focused on my plate, nodding every now and then to make it look like I was listening.

I'd called Naomi a bunch of times, but she didn't answer. I'd even walked across campus to the cottage to see if she was there before I left school, but the place was dark. So I went home.

"Kyle?"

I looked up at the sound of Mama's voice. She and Uncle Coby were both staring at me.

"Yes, Mama?"

Uncle Coby laughed. "The boy's got a girl on his mind, Olive. Ain't no use trying to get a lick of sense outta him for the next month." I was glad I hadn't told him anything about Naomi at the bar. "'Course, it'll pass."

"Oh, a girlfriend!" Mama clapped her hands together. "When will we get to meet her, Kyle?"

I pushed my peas around my plate. "There's no girlfriend, Mama. Just thinking about school is all."

"Oh," she said.

"I'm glad you're liking the Academy," Uncle Coby said, and started attacking his mashed potatoes. "It's always been a good school."

Uncle Coby had been kind of quiet ever since he'd arrived, like he used to get when things were bad at the office. But he hadn't said anything about work like he used to, about how Dad had left him to deal with all the mess by himself. He never grumbled about it, but he didn't try to hide all the shittiness my dad had left in his wake the way Mama did. When you heard people talking every day—at school, at the store, on the street—and then went home to a person who acted like nothing'd happened, it made all the other stuff ten times worse.

"Right, I'm heading out," he said once he was done eating.

Mama's fingertips pressed white against the tablecloth. "So soon, Coby? I thought you were staying a couple of days."

He sighed. "I'm not leaving town, Olive. I took a lease on a house up here so I got someplace to stay when I visit."

"A house where?" I said.

Uncle Coby gave me *the look*. "Look who's a Chatty Cathy all of a sudden." He got up and set his napkin next to his plate, kissing Mama on the cheek. "I got some unfinished business to deal with this evening, so I'll clear that stuff out of the shed and come by in the morning. Y'all have a goodnight." He put a hand on my shoulder. "Unless you want to come along for the ride, son?"

I shook my head. The only thing I could think about was Naomi, and I didn't dare talk to Uncle Coby about her. I'd say too much, and he'd know who she was, and then all the shit about Jackson and those brass knuckles would come out and he'd tell me to back the hell away from Naomi like she was on fire.

I heard his car pulling away outside and cleared the dishes to the sound of Mama's tunes on the old CD player. The news that Uncle Coby might be spending more time with us had obviously put her in a good mood.

My phone beeped, and I wiped my hands on the dishrag before I checked it. It was Kit.

Sorry, had to tell Naomi. She's @ home. Grandpa doing OK, off vents now. U should call her.

Shit.

"Whatever he had in there, it looked real cumbersome," Mama said.

"What?"

She jumped, and I realized I'd snapped at her.

"Whatever Coby was keeping in the shed," she said, the dirty dishes dripping in her hands. "The things he brought up with him last time he came for a visit, and asked to put in the shed for safekeeping until he got his own place sorted out. But whatever it was, it looked to be leaking something awful all over the trunk of his car just now." She shook her head. "They ain't gonna give him his deposit back if he returns it looking like he put garbage in the trunk, especially after the ding he got in the last one."

"Mama, what are you talking about? What deposit?"

"For his rental car, silly!" Mama said. "They gave him a much nicer one this time, after that idiot ran out in front of him and bashed up his fender."

"He told me another car ran into him."

My palms got sweaty. But I was just being an idiot. This was Uncle Coby, not my father. But *someone* had killed Jackson. Was it someone who thought they were looking out for me? The last time I'd seen Jackson alive was right before Uncle Coby showed up for a visit.

Wait.

When I'd seen him in the principal's office, he'd mentioned flying up the day before. That put him in Killdeer at the time Jackson disappeared.

What *had* he been keeping in the shed?

I went out back and crunched across the lawn that had just about started to sparkle with frost. The shed's side windows were dark, with something pushed up against them on the inside, and a heavy lock secured the door.

Two sharp cracks from my boot and the lock skittered across the path and onto the lawn.

The shed door swung open. There was no light in there, only what spilled in from the house. I stepped inside, then backed right out as the smell knocked me sick to my stomach. Covering my nose and mouth with my sleeve, I forced myself to look back inside.

Deep in the shadows, I could see a long, dark patch on the floor of the shed, with fainter tracks where something had been dragged out. I sucked in a breath, and the stench hit me so hard I could taste it, like iron and rot. It was the same smell that had filled the tower when I had heaved Jackson's body down from the bell rope.

I stumbled back out and emptied my stomach on the lawn, heaving until there was nothing left.

I want to be wrong. I have to be wrong. I can't do this again.

CHAPTER FORTY-ONE

BURTY CUTS THE CORD

Naomi

Addy had been at the cottage for almost an hour, and she was irritating the crap out of me. From the minute she arrived, she'd been restless, like I was keeping her from something more important.

Heavy clouds had rolled in, making the early evening look later than it was, thunder threatening somewhere off in the distance.

"Did Kit tell you? About Jackson, I mean? I'm really sorry," I said.

Addy waved her hand. "Yeah, that's some messed-up stuff all right. It was bad enough when that girl fell off the roof, but a dead body, right where we go to hang out? That's so gross."

"Gross?"

She stared at me just a second too long. "Oh, yeah, I mean it's just awful. Terrifying, really, to think someone was killed right inside the tower!"

"But aren't you seeing Jackson? Weren't you, I mean?"

"Seeing Jackson?" Addy said, like I'd insulted her. "Where the hell did you get that idea?"

"You said you were going to invite him to the tower."

"Oh, that. Yeah, I was just goofing around. I saw you and him arguing in school, and thought it'd be funny. I never actually *asked* him." Addy nudged me with her shoulder. "That's what we do, isn't it? Find out each other's secrets, then needle each other with them."

I couldn't wrap my head around her *so what* reaction to Jackson's murder.

"I can't believe you're still doing this," she said, flipping open Grandpa's scrapbook on the coffee table. She handled the pages roughly, even though she knew the hours I'd put into making it. "I mean, it's kind of skeevy, isn't it? To get dressed up as a boy and take photographs to show your grandfather?"

I took a breath. And another. "It jogs his memory."

"It's not really working, is it?" She looked at me, a flash of sympathy in her eyes that hadn't been there in a long time. Then it vanished. "He doesn't even know who you are anymore, does he?"

I grabbed the book from her and slammed it shut. She had picked the wrong time to come over and start chipping away at me.

"Maybe you should go, Addy."

She looked at the old carriage clock on top of the TV. "I'll stay a while longer. Keep you company and stuff."

I shrugged. "Do whatever you want. I'm going to put this upstairs."

wwwwww

I placed the scrapbook on the dresser in my old room. The cover was plenty faded now, even without me tampering with it. I must have thumbed through the pages hundreds of times with Grandpa over the last year, trying to stir up whatever memories he could still grab on to. There was a glimmer of his old self when he saw the photographs and relived whatever mischief he had gotten up to.

I missed that glimmer already.

When I went back downstairs, Addy was leaning against the windowsill, looking out over the front yard.

"Do you want a drink or something?"

She shook her head, then pointed at my phone where I'd left it charging. "Can I use your phone? I forgot mine, and I need to call my boyfriend to come pick me up."

"Boyfriend?"

Addy didn't answer, and I was a teensy bit relieved. Her coming over was a small step toward us being friends. Or at least not hateful to each other. If she started lying again, making up fake boyfriends because she felt starved for attention or whatever, I wouldn't give her another chance. I'd had enough.

I passed her my cell and wandered into the kitchen while she made the call. A couple of minutes later, I heard her hang up and went back through.

"He's on his way over now. I'm going to go meet him at the school gate."

She was already on her feet and heading for the front door, like visiting me was something to check off her list, and now I was done.

"Who is he?"

"He's a really hot, rich, older guy," Addy said. "Why, are you jealous?"

For a stupid second I thought about Kyle, and how glad I was that we were together. And then I remembered.

"Why do you even care?" I said.

Addy's expression softened. "I always care what you think of me, Nai. And I hate the way you look at me now, like I'm . . . "

Whatever she'd been about to say, she shoved it back inside the Addy locker. She walked out, not bothering to shut the front door behind her, and almost crashed right into Kyle walking up the dark front path.

"Watch it, dickhead!"

And then Addy was gone.

I slammed the door and grabbed my cell phone from where Addy had ditched it on the coffee table. Kyle pounded on the door.

"Naomi! Let me in!"

"Go to hell, Kyle! And yeah, I know who you are, you lying sack of shit!"

"Naomi, I'm sorry! You have to believe me."

My finger was already poised to dial the cops, although I didn't know what the hell I'd say. He banged on the door again.

"I mean it. I'm calling the cops right now!"

"Please! I think I know who murdered Jackson. Who's been doing all those crazy things to you."

I leaned in toward the keyhole in the old door, trying to catch a glimpse of his face. I couldn't at first because it was so dark out. Then he moved under the electric lantern above the door. He looked like hell.

Thunder sounded, louder than before, and all the lights flickered a couple of seconds after it.

He's a liar. The son of a monster. You should hate him.

But he didn't look monstery. He looked like Kyle. My chest hurt.

"It wasn't me, Naomi. I swear it."

My hands shook. "You think you can show up at my grandparents' house like this? I'm calling the police, you goddamn psycho!"

"Call them!" he yelled back through the door. "Tell them to get down here now! You're not safe here."

I hesitated. Then I spotted something that might be useful

sitting next to the stack of unopened mail—the old hunting knife Grandpa used as a letter opener. I gripped it at my side and slid back the bolts. When I opened the door, Kyle barged past me.

"Hey!"

"Lock the door," he said. "Please, I think he's coming over here. He said something about unfinished business."

"Kyle—"

"*Please*, Naomi."

Kyle locked and bolted the door himself, then sat on the edge of the couch.

"What the hell do you think you're doing? Who's coming?" I said.

"Your grandparents aren't here, are they?"

"They're still at the hospital."

He raked his hands over his scalp. "I'm so sorry, Naomi. I think you *should* call the police—where's your phone?"

It was in my hand, but I wasn't about to just hand it over.

"My uncle, well, not really my uncle, but my father's business partner, Coby. I think he was involved with what my dad did." He looked at me, eyes raw. "What he did to your mama and all those other women. Or maybe he's picking up where my dad left off."

I sat down on the chair facing him. I couldn't pretend anymore.

"I've been going over it all in my head—that night I saw Jackson all beat up, Uncle Coby's car with that big dent in it. He must've done that to Jackson, chased him down after I left him like garbage out in the rain. But those texts you got, I thought that meant Jackson was all right, except they can't have been from Jackson, can they? It was *him*. He was trying to lure you out."

His words kept pouring out, but it was too much to process. "Why did you do all this, Kyle? Why did you move here and insert yourself into my life? Was it to hurt me?"

"No! I didn't know you'd be here before we moved, I swear it. And when I recognized you, I did my best to stay away, and I thought I wasn't hurting anyone by keeping it a secret. But I couldn't stop wanting to be near you. Maybe I'm not right in the head, only the more I got to know you, the easier it was to forget you'd been that girl in the news." He reached out toward me, but I brushed him off.

"I couldn't be more sorry for hurting you like this," he said. "Please, I'm not like him, Naomi. I could *never* be like him."

I lost the battle. Tears streamed down my cheeks and I swiped them away with the back of my hand. Then he was holding me, wrapping me up in his arms, letting me cry and snot all over his T-shirt.

"I hate you, Kyle."

"I know," he said, but I could tell he didn't believe me, either.

"I hate your father. I'm glad he's dead." I wanted to hurt him, to cut deep so he'd yell and scream back at me. But he just exhaled slowly, like he was resigned to another beating.

"Me too," he said. "But it's not him we have to worry about right now."

I stared at him. He looked blurry.

"Uncle Coby's got some twisted idea in his head that he's protecting me, near as I can figure. Or—"

"Or?"

His arms tightened around me, like he needed the contact as much as I did. "Or he was in on it with Dad all along, and you're some part of what they had planned. I guess Jackson got in the way, maybe even Casey. But it has to be you. Coby said he was taking care of unfinished business—tonight."

"Coby?" My brain was finally rebooting, everything Kyle had said slowly processing.

"Yeah. Uncle Coby—Jacoby Wickes. He's the CEO of Big Blue. I think he might have been a student here when he was younger. At least, he seems to have some connection to the school."

"Wait, Jacoby? Like, can be shortened to Jake, Jacoby?"

Kyle drew in a sharp breath. "Well, *shit*."

"Grandpa's been talking about Crazy Jake lately, but I thought it was just his illness. Could your uncle seriously have been that kid?" Kyle didn't look any more certain than I felt, although every time I closed my eyes for a second, I saw those initials from Jake's cave, like they'd been seared inside my eyelids.

JW. Jacoby Wickes . . .

JW + AS . . .

There was no way he could be my father, was there? I'd only ever seen photos of him.

No. Mom had been twenty when she had me, two whole years after she graduated from the Academy. I breathed out on a long, shaky sigh.

"He always hated being called Jacoby," Kyle said. "Told me he used to get shit for it at school."

"Maybe Grandpa saw him and recognized him from all those years ago," I said, my head aching.

"I've been trying to figure it out, how I got to be at the same school as you. I thought my dad had a hand in it, but that just didn't add up. It was only over dinner that I started to wonder how Coby knew so much about the school, like he's got connections to this place he shouldn't have had. I knew his family had money, but I didn't know that he'd been *here*."

The lines were forming. Old ones, new ones. The cavern, how Jake—Coby—had been obsessed with Annabel, the girl he couldn't have. I saw how what had happened at the Academy twenty years ago had led a psychopath to track down my mom and leave her bloody and broken in North Carolina years later. And it hadn't been enough to kill her. It hadn't ended with Mom. I could feel it as surely as I could feel the storm bearing down on us.

It was only just starting.

CHAPTER FORTY-TWO

BURTY WITH THE OLD GANG

Kyle

The main line was dead, and I didn't think it had anything to do with the storm. When Naomi tried her cell and found it wasn't working, either, I knew for sure something was wrong.

"I left my phone in the car," I said, already heading for the door. Naomi stood with her arms folded in the doorway while I walked around the driver's side. "What the hell? Someone's slashed the tires. They're totally shredded."

I looked up and down the path leading from the cottages to the school, and the side road off the campus. There was nobody there now, but that didn't mean much.

"That spiteful little witch! I can't believe Addison would be so petty." Naomi came and stood next to me. The light from the cottage spilled out along the path, barely touching the side of Mama's car, but I could already see through the side window that my phone wasn't where I'd left it. The door clicked open when I tried the handle. I'd forgotten to lock it.

"Looks like my phone was taken, too." I looked up and down the path again.

"Could Coby—"

"He could've done the tires and taken the phone," I said. "If it really is him behind it all."

"What do you mean, *if*?" Naomi said. "I thought you were sure."

I raked my hands back over my scalp. "I'm sure. I think. Dammit, I'm not sure about anything right now."

I'd known Uncle Coby my whole life, and he'd never done or said anything that'd make me think he could be a killer before tonight. And the cops were so sure my dad did it alone—murdering women who looked just like Mama, all with short blonde hair that ended up red when he was done with them.

Except for Annabel Steadman.

She hadn't looked like Mama, but she'd gone to Killdeer Academy. I couldn't think of *any* connection between Dad and Naomi's mama. I ran back over the conversation at dinner, and what else Uncle Coby had said: *It always was a good school.* Could Coby really have been the Crazy Jake from the old story Naomi had told me? Had he been killing since he was my age?

"Kyle, you don't think he'd hurt Addy, do you?"

"I can't see why he would. She was already leaving. Anyhow, he couldn't have gotten to your phone, could he?" I watched that sink in. "Addy either did something to your phone out of mean-ness, or she's somehow involved with Uncle Coby and what he's got planned. And the timing feels awful convenient for her to show up and break your phone for no good reason."

Naomi looked like she might throw up. "She said she's been seeing an older guy, and I assumed she was lying again. But why? Sure, she's angry with me, but this goes beyond trying to piss me off."

I closed the door and looked over to the school, a black shape against the darker web of the trees beyond it. "I'm thinking we need to find a phone that works."

We ran, trying not to stumble on the path in the dark. Naomi knew it better than I did, so I kept close to her as we headed for the school. I caught Naomi's hand, slowing as we came to the quad.

"This doesn't feel right. There should be lights on."

"You think he cut the power?"

I'd thought he must have somehow gotten rid of the few people who were still at school, but what Naomi said made more sense.

"I guess. He'd need to shut off the breaker box is all."

I kept Naomi's hand tucked in mine and we walked around the outside of the building instead of heading into the quad. It felt too walled in, too easy for Coby—or whoever—to come at us. We rounded the corner to the front of the school building. The rain was holding off, but there, in the distance, the glimmer of lightning was railing it our way. A flash, then another. Heading closer every time, thunder snapping at its heels.

Naomi made a strangled sound before she clapped her free hand over her mouth. She was looking up at the outside wall of the Academy, at the clock above the front entrance.

There, hanging from the rusted dial, was the dark outline of a body.

CHAPTER FORTY-THREE

BURTY TAKES OUT THE TRASH

Naomi

I first heard the story of Crazy Jake and the clock the week I started at Killdeer Academy. The kids in my class played a game to scare each other, where you had to stand under the clock with your eyes closed and ask the ghost of the murdered boy what time it was. Then your friends counted all the way up to nine o'clock, when the ghost was supposed to come get you. Nobody but me ever made it all the way to nine.

Had I been a normal, well-adjusted seven-year-old, it would have scared me, too, probably. But it was easy to picture a dead body when you'd already seen one, easy to adjust the details so it was a boy's body impaled on a clock instead of my mom's body lying broken on bloody sheets.

Dead people weren't scary. The people who made them that way were the scary ones.

"Do you think it's Jackson?" Kyle whispered next to me. It seemed like a stupid question for a moment, but then the impaled boy dissolved, and I could see the very real body hanging above the Academy's front door. If you believed the story of Crazy Jake— Coby—and the boy he'd pushed from the window, this was the second corpse he'd left hanging from the dial.

It was wrapped in something. A black tarpaulin, or a garbage sack, maybe. Legs bound at the ankles, rope around the neck holding it to the minute hand of the clock. But one arm had flopped free of the tarp, with a dark splotch visible just above the wrist, and I knew. Jackson hadn't even realized his tattoo was a Rolling Stones logo until I'd pointed it out. How could you mark yourself like that, permanently, and not know what it meant?

"It's him," I said. It sounded like someone else talking, too calm to be my voice.

"He wanted us to see the body here," Kyle said. His face was shadowy in the near darkness. He stared at the body a while longer. "We'd have to go up to the room above the clock to cut him down."

"You seriously think we should go inside?" I pulled my hand free from his, and wished I'd hidden my suspicion better when his jaw tightened.

"I'm not a part of this, dammit! Coby left the body there to make sure we go inside. I'm not saying we should, just that he's steering us that way."

"And you know this how?"

Kyle turned his back to me and dragged his fingers over his scalp. When he looked at me, he was still shaking-angry. I had every reason not to trust Kyle, or at least to think he might have been influenced by his uncle to go along with this in some way, but I could see my doubt getting to him.

"He's playing us, Naomi. He's known me my whole life, knows how I think. I'm trying to figure this thing out so we don't walk right on into his trap."

"So why did you bring us around this way, Kyle?"

"I wanted to see if all the power was off, or if the building is empty." He frowned. "If it was the power, the little red lights from the security cameras would be dark, too. And it could be that someone tripped the circuit for the lights, or even just the lights in the dorms, except I don't think they did. The place seems empty, and I think he made it that way because he was expecting you."

"And how would he know where I was?"

Kyle pointed up at the little red eye pointing at us from above the main entrance. "Because he's watching us."

I shrank back, away from the building that was my home. He was in there now.

"So he knows you're here, too."

"Does it matter? He's setting this up as some kind of trap for you to walk into. If me being here was going to throw him off his game, he'd have done more than slash my tires at the cottage."

The camera above the door hadn't moved. The red light blinked once, like it really was an eye. "So he's in there, waiting for us to walk in so he can kill me?"

"I'm not going to let that happen," Kyle said.

The first drop of rain fell and hit my cheek. I looked up at Jackson's body, hanging there like a discarded rag. I felt Kyle next to me, even though we weren't touching. It kindled something inside me, some feeling I'd lost ten years earlier, and I believed him. He was on my side. I wasn't facing this monster alone.

"Let's go. Run. Get out of here," I said.

We took off back the way we'd come, skirting around the outside of the Academy to take the shortest route toward the main road.

Then a sound of pain and terror echoed all around us. It bled through my ears and my skin, piercing deep down into my heart. The scream kept coming in waves, echoing from somewhere inside the building.

"That sounds like Addison," Kyle said as he looked up at the dark windows of the Academy. "Naomi, I think you should keep going, get out of here. I'll go in and find Addison."

I gripped his hand tighter. "Kyle, no! I'm not letting you go in there by yourself. What if he hurts you?"

He shook his head. "It's not me he wants to hurt."

"You keep saying that, but you don't know. You're obviously a part of this for him, or he wouldn't have sent you here in the first place. I mean, he didn't need you here, did he? And aren't you kind of getting in the way of things if he wants to get to me so badly?"

"Maybe I am a part of it—in his mind, anyhow. I don't know. But I do know that our best chance is for you to run and call for help from somewhere safe. I'll be fine. I don't think he'll—"

The scream reached a crescendo that rattled the windows in front of us. The sound was obviously being amplified somehow, but there was no way to know if it was a recording or if Addy was being tortured while we debated.

"We need to get into the panic room," I said. "If he's watching us, it has to be from in there, and between the two of us we can knock him out or something." Kyle looked unconvinced, but I continued. "If he's not there, then we can see where he is on the monitors and call for help. The whole point of a panic room is to keep whoever's inside safe, so the phone line in there'll be isolated from the main one."

His eyes widened before he could hide his surprise.

"I saw it in a movie, okay?"

"And what if we get there and he has a gun?"

The screaming had become sobbing, broken by gasps of pain. I hated how that sound took me back to the house in North Carolina. My mom had screamed like that. Cried out for me to run.

Shhh, don't make a sound.

"A gun was never used in any of the murders your—in any of the other murders," I said. "And Jackson looked like he'd been beaten to death. I didn't see any bullet holes or knife wounds, did you?"

"You're right. And Jackson and Casey both had their hands shattered." He cleared his throat, like he felt weird for noticing that. "I thought Casey's hands just got hurt when she fell. But it was what my dad used to do. To stop them fighting back."

"Exactly! If he was your dad's killing partner, or whatever it's called, then it would make sense he'd have a similar MO."

"It's a hell of a thing to bet your life on," Kyle said as another shriek echoed from inside the building.

The last time I'd heard screams like those, running away had saved my life. But I wouldn't leave this time, not if it meant letting Addy die.

"Come on," I said, and started running toward the sound that had haunted me since childhood.

CHAPTER FORTY-FOUR

BURTY GETS BIG NEWS

Kyle

This was a bad idea. Every part of me knew it.

"It's a dead end that way," I said. "If he dead-bolted the two staff entrances, all he'd have to do would be to block off the way into the quad, and he'd have us cornered."

Naomi slowed beside me, then stopped. "I wouldn't have thought of that. Which way do we go in, then?"

The screams were still coming from inside, and there was a pattern to them. Loud, awful hollering for a minute or so, then a sound like choking and crying, then more screaming—softer, like she knew by then she was beat. And then the whole thing would start over. It was a recording. It had to be. I knew what that probably meant, and I couldn't put that idea in Naomi's head without being sure.

"Whichever way we go in, he'll see us, so we might as well go in the main entrance," I said.

It wasn't locked. It was too easy. But we had to get to Addison. Even if it wasn't already too late, he wouldn't leave her alive for long. The Bonebreaker killings hadn't been gunshot-quick, but my dad, and probably Coby, hadn't hung around, either. There were lots of places they could go—work sites, warehouses, and such—where they could have spent days torturing those women without anybody finding out. Except that wasn't what they'd done. They'd wanted to hurt those women real bad, but that was a means to the end. What they'd really wanted was to break them.

The hallways of the Academy echoed Addison's screams. From inside I could tell they weren't coming from anywhere nearby. I followed Naomi, much less sure of the way to the tower staircase that led to the principal's office in the dark. Instead I focused on the dead eyes peering down at us from the high shelves lining the walls. Eyes that were probably feeding our whereabouts up to Uncle Coby.

No, not "Uncle" anything.

A gnawing spread through my gut. Was I really so sure it was him? What all was I basing this on—the fact that he'd leased a cottage on campus? And he said something that made it sound like he'd been a student at the Academy? And his first name happened to be the same as some kid who'd pushed some other kid out of a window once?

Yeah, that, and he'd been keeping something corpse-smelling in our garden shed.

Something crackled above us, and Naomi stopped so suddenly

I walked right into her. The screaming had cut off. A moment later, a new voice replaced it, crushing the doubt I'd been clinging to.

"I'm glad you came to play, Kyle. The cards were laid out in front of you the whole time, but I wasn't sure you'd choose the right hand."

"I remember his voice! He was there, the night Mom died. He was the one who told me to run. Everyone said I must've imagined it," Naomi whispered next to me. I didn't think he could hear us through the security system, but I understood her wanting to whisper.

"You're heading the wrong way. You don't want to keep her hanging around, do you? She's almost at the end of her rope already."

The PA crackled again, like even the old wiring was laughing at us.

"The tower. He's steering us toward the tower," Naomi said. "He's already shown us what he was planning when he left Jackson's body there for us to see. Or maybe that was like a dry run, and we stumbled on the body too soon. Either way, I'm betting that's where Addison is. He's got to be in Principal Kincaid's office to be using the PA."

I shook my head. "Not necessarily. He could have patched into it using a mobile transmitter, like a walkie-talkie."

She gave me a *look*.

"Is that something you think he'd know how to do?" Naomi said.

"Yeah, maybe." Coby used walkie-talkies when he went on site visits at any of Big Blue's depots.

"So he could be anywhere. He could be watching us through a window, or hiding in the shadows right next to us for all we know."

I wanted to get Naomi as far away from the school as possible, and then go find Coby myself. I had twenty pounds and a few inches on him, so I didn't think he'd take me in a fair fight. But that wouldn't do me any good if he was armed.

"I need to find something to use as a weapon," I said.

A fire extinguisher? Too bulky and awkward. The desks and chairs in all the classrooms were the hollow, useless kind, so I couldn't break off a leg to use as a club or even slam the weight of the thing around, the metal was so light. I even weighed up some of the stuffed animals still staring down at us, but that was just dumb. They were all dumb ideas, and we were in a school— of course the hallways weren't going to be lined with things I could use to beat someone.

"Kyle?" Naomi's voice was just a whisper.

"I guess we go to the tower. I'll go inside, see what's going on. If I get into trouble, you can run like hell."

She looked at me like it was the craziest idea she'd ever heard. "Or how about this: we both go to the tower, one from the top, and the other from ground level. Take him by surprise."

"No."

"No?"

"No. What are you going to do if you go in there—and it doesn't matter which way you go in, because he'll probably see us coming, anyhow. And he's not surprised, but he's armed, and I'm at the other end of the damn tower?" I said.

"I'll stick a knife in his gut."

It took me a second to respond to that. "You have a knife?"

Naomi nodded. "I grabbed Grandpa's hunting knife when you started hammering on the door earlier. It's in my pocket."

"You were going to *stab* me?"

Even in the dark, I saw Naomi roll her eyes. "Only if I had to. What? Don't look at me like *I'm* the one who's crazy."

Separating was probably our best plan. If we stayed together, we made an easy target.

Except I didn't want her anywhere near Coby. And if Addy hadn't been mixed up in this, I could probably have convinced her to run.

"I'll head up to the attic, go in that way," I said when we reached the tower door. "I'll try to find something I can use as a weapon on the way there. Promise me you won't go inside until I yell it's safe, okay?" I was hoping she'd forget about the door not opening from the outside, and that she'd be safely on that side of it until I'd dealt with Coby.

"I promise." She looked me right in the eye. Then she kissed me, and was gone.

CHAPTER FORTY-FIVE

BURTY MAKES THE CUT

Naomi

I'd planned on using the knife to jimmy the lock if I had to, but the tower door stood open, inviting me in.

The finger of moonlight stretched in through the doorway, then it was swallowed by shadow. I took a deep breath and walked in, holding the knife at my side, out of sight. If he was in there, waiting for me, I wasn't going to give away my only advantage.

I could only see the neon painted faces glowing dimly up the wall of the tower. I listened carefully, but didn't hear any movement nearby. I gripped the knife like I was trying to snap it.

"Naomi? Is that you?"

Addy's voice was hoarse, and echoed down the tower shaft from somewhere above. I spun around, expecting *him* to leap out at the sound. Nothing moved.

"Addy? Where are you?"

I peered up in the dark, the knife gripped in front of me now.

"Naomi! Thank God. I'm on the rope. Get me down!"

I could see her, now that I knew where to look. She was some way above me on the pulley rope, dangling there. My hands were sweaty, and slid on the rope the first time I tested it. It was locked in place. I'd have to climb up to her. I closed the blade of the knife and tucked it in my pocket, then grabbed hold of the rope hanging parallel to the one she was hooked to. I began the climb.

Addy screamed. "Please, don't touch me, it hurts so bad . . . "

"What does?"

"My hands and my feet, they're . . . they're . . . "

I knew what the Bonebreaker did to his victims. I'd known it even before Kyle spelled it out for me, because I'd seen it. I saw how he started with her hands and feet so she couldn't fight back, couldn't escape. She tried so hard to crawl to me.

Shhh.

"Are you hurt anywhere besides your hands and feet?" I said.

"No."

"Good. I'm going to climb right up next to you, and I need you to wrap your arms and legs around me and hold on, okay? I'll hold your weight, but I need my hands free to cut you loose."

She made a sound that could have been a groan or a yes, so I climbed the last few feet up to her. The second I touched her, she screamed, and I jerked away.

"Addy, please be quiet! I'm sorry, I'm not trying to hurt you."

She didn't answer, but reached for me in the dark. I stayed still while she wrapped herself around me, even though her hold felt too weak to take her own weight.

"Tighter, Addy." She did as I asked, sobbing against the back of my neck now. I did my best to steel myself, using one hand to saw at the rope connecting Addy's waist to the pulley system. The knife was sharp, but it still took a while to hack through the tough strands.

"Where is he?" I whispered, partly because I needed to know, and partly because I was worried Addy would pass out and drop to the stone floor of the tower. I passed the rope between my hands, inching us lower.

"He went outside," she mumbled. She sounded drunk, but I knew it had to be from the pain. "I never knew he'd do this, Naomi, I swear. It all got so out of hand. I told him about what happened between us. That I hated how you acted like it was all my fault when you didn't even take my side over Paolo, and he said he believed me, and I . . . he said I needed to show you you're not always right. . . . It was only meant to be a prank, just messing with you and Kyle a little . . . like the owl in your room and the brass knuckles in his locker. . . . And then I took the SIM out of your phone earlier tonight because he said he had a prank planned that'd scare the crap out of you, and couldn't risk you calling the cops. I'm so sorry, I only wanted to . . . wanted to . . . "

"Wanted to what?" I snapped at her. My hands burned from gripping the rope, and I struggled not to slip as I lowered us down.

"I wanted you to need me again. I thought when you found out I really did have an older boyfriend, you'd finally believe me about Paolo. That he'd lied to my mom and Alana, and you should have believed me. You should've stuck up for *me*. You were my best friend, Nai!"

"But you said yourself that you made it up!"

"You'd already decided that, though, hadn't you?" She sobbed, breath catching. "Coby said he'd help me. . . . I had no idea about . . . about any of this!"

I closed my eyes for a second, breathed through my nose the way I'd seen Kyle do outside the school.

Addy shuddered against my back. "Then tonight, I saw Jackson's body in the trunk of his car, and he shoved me in with it!" The rope jerked as another few strands broke free, and Addy's teeth clacked together. "He told me he'd fooled you with a mannequin. I didn't know he was dead, like, for *real*. I'm such an idiot!"

"Addy, stop." She *was* an idiot, but I could feel her tears soaking my shoulder, and I had no fight in me to spare right now. "It doesn't matter."

"Please don't let him kill me!"

I gritted my teeth. I was holding almost all of her weight, and the section connecting her to the pulley rope was about to give way. If I couldn't hang on, we'd both be a mangled mess at the bottom of the tower.

"I would *never* let that happen. Don't let go," I said.

Her arms tightened so that she was almost choking me. Still, I carried us down until I felt the ground beneath my feet. Addy felt it, too.

She screamed in my ear when her shattered feet touched down. I held her up, struggling to maneuver us both in the dark, until she was curled on the floor next to me, sobbing.

It was pitch-black. The door behind me had closed, and I still hadn't heard Kyle up at the top of the tower.

"Addy, I need you to be really quiet for a few minutes, okay? I'll help you move over behind the door, so if he comes back he won't see you if you're quiet. Do you understand?"

She whimpered. "You're leaving me? You can't!"

I crouched next to her, smoothing my hands on her face because I didn't dare touch her anywhere else.

"Kyle's going in from above, and since Coby isn't down here I'm betting he's up there. I can't leave Kyle to deal with him solo."

Addy leaned her cheek against my hand. It was damp from her tears, and hot where the rope had burned my palm.

"What about me, Nai? What if he comes back for me?"

I felt my knife in my other hand. "Can you grip at all?" I said. She probably couldn't, but I needed to reassure her somehow. "I've got a knife, and I'll leave it with you. He won't know you've got it, so all you'd need to do is stick him with it once, good and deep."

Addy sniffled, then stifled a moan. "If I put my hands together, I think . . . I think I could."

I squeezed my eyes shut, glad she couldn't see me. She didn't need to know how terrified I was of facing him, especially without any way of defending myself.

CHAPTER FORTY-SIX

Kyle

The attic crawl space felt like a tomb. The roof seemed to be pressing down, crushing me.

I'd picked up my baseball bat before climbing up into the attic, and it pressed against my back, tucked under my belt.

I tried to ignore the dead animals tucked away in the eaves, watching me. It didn't seem likely those little cameras were fitted up here, but then it'd seemed pretty damn unlikely that Coby was a murderer just a few hours ago. Still, I didn't think he was sitting in the principal's office watching us on those black-and-white monitors with a bucket of popcorn. The Bonebreaker was particular about his victims. They'd all looked like Mama until Annabel Steadman. But he hadn't spent a long time stalking them. He'd chosen each victim only because of how she looked, and the rest was done by force.

The beam creaked under my weight, and I stopped. The last thing I wanted was to go crashing through the ceiling below me, but I needed to hurry.

I reached the grate leading into the stairwell at the top of the tower. Except it wasn't a grate now—the grille was blocked off with some kind of metal sheet, and when I shoved against it, it didn't budge.

What the hell?

My chest was tight, like I was suffocating. I could smell something strange in the musty air of the attic. Something chemical, and it was making me want to hurl.

I shifted around and brought my feet up to kick at the covered grate. Each time my heels connected, it made a clanging metal sound, but didn't give way.

My head swam. My legs were like lead. I sank down on my back in the dust, wondering what the black dots were in front of my eyes. Then the dots grew bigger and joined together, and I didn't wonder any more.

~~~~~~~~~

When I blinked myself awake, my head felt like it had gone another round with the bathroom tiles. I was lying on a hard surface, sick to my stomach, but I didn't have all the regular hurts. I hadn't been in a fight, then.

I looked around, and my relief died. Coby leaned against the door, with something in his hand that looked like a relay baton. I scrambled backward until my shoulders hit the wall of the tower.

My bat was gone, and it wasn't lying anywhere handy.

If I'd been expecting him to look different, to have some crazed look in his eye or something, I was wrong. It was just Uncle Coby, same as ever, waiting for me to wake up.

"Is your head sore?"

"What did you do?" I said.

"Just a little knockout potion." Coby waved his empty hand like it was nothing. "Had to get everything ready for you."

"For me?"

"Of course for you!" he said. "You think I set all this up for kicks? I got it all figured out real nice. Got your mama set to thinkin' Killdeer was all her idea, a way to honor your daddy, and of course she was happy to leave all the arranging to me." Coby sneered. "Just another dumb bitch can't do nothin' for herself. Like that Steadman girl, crying down there in the dark right now. I know you think you're friends with her, son, but she ain't your friend. She's a mistake I made ten years ago, and I been waiting to set it right."

"You mean her mother, Annabel?"

Now I saw the change in him. His features twisted into a look of absolute rage, and I shrank back.

"She was meant to be mine! But then she recognized me, called me by *that* name, and it was like I was right back at the Academy, with everyone laughing at me. Your daddy didn't think

I could do it." He shook his head. "I thought Annabel was the one. I thought I loved her, for a time, until I realized it was a different kind of love. She was meant to be my first real kill."

I strained to hear Naomi in the tower below. I wasn't gonna ask him what he'd done with her. If I could keep Coby focused on me, then maybe she would go get help. Maybe she already had, and that was why everything was so quiet. Or maybe he'd already killed her.

No. I couldn't let myself believe she was dead. I had to keep him talking.

"I thought you pushed that boy out of the window?"

He snorted. "That wasn't planned. It wasn't something I'd worked for. Your daddy showed me that, you know. If you work for it, there's so much more to it, so much satisfaction. You don't know how hard it is to go for years without feeling it, and then when that girl ran into me up on the roof a couple weeks ago, it was like your daddy giving me his blessing, sending a gift, for me. I was only up there waiting for you to see my message, to see how that girl was already marked."

Casey. He killed her.

This, everything he'd said, was too much. This wasn't the man I'd known my whole life.

"I knew you'd understand," he said. "It's like you told me when you was a kid, about the owl and the mouse, and how there ain't no changing what it is, what it's meant to be. The owl is always gonna kill that mouse. The mouse is always gonna die. And then that girl just walked right up to me on the roof. She hollered some when I did her hands, but she didn't make no sound when she dropped, she was so scared. Quiet as a mouse, she was."

He crouched in front of me, elbows on his knees and that baton still held loose between his fingers.

"And it helped me figure something out. Now, I'd always believed it had to be done the way your daddy showed me. But killin' is a craft, son. And to master it, you need to find your right way with it. For me, it's not the knuckles. Bobby liked to feel 'em breaking under his fists, like he was battering his way into their souls, he said. But it ain't that way for me, and killing that custodian guy just showed me for sure. I needed to get him outta the way, stop him hanging around her all the time. I beat him good, but when he tried to run, I let him. It wasn't doing nothing for me, see. Then I saw you run into him, and it was like fate stepping in—I didn't know if you'd call the cops or finish the job for me, but I guess it was too soon for you. And then you left him like the sack of shit he was, and I knew it was the right thing. He wasn't the one for you."

I could have saved Jackson. Instead I left him alone to die.

Those words sank deep, and there was no taking them back.

"I had to track him down in the car and finish him later, of course," he went on, "but it showed me I needed to do things my way, not like your daddy. I like to break 'em, but I *love* to watch 'em fall."

I closed my eyes, like I could will myself away. Any place else, just away. But the darkness only made my head spin harder.

"I was going to finish her that night, too. Tried to get her to come meet me, but the bitch didn't answer. Turned out for the best, though, because you were meant to be a part of it—I see that now. I brought you a gift, Kyle. We're gonna end something I started all those years ago. It's a beginning for us both, too. We'll do them together, like your daddy wanted. He wrote you a bunch, you know, from prison. Your mama was going to throw the letters away, but I kept them safe for you. I have them right here, in my pocket." He gave me a serious look, like he did whenever I brought home a bad report card. "I had to wait until you were ready to be a man. A real man, Kyle. Is that what you are?"

It felt like I was watching him say all this insane bullshit on a TV screen. I could see he wanted something from me. Some sign of agreement.

"I don't understand why you're doing all this."

"Because they're all liars! That little bitch I brought here—Addison—do you know the lies she told me, the things she said and did to try to convince me she was worth even a second of

317

my notice? The things she told me about *you?* She said she rejected you, Kyle. Like she was better than you, like she wasn't some sniveling little worm that you could crush under your shoe. She's *yours*. Your first. For a long time, I thought it was gonna be your mama, but I guess she comes later. Don't you see how perfect it is, that those two girls are right here, in the same place where it all began?"

I heard something, like a shout, only really far away.

"I see that little Steadman bitch got to you. I know how tempting it can be to believe they have real feelings for you, just because they put out. They're liars, Kyle. All of 'em. Even her granddaddy told me what a liar she is. I been talking to him since I came back, catching up with the old fella. He's gone cuckoo now, though, can't see what needs done. Do you, Kyle? You got a choice to make right now. Are you gonna be a pussy-whipped little nothing your whole life, or are you gonna take charge and be a man?"

I didn't get how he could think like that, how I'd never known what was going on inside him all this time.

"This is no way to be a man," I gritted out, keeping my head flat against the wall. Even moving just a little made it spin like crazy.

"This ain't the time to sass me, Kyle. I got them both trapped at the bottom of the tower. And you can decide how we do 'em.

Maybe you take after your old man, and wanna do it up close and personal. Or if you're like me, then all we have to do is drag 'em up here, and we can send them right back down again. Pow! Like bugs under your shoe. What do you say?"

Coby stood up, held his hand out to me, and I glanced at the trapdoor.

"Come on, Kyle. It's time for you to step up."

CHAPTER FORTY-SEVEN

BATTER UP, BURTY!

Naomi

I stared at the howling faces as I climbed, emptying my head of everything else apart from getting to the top of the damned rope. If I didn't focus, I'd feel it digging into my burned hands, the fear making my muscles cramp. And Kyle's life might depend on me reaching him before that maniac figured out Kyle wasn't on his side.

Then something hit my forehead. When it trickled down my cheek, I realized it was only water. The rain must finally have hit. I forced my arms and legs back into a rhythm, focused on the glowing faces again, going higher, closer to the trapdoor.

Only a few more feet.

The last painted faces were above me now, and I could have cried with relief. I'd left about ten layers of skin behind, and was shaking with exhaustion.

Don't scream, don't scream!

My grip slipped, the rope like a firebrand.

I had to be quiet. If Coby was up there and he heard me, I'd be dead before I could even see if Kyle was still alive. I pushed on.

One hand up, pull.

Wood crashed against wood like a gunshot. Clambering up through the trapdoor, I spotted Kyle across the dropout room of the tower, but the man who had to be Coby was nearer. I looked up into eyes narrowed in anger, and saw nothing familiar in them, just the cold rage of a monster.

"You little bitch."

The baton in Coby's hand telescoped out, and he raised it, ready to bring it down on my head. Kyle lunged at him, tackling Coby against the wall. The man beat Kyle with the handle of the baton once, twice, and I could see Kyle starting to slump. I scrambled over to them.

Kyle somehow still held Coby pinned against the wall, but just as he seemed on the verge of passing out, Kyle headbutted him in the face. They both crumpled.

"Oh my God, Kyle!"

He was barely conscious. Coby groaned next to him, rolling up onto his hands and knees. The baton he'd dropped was somehow in my hand, like the metal had sprung right out of my arm.

I lashed down at Coby. Over and over while he curled in a ball, his arms covering his head.

"You bastard! You sick, twisted fucking psycho!" I held the baton in both hands now, moving in sharp jerks, each strike landing harder than the last. "You took her from me! You killed her, you fuck!"

I screamed at him the way I'd wanted to scream back then, the baton growing slick in my hands. His blood mixed with my sweat, every impact ugly and raw and perfect, all at once. Each time I drew back my arm, I was taking something from him, something he'd stolen from me years ago.

I didn't let the baton drop from my hands until Coby stopped moving.

Had I actually done that? He was barely recognizable now, seemed barely human.

"I'm sorry," I said as I knelt over Kyle, breathing hard. I reached out to touch his face, until I saw the blood covering my hands. "Are you okay?"

He nodded, though he looked far from okay. "Are you?" he said. "There's blood. Did he—"

"It's not mine," I said, jerking my head to where Coby lay on the floor. "He's out cold, I think. Kyle, Addy's hurt, and I don't know what to do. The door won't open down there. I need to get to a phone, but I can't leave you here with him."

"Go," he said. "Over the roof. Attic's not safe, he used some kinda gas." Kyle coughed, then groaned. "There's a phone in the principal's panic room, remember?" His eyes started to roll, but he fought to keep them open as he struggled up onto his knees. "I'll watch him."

Coby wasn't moving, but he might wake up at any moment. I pressed the slippery rubber grip of the baton into Kyle's other hand.

"I'll be as quick as I can," I said, and hurried up the steps to the window looking out onto the roof.

I heard footsteps behind me when I'd gone no more than a few feet onto the catwalk. I'd crossed it a hundred times before with no problem. Now my legs felt heavy and slow, and I slipped, landing hard and clenching my teeth when the tiles bit into my sore palm.

No choice. I had to get up, had to run.

Thunder clashed overhead, and I looked over my shoulder in time to see Coby lit by the lightning flare. A shudder ran through me.

"What did you do to Kyle?"

He shook his head, like my question confused him. "You shouldn't have cut your hair, you know. It was so beautiful. But at least you're wearing the necklace again." Coby stepped toward me, and I backed up. "I gave it to her back when we were in school here together. Did she tell you that?"

Another step closer. I clutched at the sunflower pendant, like I could hide it from him, like I could keep him from ruining it. *He'd* taken the necklace from the cottage. *He'd* been the one to leave it in my dorm room. The thought of him in there, touching my things, made me want to throw up.

"No, she wouldn't have said that, I guess," he continued. "She pretended that no-good boyfriend of hers had left it in her locker. Like he'd have known what she liked the way I did." His fists clenched at his sides, and I inched away from him. In the moonlight, the whites of his eyes gleamed too brightly. "She wore it every day, and I knew she felt it. I loved her, and she loved me back, deep down."

"She didn't love you! You killed her!"

I turned my back on him and ran, my sneakers skidding again. I kept my balance and pushed forward, the tiles rattling under my feet from Coby's heavier steps.

"Annabel, come back!"

"I'm not her!" I screamed as his hand landed on my shoulder.

"Stop fighting me!" he hissed, his fingers curling around my neck.

Stop fighting.

He'd said those same words to my mom ten years earlier, even as he was holding me so I had to watch what was happening.

I wrenched free of Coby's grip, feeling the chain snap at my throat. My legs snaked out from under me and down the slope of the roof, and the necklace slithered past me and disappeared over the edge. I clawed at the tiles, scrabbling to get my knees under me, but still sliding down toward a drop that would surely kill me.

No!

I lay flat, willing myself to be heavy, to grip the slick tiles, until I started to slow. I finally skidded to a halt with my feet hanging over the lip of the roof, too breathless to scream. My hands throbbed, but I ignored the burning pain as I slowly, carefully, dragged myself away from the edge, almost losing my grip twice before I made it back to the apex.

He was there now, his own blood dripping off him like rainwater.

"Why are you doing this to me?" I yelled.

"You shouldn't have run from me, Annabel."

"You're sick! Can't you see that? Don't you realize I'm not her?"

"Shut your lying mouth!" He lifted one foot and brought it down with a crack on my fingers. I screamed, the shock followed by a burning, seizing pain rushing through my hand. I pulled it in tight to my chest. "I told you to BE QUIET."

He stepped toward me and I kicked at him, but my balance was off and I slipped again. I rolled, still cradling my busted hand. Then a shadow rose behind Coby.

There was a thud, and Coby went down, sliding past me and straight over the edge of the roof.

"Naomi!" Kyle stood over me, and I caught his outstretched

hand. Relief surged through me for a millisecond before some-thing clawed at my leg, tightening like a vise around my ankle.

"Kyle!"

Coby grabbed for me with his other hand, and I kicked at him, a low, animal noise rushing out between my teeth. I might not be my mother, but she'd never stopped fighting this monster, and neither would I.

Lightning split the sky again, glinting off the baton in Kyle's hand as he smashed it down on Coby's arm. The man howled, and my leg was free. I scrambled back up the roof, out of reach. When I turned, Kyle was still at the roof's edge.

"Don't let me fall, boy!" Coby yelled. The rest of his words were lost to the bellow of thunder overhead. Kyle was straining against something, and I saw that Coby had caught hold of Kyle's jacket sleeve and was pulling them both down over the edge.

Kyle looked back at me, jaw clenched, with the rain lashing against his skin. He looked like a statue, as if the rain had been beating down on him forever.

I lunged for him, clutching at air.

"Kyle!"

But they were gone.

CHAPTER FORTY-EIGHT

BYE BYE, BURTY

Kyle

My eyes were closed, but I could hear the news report on the TV.

" . . . Jacoby Wickes died of his injuries the next day, and the missing Killdeer Academy students were found locked in the school basement. Police have issued a statement saying that they are not looking for any further suspects in the murders of Jackson Pritchett and Casey Grimshaw. Wickes is also believed to have been responsible for the assault on another student at the school—Addison Mendez—and the attempted murders of Kyle Bluchevsky, son of Wickes's late business partner who was convicted of the so-called Bonebreaker killings that shook North Carolina more than a decade ago, and Naomi Steadman, whose mother was the final victim of the Bonebreaker. Wickes is alleged to have been an accessory to those murders as well, and police are reopening their investigation into—"

The sound clicked off, and I opened my eyes to find Mama sitting next to me.

"Mama," I said. The word came out on a croak.

She looked at me nervously, then held a glass of water while I sipped from a straw.

"How do you feel, Kyle?"

My head felt like someone had played Whack-a-Mole with it.

"What happened? Is Naomi okay? And what about Addison, and—"

Mama's eyes filled with tears and I tried to sit up, struggling against the pain that wrapped around my head, my feet, and every inch in between.

"Mama, *tell me*."

She held my hand, and when I looked at her properly, I saw she was really smiling.

"You're all right, aren't you? They said you'd fractured your skull weeks ago, and that the fall probably woulda killed you if you hadn't landed on . . . "

If Coby hadn't broken my fall.

Mama wiped her face with a tissue from her purse. "I was so scared it would be like my accident. All these years I worried you'd end up like your daddy, but Coby said sending you away from me would be a good thing, would make you your own person, and he was lying the whole time! I didn't want you to wake up wrong, like I did. I never wanted that for you, my boy."

The tears were coming too fast for her to catch them, so I just held her hand. A uniformed cop knocked on the door a short while later.

"Good, you're awake. We've got some questions for you, son."

Another cop joined him a few minutes after that. They questioned me for hours, it seemed.

"When did you realize Naomi Steadman was the daughter of the woman your father murdered?"

"How did you happen to be at the same school as her?"

"Whose decision was it to move to Killdeer?"

"Why did you change your last name?"

Mama was with me the whole time, being as I was a minor and all, although she might as well have not been there. All the questions pushed her back into her head where there weren't any dead bodies, just Disney tunes and poppyseed chicken.

"I told you already. I knew the second she told me her name, but I figured she didn't need to know who I was. I asked Mama to get our names legally changed after my dad was executed last year. The paperwork came through the week before we left Whistler, and my mother chose the new town, didn't you, Mama?"

Mama stared straight ahead, unblinking. I shrugged at the two cops facing me. "I appreciate how it looks, really I do. But I didn't try to kill Naomi, I didn't kill Jackson, and I sure as hell didn't kill anybody ten years ago. I had no idea what Coby had planned. If I had, I'd have made sure he never got anywhere near Naomi."

The two cops—a man and a woman who looked sort of the same—stared at me like I was full of shit.

"And what about Jackson Pritchett? We have statements from three students who claim they saw you in an altercation with him."

"I didn't like the guy," I said. "But I didn't kill him. You've gotta know that I didn't hang his body from the clock, either."

I got a head tilt from both of them, and it reminded me of an old film I'd seen about giant man-eating lizards.

"From the security footage," I added, being as they were bound to ask.

The male agent sighed like I was being a pain in the ass. I didn't care. Coby had deleted the footage from the night we'd found Jackson's body hanging in the tower, but the cops had to have seen Coby hang him up on the clock dial. He'd had no time to get into the principal's closet to erase it.

Someone knocked on the hospital room door and popped their head around.

"Sir, can I have a word?"

The male cop left the room and came back a few minutes later looking thoroughly annoyed.

"Seems Miss Steadman's story matches yours," he huffed. "So

it looks like we have everything we need here."

The two cops left, and Mama finally looked up.

"Where did those nice police officers go?"

~~~~~~~

It felt like I only blinked, and I found Naomi sitting on one of the hard plastic visitor chairs, her feet up on the bed next to me and one hand fat with bandages. I didn't know where Mama had gone to, but I didn't have much mind to think on it.

"I wasn't sure I'd see you again," I said. "At least, not outside a courtroom. Are you all right?"

She smiled at me, and it looked sad.

"I would've come sooner, but what with Grandpa going back home and having to deal with the police and everything, I couldn't." She sighed. "And I didn't know what to say to you, Kyle. I mean, you lied to me, and I'm still mad at you about that, but when they loaded you onto that trolley and took you away in the ambulance, I . . . "

"I can't believe you're even here," I said.

"We all are. Fletch is out in the visitors' room, and Kit is down the hall checking on Addy. The guys have both been in to sit with you while you were out."

She bit her lip, but I'd seen it tremble.

"I missed you," I said, reaching for her unbandaged hand on

top of the thin hospital sheet.

"You were unconscious." Naomi laughed, and a couple tears broke loose, but she didn't push me away. "I was so scared you weren't going to wake up, and I was so . . . so *angry* with you for lying, but when you fell from the roof and I thought I'd never get the chance to tell you—"

She was crying for real now. I wanted to get up, to wrap my arms around her, but I wasn't even fit to sit up. So I lay there and squeezed her hand. "Don't you hate me after everything that's happened? Now that you know who I am?"

She shook her head, wiping her face with her sleeve. "Finding out who your dad was, well, that wasn't easy. But I know who *you* are, Kyle, and that's not the same thing. You aren't him, just like I'm not my mom."

"I could've saved Jackson, you know. Coby told me that." I waited for her face to change, to get that look people got when they slapped a "no good" label on me. But her face didn't change.

"You didn't know what was going on any more than I did," Naomi said. "Saying you could've saved him is like saying I could've stopped Coby sooner if I'd answered his texts, or if I'd paid more attention to Addison. You can't go looking for evil."

I'd been surrounded by evil my whole life, and I still hadn't recognized it in Coby.

"I spent so much time trying to figure out what kinda guy I wanted to be when we moved to Killdeer," I said. "I didn't want people to look at me and see my dad, see the things he did. But I'm no different. I hurt you, and I messed everything up. I'll always be sorry about that. But being with you wasn't a mistake. I won't ever believe we were a mistake." I hadn't had the time to get the words straight in my head, but they felt right—and necessary.

Naomi's gaze was clear and steady, and I knew her mind was made up. "We're nobody's mistake," she said. "And you can't keep paying for what your dad did, or Coby. We can't change what happened. The only thing we can do is let it go."

She leaned in and kissed me real soft, the taste of her tears on her lips. I held her, ignoring the searing pain shooting through damn near every part of my body, kissing her and holding her so there was no way she could take it back.

"Scooch over," she said. Naomi slid in next to me on the narrow bed, tucking her head under my chin. I smiled into her hair and closed my eyes.

Lying with Naomi in my arms, I finally saw the things I needed to let go, and what I had to hold on to.

[Letter from Robert Bluchevsky to Coby Wickes]

Coby,

It looks like this is finally it.

Look out for my boy until he's of a right age to know what needs done. Teach him, just like I taught you, and our business will go on how we planned. Show him that everything starts back at the beginning, like it always has, and he'll find his true path.

It breaks my heart that I won't be there to walk it with you both.

Take care of Olive for me when the time comes. That final chapter wasn't meant to be mine, I guess.

Bobby

ACKNOWLEDGMENTS

Without my amazing editor, Lisa Cheng, and the team at Running Press Kids, *Breaker* would've been broken. My immense thanks to you, Lisa, for your insight and expertise, and for letting me keep "masturbatoire."

T. L. Bonaddio—you gave this book the perfect cover. I am still staring at it, wide-eyed and awestruck. Thank you!

My critique partners/beta readers/lifesavers—Jani, Bridget, Erin, and Jeanmarie; I owe you oceans of cocktails. And Dawn, who adds a little crazy into my life when I need it—as always, you shall have payment in cake. Also Gabrielle—thank you for the excellent photographs.

My wonderful family and friends—thank you for all your encouragement, support, and general touting of my books. And especially Ian, who puts up with me every day: I love you always.

Finally, to Molly Ker Hawn, my most kind, smart, and in all ways stellar agent: thank you for the immeasurable work you do on my behalf. Without you my books just wouldn't happen.